ARRIBADA

ARRIBADA

A NOVEL

Dear Anna:
Here's to the pleasure
of having met you.
Enjoy my stories!
estela

Estela González

cennan
chester county,
pennsylvania

Published by Cennan Books of Cynren Press
101 Lindenwood Drive, Suite 225
Malvern, PA 19355 USA
http://www.cynren.com/

First published 2022

Printed in the United States of America on acid-free paper

ISBN-13: 978-1-947976-31-3 (hbk)
ISBN-13: 978-1-947976-32-0 (ebk)

Library of Congress Control Number: 2021944516

This novel's story and characters are fictitious;
the characters involved are wholly imaginary.

Download a playlist curated by the author to complement your reading:

Cover and interior art by Ariane van Driel van Wageningen, copyright 2021

Cover design by Kevin Kane

Ernesto Alonso—your music never fades

Let this darkness be a bell tower
and you the bell. As you ring,
what batters you becomes your strength.
—Rainer Maria Rilke, *Sonnets to Orpheus*

Earth took a step
It sounded loudly
Touched infinity

Those who speak of ancient things
Carry history
—traditional Comcáac song

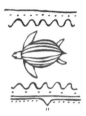

Moosnípol y la Mar

All because the sea ate the beach.

Careyes. Hundreds of meters of sand in all directions: warmth of talcum powder between our toes where we dug ourselves up to our necks, played war, climbed on black cliffs, and dove from them; where we rode the waves, our parents unaware, to where our feet could no longer reach. The sea rocked us. It held and sustained us. The sea was always there.

But one day the machines arrived. They drove piles and built walls dressed in hibiscus and bougainvillea. They erected towers, dug pools bluer than the ocean blue. They named Hotel Careyes after the last hawksbill nesting on its beaches. The paradise of delight was open to all. Who could pay.

Everyone smiled and dispersed pictures of the nation's heroes on little papers.

And the sea churned. It bellowed its ire at the stone that was not stone, the glued-up gravel. It licked the cement, it spat at the walls, spewed insults of seaweed and jellyfish. It rose and climbed, ate a centimeter of beach. The next year, one more. Erosion, pronounced the solemn engineers, rushing to reinforce the levees, build retaining walls, burrow deeper.

The sea hurled waves. It invaded the lobbies of luxury hotels; its irate hurricanes inundated the polished parota floors, stole Persian rugs. When it shattered the windows of jewelry stores, rivers of pearl and coral returned to sea. The wind kidnapped dogs from the laps of distinguished ladies who, ¿de dónde nos visitan?

Such was the clamor in the paradise that was Careyes Hotel and Resort.

Until one day, exhausted from holding tons of steel and cement,

1

the Sand renounced her destiny as blond Atlas, abandoned herself to the depths, and let the Great Blue cover her. Under it all, Sea and Sand remembered that before time was time, She, the Enormous, had been alone, round, weeping her blue solitude.

The Sand's return also saddened Moosnípol, the oldest turtle in the world. Because in the beginning only she, Laúd, had pitied the Great Blue. Old Moosnípol with seven lute strings on her Leather Back, the lone mariner who in the beginning had descended to the depths and murmured distant songs into the Great Blue's ear. The Leatherback promised the Sea a companion, firm and joyful, sunny and sweet. She took a clump of sand and carried it to the surface. She took another clump. And another.

Clumps created mounds, hills, mountains.

That is how Mother Moosnípol presented the Great Blue with a warm companion to caress with her waves. She gave us a home where we could walk and climb and dwell.

She gave us Earth.

But we broke her, and Earth returned to Sea.

Part One

La Perla del Pacífico

1990

One

So you're back, they surely said. As if she had been gone for the weekend.

It was hot when Mariana returned. She stood at the Ayotlan airport surrounded by the kiddy guitars; the paper flowers in Mexican pink; the coconut and tamarind candies for tourists to take with them, the aromas of this far-off land. One o'clock in the afternoon, and in the waiting room stood only the sleepwalking workers with no lunch break but yes, a promise of better pay next year. Their gray necks glistened, their shirts stuck to their backs like the drenched sails of a sinking boat. A bit uppity, a bit shy, they smiled at Mariana and she smiled back, airing herself with her lace fan.

It was all so familiar.

But not everything was the same. Remember the day she left.

Then, the airport had been a market sweltering with laughter and the last-minute recommendations of relatives wishing Mariana a safe trip. Everyone had been there: the vociferous neighbors, the Rotary Club dignitaries. Alonso, the young uncle, really a brother: guitar case in hand, absentminded smile, his quiet hugs for Marianita. Little sister Luisa. And doña Clavel, standing stiff and tall, as if someone had taped a sword along her spine. Mother to the most admired girl in Ayotlan, commanding attention as she slapped herself on the hip. Her proud, cobble-stoned voice: Mariana, high school in New York, the Rotary scholarship.

That was the first of many goodbyes. Then Mariana found a way to extend her studies and came back only for vacation, to leave us again heartbroken. Pianist. collecting so many feathers in her cap she might turn into an ostrich. And the dazzled family, the acquaintances and neighbors again congregated to wish her happiness: write soon, child, study, eat. Pórtate bien.

Places preserve odors and echoes over the years. This decrepit lobby, drenched in the fragrance of coffee and pineapple juice, more market than airport, the hallways resonating like a tuning fork with the sounds of the runaway city—Mexicana de Aviación, announcing flight 558—

The laughter and the merriment that accompanied Mariana on her many departures. Where did it all go?

Now, sweat and silence.

How pretty, how alone, standing in that lobby with her black trousers and silk blouse, her lion's mane. A few droplets on the bridge of her nose, a bit of red on her cheeks. She was an Ayotlan girl, would not complain, though the shock was mighty. Mariana and her high-heeled sandals, her freckled feet.

A carcajada boomed from the paper flower stand, where Fernanda sat on the counter framed by a garish wreath like a pagan Madonna. Her splayed thighs pushed aside the many-colored boxes and jars and pots and trinkets. Her ruffled skirt barely covered what it was meant to cover.

She jumped off and rushed to hold Mariana. Ay chiquita, I heard—tu tío Alonso. Qué tragedia. She stroked Mariana's cheek.

Thanks, Fernanda. So glad to see you.

The embroidery on Fernanda's frock brushed through Mariana's blouse. Fernanda was black coffee all over: her almond eyes, her cheeks, her chest. Coffee crowned by a torrent of black hair. She smelled of sage.

Are you selling crafts? What happened to the PhD?

No, linda. Just taking care of Belisa's stand. My PhD is done. I'm back from México City, ready to play con el mar y sus pescaditos.

She glanced at Mariana's lips.

What's the shortest way to the parking lot?

Fernanda pointed. She said Saludos a Luisa and the mothers.

Such a good friend. Mariana was lucky to have some left.

She walked, then waited.

In picking her up, Luisa and Madre stopped for an instant, drawing a triangle: on the center, Mariana shepherded her little suitcases. On the right, doña Clavel sat in the taxi outside. And on the left, Luisa stalked Mariana from behind a column. Then she reached her in a few strides. They held each other: chins resting on shoulders, eyes closed. Luisa leaned over to help with the bundles.

That's all you brought? So let's go home. Quick quick, or you'll melt on me.

Poor Mariana was back to stay at her mother's house. Her uncle Alonso—more than an uncle—her anchor, her brother. The boy who taught her music and to give her heart. Disappeared, Luisa had phoned. His tracks lost in the sands. Mariana must find him. Share his story with the town. Alonso, his music flowing into her ears. Hers and no one else's.

No more. Not now.

We'll find him, Luisa said. And if not, he'll rest, and we will too.

Santo Cristo.

Outside, Luisa waved at an elderly lady bobbing her head inside a taxi. Their mother. Where was the black chignon, the arrogant eyes?

Mariana held Madre's face, her brittle white hair. Her skin, bereft of makeup, dark and defenseless. Her unlined eyes seemed blind.

Maaa. Maaaar.

Luisa glanced at Mariana. That is right, Madre. Mariana is finally here.

It was good to be back. Mariana was coming to help doña Clavel recover. It would do them good to be together again. Luisa had kept their mother company for years, and lately with help from no one but Amalia. Doña Clavel would enjoy her elder daughter.

She was barely a woman when she left. She couldn't stand this backward town, they said. Rotary scholarship for a year of high school, then the conservatory; the competitions. Freelance accompanist. Agile, enterprising, fearless girl-woman, little breasts free of the tyranny of any bra, freckled-faced Muñeca. Every so often a newspaper clipping would spill out from an envelope and do the rounds of family and friends. Descriptions of a full-house concert would evoke a child's recital dazzling the cream of Ayotlan Country Club. Her wild, blonde hair forced into a mass of tubelike locks, the organza dress, the blue sash, the Clementi sonatina, the twelve years. But with the recent pictures, one had to free her curls, adjust the size of her chest, modernize her attire. Hear the Schumann in her. And it hurt.

The taxi drove down Mariana's favorite road, retracing her steps from the day of her first goodbyes. The twelve-mile malecón with the tiled sidewalk beginning at Punta Farayón and ending at Cerro de la Nevería: black cliffs and jungles, beaches blushing in the sunset, all of us skipping a heartbeat with each acrobatic diver's leap—it was the slowest road in Ayotlan, and Mariana would not take any other. The site of the Belmar Hotel where the Belle Jeunesse of the great-aunts and -uncles had danced Saturday and Sunday afternoons. Back then, tía Laura, whom nobody knew but everyone knew of, wore the heaviest sequin dress in Ayotlan. Laura, whose coronation as queen of the Carnival ended with a firecracker turning her into a human torch.

Despite the traffic, the driver honored Mariana's request and drove past the Devil's Cave to the beach where she, Alonso, and Luisa had camped. Careyes, that beach inhabited by friendly crabs where high-tide waves would rise like towers, then fall inoffensively at the feet of toddlers and tipsy adolescents.

Mariana peered, breathing in the iodine air, but the places were not familiar. Where was the Belmar, and Careyes Beach? The three islands floated across the bay: Deer, Wolves, Birds. But here were no dunes—nothing but waves licking at the Malecón wall. She must be mistaken; in her distraction she surely missed it. It hid behind her tears, her sister's words, her mother's babbling.

That seaside road saw Mariana and Alonso grow into themselves. At his four years and her zero he sang to her, and she learned music before words. This language grew to keep others out. During Easter preparations the family would feed the tamales assembly line at the brown-paper-covered table. Amalia kneaded the corn meal; doña Clavel spooned out the chicken stuffing; Luisa the pork; one guest or another the olives. But not Mariana or Alonso: we need more tomatoes, Mariana would sing. Hours later, they would return, sunburned and sandy, with a sack of seashells in one hand and a few tomatoes in the other. We're back! they would sing. And so it went.

The two walked Careyes Beach singing tales of sea turtles and hermit crabs. As they grew, the guitar and the piano rounded out songs everyone memorized.

Now, here rode three silent women and a taxi driver pestered by a loudspeaker truck, a rolling advertisement for habanero paste or election candidates or the day's news. Illicit lovers, hollered the loudspeaker. Stabbed to death when surprised by her husband, who was his brother. ¡Andale! Buy the evening edition of *El Heraldo del Pacífico*.

Why advertise other people's tragedies as a public spectacle? Who would tell Alonso's story? And how?

The women rode toward the stone fortress that was their house. In past years the family had dwindled. Tía Laura, abuelos, padre: all gone.

And Alonso, who liked to accompany their evenings with bossa nova and childish jokes. He left work one night and took the malecón, never to be seen again. As if the waves had swallowed him whole. How could they?

Mariana was about to plunge into a silent house with a sister and two mothers. Twenty-two, her womb as barren as the house: since she had sent Osvaldo away, no one had heard of another man. But she was young. She would soon smile, and someone would take her out of here. Blue eyes, translucent skin—no need to put San Antonio upside down.

Luisa was another story: dark, feíta. Dry like a brick. She would rather draw or paint than go out. Madre complained of her paints and solvents in the courtyard. Under the unkempt fronds of the limonaria tree sprung paintings of jungles and hallucinated animals; tapestries with yarn bulges in insane purples and reds. At night the fruit bats took over the courtyard corridors, mesmerized by the limonaria scent. Madre and Luisa argued over it all. In the heat of the battle Madre would threaten the limonaria: useless tree; all flowers, no fruit. Get rid of it. And go out, child; life is passing you by.

Now with the stroke Madre seemed to have pardoned her. She nodded and smiled: you keep the tree, and I keep you.

They got home and eyed the clock. Night should fall soon enough—what are the tropics made for?

They had supper and small talk. The sisters propped doña Clavel on her pillows and climbed the stone staircase. Mariana took her sandals off to receive the consolation of the polished rock in the torrid night.

Luisa asked what else she needed.

Just a bath, nena; I'm a soup.

Mariana brushed her hair while Luisa poured flowers and herbs in the ancient tub. Dark clothes fell on white tiles, liberating two slender bodies. The ample bathtub received them as it had scores of others: so many women had scrubbed their husbands' backs. So many children had enjoyed the caress of bubbles and sea sponges. The sisters stayed for a long time submerged in the aroma of limonaria, rose, and lavender. Their tresses floated and tangled—blonde; black.

They toweled off, and Luisa started off to her room. But Mariana, Come over here, Luisín. There's room for both in this bed.

Chiquilla.

They lay on their backs, legs folded, knees parted to catch the air. They held hands as when they were little.

Back then Madre would host guests for long weekends, and the girls gladly gave up their rooms to sleep in the chaise longue in the open corridor. In the festive chaos no one remembered to monitor their sleep. Covered with a gauze sheet, more protection against bugs than the weather, they would talk for hours, watch the moths' suicidal dance around the lightbulb. While the adults indulged in canasta and conversation, the sisters whispered the discoveries of the ten-, twelve-year-olds they were.

They told me, Mariana said. If you want kids you open your legs to a man. There's a little hole where a seed goes in, and later the baby comes out.

But how does the seed go in?

Para eso tienen el pito. The men use it like a syringe. The seeds swim like tadpoles in a white broth.

Over the guests' laughter, they breathlessly explored the transformations in their bodies.

See? Mariana said. My chichis are growing. Just you wait. One day you'll wake up with like two mosquito bites on your chest. Then they get fatter and fatter every day.

Steps in the hallway had them draw the sheet up to their throats. But it was just Alonso.

He was seventeen and spent his time filling the house with Bach, Villa-Lobos, bossa nova, always in the room next to the girls'. On his breaks he talked to them. One hand holding the guitar, the other his cigarette. And he was the authority.

You girls, no need to worry. When the moment comes you will see what there's to see; and you will know what there's to do.

Did those maxims address the love of romantic novels and soap operas, or the news of orifices and body fluids they had just shared?

No. He would not talk to them about *that*.

He finished his cigarette, said good night, and presented them once again with quiet melodies from next door.

I'm getting dizzy with the bugs flying around the bulb, said Mariana. Lights off, Luisín?

And nighty night. They looked away, either at the plants in the courtyard or the paintings on the wall. The other always fell asleep first, each thought.

The night deepens. Over Alonso's music Mariana explores her little torso, her square hips. At her chest she seeks the protuberances she just lectured Luisa on. And today there is something—a raw tenderness like the one on your lips after a day at the beach. That lightning bolt connecting her little chest to the rest of her body. Mariana wets one finger, strokes her nipple, makes it stand like a raisin. The finger and the breast play this game for a while. Then the child's eyelids droop.

She tries to sleep, but the heat is unbearable. She tosses and turns as Luisa's breathing slows. Then Mariana commits her most daring act. She wants to feel the difference between her sister's breast and her own. The gossamer nightgown is no obstacle; neither are Luisa's splayed arms and legs; nor her eyes, half open. She is asleep, Mariana knows. Her heart drums on her temples; the sound of her rushing blood overpowers Alonso's music. With all tenderness she places one fingertip on Luisa's nipple.

It hardens.

Mariana drops her hand like a cotton cup on Luisa's flesh.

She uncovers it. She leans, then tastes her bittersweet sister.

She tucks her hand between her legs.

The sigh Luisa responds with could double as a sob.

That old night of the end of their childhood was in their minds *tonight,* as the sisters slept together after many years, protected from the insects by gauze sheets. Just the same, they pretended to sleep as soon as the lights were out.

Two

How was I to find him—if I could hardly recognize my own mother?

As I flew from Europe, the phone conversation with Luisa echoed in my mind—missing, stroke, wheelchair. At the lobby she warned me again—Madre está muy disminuida. Still I could barely control my alarm as I saw her bobbing her head, her gaze as though frozen on the family photos Luisa had found her clutching the night a red flood nearly drowned her.

What could I do? I placed my hands around her face and kissed her wet cheek.

Maaaa. Maaaar.

The strongest woman I knew, a beautiful, forty-something woman, all lustrous black hair and intense eyes just a year ago. Now her hair was a brittle white. Her dusky skin, naked in public for the first time, clean from the polvos de arroz that had always lightened her complexion. White hair, formerly black; dark skin, formerly pale: she seemed a negative portrait of herself.

Maaar.

I would need time to learn a new language of gestures to communicate with this ghost of the commanding woman I had always known.

There would be time to hear the details about Alonso too. The last person to see him was the hostess. Alonso locked the restaurant as usual, then stayed in his office to practice guitar for a few hours before taking the long walk home on the Malecón.

He never arrived.

Earlier that year, the news of the restaurant job had shocked me—how was managing a restaurant better than teaching at the Conservatory?

Lana, he said in a neutral tone. We need the dough.

It sounded like Swedish.

¡Muñeca! How's the piano? the taxi driver asked as he loaded the luggage in the trunk. Doña Clavel is surely glad to have you back. ¿Eh, señora? All will be fine now.

I must get reacquainted with everyone knowing me, and volunteering their opinions.

As we rode by the sea, I watched for slices of blue between the buildings. I tried to recall the driver's name.

There is so much you can do, he went on. Your music, your—

Don Gualberto is right, Luisa said. Alonso will turn up in no time.

My stomach turned at the archness in Luisa's tone. Had she not begged, Come, Mariana, take the next flight?

Muñeca, they called me. A doll who could magically—do what? To some I was achievement and fearlessness; to others I was an ornament or a princess, too good for this backward town. Ayotlan's talented daughter, the memory of a child. A vessel of dreams.

A chill came down my back. What was I, really? Who?

Please take the Malecón.

We'll be crawling with the midday traffic, Muñeca. I can take you home through the Libramiento in no time.

I scanned the sidewalks. I searched.

Luisa glanced at me. The Malecón, don Gualberto. We are not in a hurry.

We rolled at a turtle's pace, and I began my search through the crowd of pedestrians.

My eyes widened. I spotted a young man carrying a music case. The balding crown, the turned-out gait. My heart raced as the taxi approached.

Then I saw his face. It was all wrong.

I looked for Careyes Beach; I saw murky water. No dunes, no umbrellas.

The water reaches the seawall?

Sí, Muñeca. It's high tide.

But the intertidal zone is two hundred yards from the wall.

The driver chuckled. Two hundred yards? That was in my grandparents' time.

I was not around in your grandparents' time, I spat.

No one answered. I sat back, ashamed. Out my window a city

bus changed gear, spewed its diesel stench onto my face. I closed my eyes, longed for my bedroom with its windows shaded by magnolia trees; my ceiling fan. Would Madre be fine if I took a shower and a nap when we got home? While I slept, Alonso's guitar music would seep in from the room next door. I would run to hug him, and this nightmare would be over.

The traffic roared.

Mariana, Luisa said. I opened my eyes into the glare. She gave me a small pillow.

Madre had dozed off, her neck bent awkwardly. Her head bounced with the car's jerks. I tried to steady her, but the pillow fell each time. I cupped her forehead in my palm. I swallowed the saliva forming in my mouth.

In the fortress of concentric squares that was my home I felt protected: the stone walls surrounding four wings of rooms; the rooms surrounding long terraces; the terraces enclosing a courtyard. We crossed the zaguán and the terrace to the courtyard, parked the wheelchair and sat under the tree, next to Luisa's looms and paintings. Among the masks hanging from the limonaria tree cooed Juana and Camelia. I called them. Juana alighted on my palm.

The clock rang three.

¡Mariana, hija!

Out of the smoky kitchen came Amalia. She walked past Madre. She touched Luisa's shoulder, stroked my hair and cheeks. Her palms were like sandpaper; yet their touch was soft and light.

¡Nana Amalia! I hugged her.

Look how little you are. Are you growing backward?

I sat in the middle, squeezed Luisa onto the side.

Have a seat.

In a moment, girls. How about some lemonade?

'Monada. Madre lifted three quivering fingers, drew a squiggly circle in the air.

Luisa stood up. You mean for the four of us. Sit down, Nanita. I'll get it.

Amalia glanced at Madre.

I pulled Amalia toward the sofa. ¡Siéntate pues!

She sat on the edge, her hands folded with mine.

The breeze swelled the muslin drapes hanging from the courtyard archways, revealing more of Luisa's art.

¡Luisa, qué bárbara! I called toward the kitchen. You colonized the walls.

The perfume of the limonaria, of guava and hibiscus, filled me.

Her—st—studio, Madre said, and her back straightened.

Our doves cooed.

Luisa carried a pitcher, glasses, and a melamine cup with a built-in straw. She placed the tray on a table next to Madre and sat down.

I'm astounded, I said. This is a completely new vision.

Amalia nodded. People say Luisa's work is inspired in Frida Kahlo's, but I think it is more a combination of Bosch and Remedios Varo. And nobody paints animals the way you do.

I squeezed Amalia's hand and felt her quiver.

Madre stared at Amalia. A deep sound came from her throat. A snort? A growl?

Amalia turned crimson. I need to check the sauce. I'm making tamalitos with tomato, cream, and panela cheese. She hustled away.

I stood up.

Luisa held my hand. Come here, she said. Amalia's been a bit nervous lately.

What was Madre upset about—the old conflicts over our art and music? Those pursuits were fine as hobbies, she had always said—too much was a distraction. Then she would call the limonaria a spinster's tree.

It is ours, we told her. Our childhood.

I picked a silk and ivory fan from the table and fanned myself. Madre smiled!

She wants you to have tía Laura's fan, Luisa said.

Tía Laura's treasures were few, and when Madre distributed them, they often fell to me. Was it a beauty queen's scepter? One more job besides bringing back Alonso, nursing Madre, clearing out whatever mortified Amalia?

What do you do with your studio during the rains? I think I smell hurricane.

It's coming in a day or two. My things are easy to move. The library is now my rainy season studio. Alonso decided to share it with me.

When was that?

When he started working at the restaurant.

Juana cooed on my hand, and I closed my eyes. I heard a faint whirring coming from behind the limonaria—a child's bicycle speeding toward us. The little black boots pumping the pedals were covered with a thin layer of dust; the socks were rumpled. The young cyclist sang an undulating melody as he rode toward me, Juana's coos providing an ostinato. I took a long breath, ready to sing back.

I opened my eyes.

Luisa and Madre were watching me. There was no child's song, no little bicycle. Just the wind whistling through the branches. Juana flew onto the tree.

Do you want to play some music? Luisa asked. Alonso hadn't—hasn't played much lately.

The baby grand piano stood paces away, under its manila shroud.

The clock chimed three thirty—time to unpack. Luisa pushed Madre's chair next to the phone and tuned the radio to the bolero station. Our favorite show, "La hora de los novios," Luisa said. She patted Madre's cheek.

Bh. Bh. Ell.

Of course, I almost forgot.

Luisa set a chrome-plated chime next to the telephone. That way she can call us. Right, Madre? It was Amalia's idea.

We carried my luggage into my room. In the center was a tall, queen-size bed enveloped in tulle. Four windows caught the crosswinds. Luisa opened the armoire with oval-mirrored doors. It was filled to the brim on one side, empty on the other.

I can make more space, said Amalia.

It's fine, Nanita. The only bulky thing I have is Alonso's old classic guitar.

He had given it to me after a study trip to Seville with Narciso Yepes, where he acquired his ten-string guitar, "la definitiva." So his old one was for me. My fingers were not very sturdy. I played bossa nova, some beginning Bach and Vivaldi. He had taught me the music, and his guitar went wherever I went.

As we organized my things in the armoire, I toppled a

cardboard box, and a pair of tiny boots fell out. I put a finger inside one. The sole was thin, supple, almost like fabric.

Whose are these, Nanita?

Yours, baby. And Luisa's, later. You both learned to walk in them.

So many things she will not part with, Luisa said.

I chuckled. You little hoarding squirrel. Why keep this clutter? If Madre hears you're stockpiling—

Niña. Do what you want with these things. They are yours. Just don't tell Madre.

Of course I won't.

I held Amalia in my arms. You can put our stuff wherever you want. You're our mother as much as she is.

She pulled away with a strength I did not know.

Out in the corridor the chime rang.

It's her, Amalia said.

She fled.

Three

A child's world is enormous. Ours was sand, salt, water.

Alonso whistled. The tide is coming up, he whispered from outside our tent.

I lifted my head from Amalia's shoulder and propped myself up on an elbow. She kissed my temple. Under the cocoon of the blue tent Luisa snored lightly.

Alonso scratched on the tent's fabric. ¡Orale!

I tickled Luisa's cheek. Come on! This is when the terns and frigates dive.

Let her sleep a little more, Amalia said. I'll stay with her.

Amalia taught me to swim. She would cradle my face up on the water until I relaxed. Then she softly dropped her hand, showing me that I was floating before I knew it.

But now she was opening the sleeping bag and peeling me off her. I clung. I had so few chances to sleep with her. Big kids sleep alone, Madre often said.

Didn't my parents share a bed?

But the outside beckoned. I balanced in the tent, put my cutoffs and tank top on. I rummaged in my sleeping bag. Amalia found my conch shell and handed it to me.

Bueno, Nana, I sang into the shell. Come when the baby wakes up.

I crawled out of the tent and slapped Alonso on the back. I mimicked a fanfare with my conch, and Alonso added some more hooting to the mix with his. We raced up powdery dunes—I won; then down to the wide, wide beach—he won. We splashed. We swam beyond where the waves broke. We shouted raucous songs.

Are there sharks? I asked.

Sure. Feel them swimming past your legs.

Not true!

We laughed. We floated. On land, our tent was a blue dot on the immense dunes. Behind all, Ayotlan climbed the hills.

When we came back to shore, our bodies were heavy. We held hands, singing melodies into our conch shells.

Adults reacted with amusement to our melodic conversations. Sometimes they lost patience. And they never understood.

Behind the dunes a pile driver produced painful thuds. The workers' shouts broke through the waves. We stayed as far from the construction site as possible. In the surf a girl splashed, a flock of seagulls hovering above her.

Alonso let go of my hand.

I've never seen eyes that big, he sang.

Let's go, I answered, and pointed down the shoreline. She doesn't know our games.

Why did he have to stare at that brat? She stuck her tongue out at us.

She swims like a turtle! Alonso whispered. He sang out: Soy Alonso. ¿Y tú?

Karina! She did a raspberry. The seagulls screeched as though feeding from her.

Nasty, I said. I plowed my feet searching for treasures, then looked back at Alonso. Come on, already!

He followed me along the shore. After a while we came upon a mound of sand as high as my knees. Something squirmed under the surface, producing little avalanches.

Jaibas, we whispered. But this crab was taking too long. We dug and found white shards and something dark and moist and fingerlike glistening in the morning light.

Slugs!

Wait, wait—a second slug dug itself out, moving with the first.

They were part of a larger creature.

A baby turtle! I picked it up. It hardly covered my palm. I could crush it in my fist.

I stroked the carapace.

Un carey, said Alonso, scanning the area. Hawksbill. So there are still some left.

Where's the mom?

In the water.

But who's going to take care of the baby?

The ocean. Come, let's give her a ride.

The seagulls hovered above the girl, so we walked in the opposite direction.

Your lucky day, little one. The hardest is over.

Are there raccoons on the beach?

The two-legged kind. They sell the eggs at cantinas. The borrachos drink them with tequila and habanero chile. They say their whistle stands up better.

What do they want the whistle to stand up for?

He shrugged. Come on. Let's bring her home.

The little turtle pressed toward the water. I turned away, and the turtle turned again toward the sea, as if pulled by a magnet. I sang a lullaby as she crawled on my palm. When she reached the edge she dropped into the air, and I caught her in my other hand. Again and again. Rocking the baby.

Ya, Alonso sang. Let her go.

I knelt and put my hand on the sand, and the turtle crawled off. When she touched water, she bolted away.

We waved goodbye, sang a long farewell, watched the little head emerge, then plunge.

The water exploded. That girl had swam underwater!

She is groping her! She almost killed her, I shouted.

Did not! I am just taking a look.

The seagulls screeched. I threw fistfuls of sand at them. Leave her alone!

The seagulls flapped and cawed. Some sand fell on the girl, and she cawed too.

A fishing trawler sailed by, wafting its rotting stench. The birds soared toward it. Carey's tiny head peeked out of the water every few seconds.

Alonso looked up at the blue sky. Good signs. No birds for now, strong Carey. I've seen the moms come out at night. They make a big old hole in the sand.

They don't fall in?

They lay their eggs there. And they cry.

Alonso alternated his gaze between the turtle and that Karina.

It hurts, huh? I sang, and stroked Alonso's arm.

They know the pinche world they're throwing their babies into.

Why don't they just go somewhere else? the girl asked. They'll be better off—

I glared at her. That's ridiculous. This is her home.

Alonso nodded. They always return to the same beach. They'd

rather end up in a stew pot than have their hundred kids far from home.

A hundred!

That way some survive. This one passed her first test.

I sang, See you when you return, little one.

Alonso smiled. By then you'll be on the other side of the earth.

No! I will always play here.

Me too, said Karina.

We turned to her. I had forgotten about her.

She shouted, You think you own this beach? Just so you know—it's mine. I'll be swimming in Padrino's hotel every day. He will keep you out!

She ran toward the construction site. Alonso followed her. I followed him.

Start the hole already, motherfuckers! A man in a hard hat yelled.

Sí, señor Menard.

Karina ran to him. The man caught her in the air and gave her a piggyback. Soon his button-down shirt was drenched.

Up on a billboard painters were dangling from ropes. They wrote "Hotel Careyes Resort." In the picture a girl frolicked in a huge swimming pool. Above, angelic seagulls hovered over a pink sky.

Swim in Ocean Blue Waters, it read.

My beach. You keep out.

Dig the hole, motherfuckers.

The man with the girl walked into his trailer office.

I brought my shell to my mouth. I sang tremulously, Whose is the beach?

Four

our hair is more pliable with this conditioner, Madre.
   As I gingerly brushed her white curls, I discovered the elegance of an aged lady.
   Arrh . . . , she had said at the breakfast table. Arréglame, I understood, and was happy to oblige. Improving her looks worked wonders on Madre's mood. Appearance meant dignity.
   I patted the chignon and tucked in a silver comb. How would you like some cream on your face now? Your skin is a little dry.
   As I rummaged through her dressing table, I recognized the jasmine fragrance of polvos de arroz—one more thing she had lost with the stroke. I applied some powder in the shade "Porcelana" on my cheeks. It made me look paler.
   What would the makeup be that matched Madre's color—"Siena"?
   I walked back to her bedroom carrying a lotion with basil extract. Her good hand hovered about her face. Poh. Vhh. Ah. Rrrrr.
   ¿Polvos de arroz? I'll give you a massage, and then I'll make you up.
   I worked a little lotion onto her cheeks and neck. She closed her eyes, parted her mouth slightly. She breathed a long, clean sigh. Absent the white makeup she had covered herself with all her life, Madre's skin had a lovely, deep glow. But I knew better than to praise it.
   I sat down and found a novel under the newspaper: *Los recuerdos del porvenir.* Shall we read this one?
   She made the stroking motion toward her face again.
   Oh yes, I forgot.
   As I returned with the makeup, Madre had a lopsided smile.

I chuckled as I applied the fragrant powder to her face. Where do you want to go, viejita?

Who is going out? Luisa asked from the room next door.

¡Madre! I said, loud and clear.

Five

No es nada. Nothing to fear.

Mariana may have grown tired of our little town, but I loved Ayotlan. I did not need to travel—as long as I had my art, I was free.

That is, until the night of the stroke. Now I was a hostage to my thoughts.

Nothing to fear, I told myself again.

A cold sweat drenched me as I caught sight of a bundle at the entrance corridor of that house. Nothing more ordinary: a load of laundry ready to fold, neatly wrapped on a table at a house's door. Yet my pulse raced, my fear unchecked.

I trusted my eyes without question. My vision was my guide, and I knew every cobblestone, the shade of every color, every tree in my neighborhood. My eyes told me it was ten in the morning, and I stood in front of the Zamoras' house, next to the bakery, in the glaring sun, and not in my darkened house at night. No!

I said no to the dark, do not swallow a healthy woman, do not spit out an invalid.

Clean laundry, ten in the morning.

No dark, no wails, no horror.

But there it was in that house's dusky corridor, bulky, shapeless, sepia and maroon. And there I was, back to that night.

It was nine o'clock when I walked into our house, the lights off. How strange for Madre to be away at this hour.

I walked my darkened house carrying a parcel wrapped in

24

brown paper under my arm. I had just framed a painting for Madre; it would take a few minutes to hang it in her bedroom. There a faint light filtered in through the shutters, casting a glow on a heap on the bed. Laundry to be folded.

I was breathing faster. Shallow.

No! I told myself. Stop. Do not take another step.

But I stubbornly walked in, put the picture down—just like that night. I approached the bed, the pile. I dug vigorously.

It was soft, it was formless. Flesh.

I shrieked. Again.

I switched the light on—the bundle was my mother. Slumped, head on her chest, shoulders off balance, eyes glazed. A trickle from her mouth wetting her dress.

I took the telephone from her hand and put it back into its cradle. I cleared from the bed a pile of snapshots and lay her down. The pictures fell to the ground. Many were wet, stained in brown. I touched her. She was warm. She was breathing.

¡Nana! ¡Amalia!

I kissed Madre's cheek. I tasted salt.

I looked around, back from the nightmare. I was standing on the street on a torrid morning, facing a bundle of laundry in a darkened entrance corridor. Next to me on the sidewalk, Mister Zamora stared at me. He seemed to be waiting for an answer.

I was nineteen the day Alonso disappeared and Madre suffered the stroke. I did well as head of a family in crisis. I was proud, and exhausted.

Using my best judgment, I waited a month before calling Mariana to Ayotlan. I spent the first hours and days of my new life with Amalia for only company, tending to Madre, hearing her mutter every possible shred of the word *Alonso.*

I learned what she had found out: that Alonso had gone missing. I consoled her, heard from the doctors about the delicate interaction between trauma and a frail cardiovascular system. I ran to the maddening precinct; I ran to Osvaldo for help.

But I did not call Mariana right away—I did not want to rush her back. With Madre cared for in the hospital and the search under way, there was no need to pry her from the concert tour she had looked forward to for years. But when I reached her in Prague, I realized how much I needed her. I could take some breaks, put my guard down. With her intelligence and energy we could expedite the search, help Madre recover. No one as optimistic and levelheaded as Mariana.

Except now, instead of receiving support, I had to console a bewildered girl who ate like a bird and sat around staring at a book. Un norte—a North Star—was what she lacked. Her tendency to get lost verged on the pathological. This morning she left for a walk a little after dawn. Three hours later, she was not yet home.

Amalia broke the news. She must be all turned around, with the changes in the neighborhood. Luisa, would you look for her?

She can ask directions. I sipped my coffee, glancing at *El Heraldo*'s front page.

Have you heard about these hooligans the newspaper is talking about?

I don't know, Luisita.

Amalia clutched at her sides.

Do me the favor. Please, baby.

I stood up with a sigh, hugged her. Because you ask me, Nanita. But promise you'll tell me what's making you so skittish lately.

I had been asking that question for a month.

Can't you say where you're going?

I had walked the streets for two hours. And there she was, staring at a ruin.

Where is Adrián Landeros's house?

I passed my hand through the crook of her arm.

He sold it and moved to the Gaviotas suburb next to his nephew. They have a family-size Jacuzzi. You should see that.

I was looking for the street vendors. Madre ran out of basil lotion.

I pointed the way to the open-air market. To get there, we walked past several mansions as old as ours. The same neoclassic style, the same square walls, the portal offering a peek of the hidden courtyard. But these mansions were in different stages of neglect. Some were turned into dumps. One was divided into single-room apartments; another was a printing press, an auto body shop, and a parking garage. An ancient tree had been pruned to free the power lines; two vultures rested on its stumps. The street broiled, covered in dust.

Demolished houses, destroyed trees. I had seen these changes over the years. Alone, each was just one sad story. But together, they brought death into our neighborhood.

Didn't Adrián push to declare the downtown a historic center?

I shrugged. He's slowed down since the pneumonia. I'll give you a little surprise. It's close to his old house.

We walked past several other mansions with for-sale signs. Mariana shook her head.

People want air conditioning, I said. Look at Adrián. His nephew said he had to move to a regular house if he wanted them to take care of him. Besides, you'll see the project they started. It made sense for him to sell and take the money while he could.

Mariana seemed to struggle to imagine our godfather making those decisions. All through our childhood, we had played in his house on the bluff, talked to his topiary trees as though they were the heroes of our fantastical stories. There Padre and Adrián argued about the town's fate as if they owned it. Padre wanted cheaper hotels, restaurants, entertainment. Adrián wanted higher prices for elegant people—less is more, he liked to say.

Then came that Menard, and Padre's way prevailed. More tourism brought jobs, cars. A little trash too. And really, where did our educations come from?

We used to play dress-up at his house, Mariana said.

I nodded. With Alonso, Osvaldo.

And Fernanda. Remember Semana de Amor? I saw her at the airport.

I shook my head. I never liked those kissing games.

I know, Mariana said. The cooties and all.

At least I don't go around grabbing those—she grimaced, and I stopped myself.

Then I wished I had not. When would I stop worrying about the effect of my every word on Mariana's mood?

Six

aca was that day's word.

When I was about eight, we had a game for practicing new words. Luisa and I alternated a hop on the green tiles of the Malecón with another on the rose ones—a word for each.

Naca-india-naca-india.

Alonso and Amalia walked ahead, while Padre and Madre shuffled behind us, consulting with Dr. Colunga on Padre's sore joints.

Naca-india-naca-india.

We caught up with Amalia and Alonso.

Don't say that. Where did you pick it up? Amalia said.

I pointed at a group of girls chasing another one, trying to lift her skirt. They call her "india-naca."

Who's naca? asked Luisa. Who's india?

Amalia lit up. It's a person with warm, deep skin and eyes like the night.

Luisa yanked at her own ponytail. Pretty? Black hair? *Blonde* is pretty. Like Mariana. And you, Nana.

She placed her arm next to Amalia's.

Don't be silly, said Alonso, tickling her nose with her own ponytail. I've told you many times how pretty you are, and kind, smart. If you were india, you'd be just as pretty. Those there think they'll feel special if they put someone else down.

But indias live in orphanages, Luisa said and ran to Madre.

The girls were a swarm running in our direction, closing in on the dark-haired girl. Her long braids lashed her hips like soft whips. The others edged closer, grimacing.

She's not wearing underpants. Indias don't wear underpants!

As she approached me, the pretty one tripped on her long skirt.

I offered my hand. That's a bad scrape.

She peered at me, then at the pack. She scrambled to her feet and ran toward a throng of tourists about to board an amphibious bus.

We lost her among the gringos with the sombreros and the shopping bags. The mean girls scattered. Alonso approached one of them, her face like a hunter's. He pointed toward the town. The girl smiled and sped off, her pack close behind. I plowed through the crowd and found the bonita crouching next to the bus's fender.

Come, I said.

I took her hand and led her toward the seawall. We walked down the steps until we reached the sand. Her throat fluttered. Her lips were full and dark like violets. Her cheeks and neck were moist. I wiped her face with my sundress.

It's hot today. Hey! Your eyes are like the night.

She looked at the ocean, then back at me. Yours are like the water.

What's your name?

Fernanda.

And I—

¡Naca! Need some panties?

A mean girl was leaning over the wall above us. She wore the Escuela Pacífico uniform. She was in sixth grade. Other girls joined her.

Mom says indias don't wear underpants so they can piss anywhere they want.

India, did you have to take a leak? Her companions cackled, then started down the steps.

Fernanda looked left and right.

I held her hand tight, sang out a few notes.

Up on the wall, Alonso sang a shrill, undulating song. Holding Luisa's hand, he followed the mean girls. I replied with my own song, keeping Fernanda's hand in mine. The wild girls covered their ears. They craned their necks up to Alonso, then down at us.

Fernanda and I took one step up. I sang louder. Alonso responded, walking downstairs one step at a time. We had them surrounded.

One of them jumped eight or ten steps onto the sand. Others followed. A younger one cried out. They scrambled away.

India lover! one stopped to shout. You'll take your underpants off too?

A fire rose in my chest.

When they were gone, Fernanda kissed my cheek. She smelled of summer rain.

I'm Mariana, and that is my uncle Alonso. And my sister Luisa.

Fernanda turned to them and said Hi. Gotta go now. See you at school.

You go to Escuela Pacífico?

Starting tomorrow.

What grade are you in?

Sixth.

Fernanda slipped her shoes off, held her skirt, and darted along the surf. It was magic—in no moment did her clothes get soiled.

What are you doing down there? Madre called.

I ran up. Madre took me by the arm. Was that india bothering you?

Luisa clung to Madre's thighs. Her little head tilted upward.

Madre, you won't send me to the orphanage, ¿verdad?

Seven

Luisa was afraid of the orphanage, but I could not feel safer. I had her and Alonso, I had two mothers. I had Padre. My doves on the limonaria. Amalia clapped handmade corn tortillas for our supper. To entertain us, she made little donkeys—a tortilla straight from the comal, a few grains of coarse salt, and a sprinkling of water. She mashed it between her hands and shaped the donkey's head and ears. A pretty, soft, aromatic thing, the most delicious.

Once I tried to make one and burned my hands by squeezing the hot dough. Amalia was so strong she did not burn.

I liked to visit her in her room, play with her doll. Her mother had made it for her before she came to live with us. Her name was María.

Like the Virgin?

Like my little sister. I took care of her, held her in my arms.

Is she like the doll?

Exactly.

How old is she?

She died, Mari. She was two weeks old. Always two weeks.

I held María the doll a little tighter against my chest.

Only once I saw Amalia with her hair all loose.

It touches your ankles. It's like gold! Why do you always tie it up?

How could I work with all that stuff hanging loose? I just washed it, and I'm letting it dry before I braid it again.

Can I braid it, please?

I took a brush from the orange crate at her bedside. So much softness.

Can I have braids too, Nanita?

Mari, your hair is too short and thick. It will fall out of the braid with your first hop.

That was Madre's answer; we had it memorized.

Amalia went to the laundry room next door. When she came back carrying a pile of linen, she found me working braids at the mirror.

I told you, it's grown.

I had plaited two or three turns on the left side of my head. More hair fell out of the braid than was secured in it.

Ay niña, so pigheaded. Give me that brush.

Don't forget to pull my bangs off my face. Like you.

I pushed the hair to clear my forehead.

After a lot of work and Dippity-Do, Nana and I stood at the broken mirror, our hair parted in the center, our foreheads free, two braids emerging from our napes. But hers wrapped around her head like a crown.

How long before I can have my own crown?

You know what Madre says—

Ay Nanita, come on! I bet the stylist will help us. It worked last time. I told her, Madre said only to trim it, so she let it almost the same length. How long did it take to grow yours?

She chuckled. Why would you want hair like mine?

It's a queen's cape! If you don't like it, why don't you cut it?

She shook her head. Es una manda.

It's a what?

I was very sickly when I was born. My mother begged the Virgin to protect me; she promised I would never cut my hair for as long as I lived.

And you won't.

She shook her head. Las mandas son promesas.

Madre was calling me.

Amalia stopped me at the door. Mari. Undo the braids.

I turned around—no use arguing. After a good rinse, the

usual coils covered half my face like a yellow cloud, just the way Madre liked it.

I love it when you call me Mari. Is that our secret?

That's what you're called in this room.

She held me, buried her nose in the crook of my neck, and took a deep breath.

Like the gata with her kittens?

She finds them by the scent.

Eight

There was no better time than Christmas for playing at Padrino Adrián's house. After the hurricanes, the protective slats came off from the art deco windows, letting the breeze perfume the drapes, the manila shawl on the grand piano. The orchestra at Hotel Belmar next door helped us celebrate the water's palpitations, the twelve-mile curvature of Careyes Bay.

As little kids we ran in a pack, we rolled on the silken dunes of Playa Careyes, climbed the slopes of Adrián's lawn, talked to the dragons and the peacocks of his topiary trees. Then we walked up the stairs to the terrace. There we stopped at the balustrade carved with seashells, dragons, and mermaids. Alonso pointed at the Nereid and sang, Venus is born. The sea horses pull her scallop across the ocean.

And the winds blow with their chubby cheeks, keep her hair combed back! I said.

A few paces away, the grown-ups made nice with that businessman, Chepo Menard.

Thanks for the lands, buddy, he said once, and everyone's smile froze like in an encantados game. Padre lay a hand on Adrián's back. He would not live to see the next Christmas, but he could still be forceful. He said, Tourism is it, compadre. You gotta hop on board if you don't want to miss the boat.

Where is the boat? Luisa asked.

Menard poured himself a glass of whiskey. The ladies shrank into their shawls.

A guitar trio crooned. Alonso and I added lines to their songs—we would later learn they are called harmonies. The singers made faces, but eventually they smiled like everyone else. Padrino Adrián and Madrina Luz stood up to lead the dance, their patent leather and high heels stroking the black-and-white tiles. We looked out to the fireworks and the valemadrismo returned, the sure-why-not joy of Christmas celebrations.

As we grew, Alonso and I helped soothe the adults' anxieties with our songs. Then, when they looked away, we liked to drink their glasses' dregs. Warmed by the strange fire, we held hands, climbed the flying staircase, walked past the bedroom into the dressing room. Some kids ran around. Some hid behind the gowns. Fernanda and I tried some on. Mine was aqua, hers was orange. She offered me a feathered tiara.

It is perfect on you.

Luisa forced herself between us and switched on an electric candle at the little shrine on the dressing table. She said, It's la Virgen de Dolores, like the one at church.

It was indeed the Madonna of Sorrows, but a precious hand-written card on her pedestal rebaptized her Nuestra Señora de Todos los Placeres.

Ouch turned into aaah! Fernanda said, and we giggled. Luisa did not.

Fernanda's neckline was so open that the blouse was really two wide straps covering her breasts. I teased her hair and let it tumble down her bare back.

Time for semana de amor, said Karina as she locked the door. Barely lit by the candle at Our Lady of All Pains Turned Pleasures, the mirrors showed us a multitude of ourselves.

She explained the rules. Sit on the bench opposite your partner, touching backs. The girls look toward the mirrors, the boys to the altar of the Pleasures.

Alonso, you with me. Mariana, you and Osvaldo. Rosana with Roberto. Luisa, you need a partner. You too, Fernanda.

I'll play with Luisa, said Fernanda.

Karina shook her head. This game is boys and girls.

Then I'll be judge.

Karina nodded. The couples sit up straight, back to back. When Fernanda and Luisa call Monday, the first couple crane your necks. If both look the same way, they kiss. If they look the other way, the girl slaps the boy. OK?

And the judges? asked Luisa.

You call slaps or kisses. Alonso, let's show them.

Monday, Luisa and Fernanda announced. Kiss!

Alonso and Karina faced each other and demonstrated how

35

a kiss lets you give of yourself and receive. The rest watched and practiced air kissing.

Then came Tuesday—Osvaldo and I.

Slap, Luisa announced.

I turned, raised my hand, then dropped it flat on his face. The other kids screeched Ouch! His eyes shone with tears.

On our second turn, Osvaldo elbowed my side, and I knew which way to turn.

¡Beso!

We stood up and turned. I propped my knee on the bench. He put his hands on my shoulders, opened his mouth, and took in my pursed one. I parted my lips inside his and tasted his warm tongue. His shudders rocked me.

After another turn the couples shuffled.

You can have Osvaldo, I told Fernanda. He stepped back.

She said, Nah. I'll be judge.

Everyone looked at her. Who would turn Osvaldo down?

After semana de amor we played hide-and-seek. Karina switched the electric candle off and we roamed in perfect darkness. We sought with outstretched arms, grazing doña Luz's party gowns, the ambassadors of our future. I found Osvaldo and kissed him again.

I kept seeking. Then my hand felt something hard, surrounded by two softnesses. It was Fernanda's chest. She kissed my cheek, said hello into her conch shell, and walked away.

When the game was over we bade the Madonna good night.

Nuestra Señora de Todos los Placeres, Fernanda mocked a mystical tone into the seashell. Take care of our shellphones. We will be back for them.

She lifted the Madonna's frock and placed the shells underneath.

Ooh! *Todos* los placeres.

We laughed. We kissed.

Paces away, Alonso and Karina climbed the spiral stairs. He waved at me, and I waved back.

That staircase led to doña Luz's mirador, her house's crowning glory: a tiny room with windows to the sea. And in it, nothing but a sofa. A monument to the pleasure of two.

I squeezed Fernanda's hand.

Nine

Padre got sick, then he was gone. That's when things changed: the house grew louder and brighter, Madre grew taller, Luisa grew colors. My piano and I became one thing, Alonso and his guitar another.

Madre showed me off like a prize. My closet had more organza dresses and silk sashes than I could admit. Luisa and Madre busied themselves washing my hair with chamomile, preening the yellow ringlets around my face.

But I wanted out. Madre sent me to Padrino Adrián to talk about high school abroad.

Adrián said, Your father, rest in peace, left enough for school, but not in the States. Why don't you ask at the Rotary? I did.

Play a recital, they said. I played the *Polonaise héroïque*.

Fill out the paperwork. I did.

I would do anything for an exit from this town I loved, with everyone in it.

When the scholarship came through, I felt I would explode. I packed and unpacked for a month.

We had a goodbye party the night before my trip: playing music with Alonso, hugging Luisa, drying Osvaldo's tears, dancing with Fernanda.

At daybreak I sneaked into Amalia's room.

Nanita, I have to give you my hug here so no one can take you from me.

Of course. You'll send me a postcard now and then? I want to see the school, your new friends. I want to hear about the recitals. Send me a picture?

A propos. So you won't forget me. I handed her a package wrapped in brown paper.

How could I forget you? It is just one year. You will be back before we know it.

I plopped on her bed.

I want to remember what we looked like now. So you see what I say is true.

She unwrapped the package and took out a picture frame containing the portraits of two girls. A pretty calligraphy read "Quinceañera." The picture on the left was black and white, the cardboard cracked. The girl in it wore her blonde hair in a braid above her forehead; her melancholy gaze reached beyond the camera. I knew the story—Amalia's mother had splurged to celebrate her daughter's fifteenth birthday.

Now you have a framed copy, I said.

Then Amalia looked at the right-hand portrait. It was in bright colors, the paper new. But it was the same. The same pose, the same tiara of braids crowning the face. The same stance. But this quinceañera smiled.

Aren't we like twins?

How did you do this?

I gooped my bangs. We used extensions so the braids could circle my head.

With my hands I performed the movements needed to convert my fluff into something sleek and long enough to weave around my head like hers.

I hugged her.

I'm taking my own copy to New York.

Ten

She is a grown woman, and yet I have to take her by the hand. Show her our town as if she did not know it.

I was in a hurry to walk down Rebaje Street—the heat was picking up. The breeze at the Malecón would cool us.

Remember camping on Careyes Beach when we were kids?

Mariana said, Yes, Karina attacked the turtle, then she said it was her beach.

Yep. Padre sold to that Menard guy who built Hotel Careyes.

Mariana stopped to look at me.

You did not know we used to own that part of Careyes Beach? Padre paid off the other houses with it.

We had more houses?

That's another story. We still own the rest: north from Punta Farayón. Let's go; it's getting hotter.

I wondered if Mariana had read Padre's will—the "small homes" and all. We walked shaded by the great wall of Hotel Careyes. Every twenty yards the roar of air-conditioning units added to the street noise, and we had to hop over the condensation puddles.

On the sidewalk, vendors hawked their trinkets on folding tables. Mariana stopped at one of the stands. We browsed over jars arranged in little pyramids.

Some lotion with basil extract would be nice. Madre looked so happy yesterday with the massage I gave her.

This one is roses and sage, the vendor said. But I do have basil. Just a minute.

And then, looking up, ¡Muñeca!

Belisa! Madre buys the polvos de arroz from you?

From my mother. The herbs are from our ranchito in Concordia. Cosmetics for old ladies, you know. But look here.

Belisa's own crafts lay on the other side of the table.

Combs, barrettes, bookmarks. Genuine tortoise shell. See through—it's translucent. That's how you know it's authentic. It's not cheap—real hard to find. But for you nice ladies, only the best.

And it is hard to find because? Mariana asked.

Se las están acabando. People are overfishing the poor turtles. Jacinto has a hard time getting to them. And then they're this small! Fishermen have to dive to find them in their sleeping spots. Poor Jacinto has to learn to scuba.

A fisherman who does not swim? I said.

Are there other options? Mariana asked.

I don't know. I just feel working in the water is safer. Anyway, you tell me where's a job for us.

She took a barrette.

Let me make you a gift. This will look beautiful in your blonde hair, Muñeca. And for you, Luisa, how about this golden head-band. Nice contrast.

To my dark skin?

Belisa pinned the items to a card.

Our calling card. Come visit one day. You can see me carve the tortoiseshell.

The card had a picture of a smiling Jacinto on his boat, holding a sea turtle by the extended fins. A gash shone on its white underbelly. On the boat's own underbelly a name was written in red Gothic letters: *Belisa.*

Nice name for a boat, I said.

Belisa beamed. Such a romantic, my Jacinto. I'll introduce you. If you come by tonight, you can try the stew I made from last night's catch.

She gathered the fingers of one hand and kissed the tips. Then she drew a graceful circle in the air, as though hurling the kiss for the world to enjoy. Mariana took the card and walked.

Thanks for the gifts, but it's not necessary.

I thanked Belisa, tried to pay, insulted her, rushed after my sister.

Mariana, really!

Left behind was the basil and rose lotion that would heal Madre.

Eleven

We stopped at the entrance of Hotel Careyes.

Is this how Menard made his millions?

His first millions, but not as many as he would like. Padre died before he could buy the rest of the lands. He says he never got enough for the resort he wanted, then others stole his idea and built first.

Mariana did not say anything.

Papá used to say, Tourism brought the goods. Other things too.

We circumvented the building and reached the sea. We sat on a Malecón bench under a coconut tree, facing the construction site. A tangle of bulldozers, diggers, and cranes sat under the billboards. "Hotel Careyes: The Dream at Last!" The main structure of the building was complete. Twenty stories of wall on the street side. On the sea side, rows of arched balconies overlooked the ocean.

Why would the wall on the town side not have windows? Mariana said.

I clicked my tongue. You think tourists want to look at Ayotlecos? They'll surely add some bougainvillea for local color. It's not all bad, Mariana. This project means jobs. It's just the idea of the all-inclusive—I wiggled my fingers like a witch luring children. Come on in, little tourists! Then I growled, Down with the drawbridge, guards!

As if they had heard me, the guards at the entrance of the site puffed out their chests, repositioned their rifles. A flock of seagulls took flight toward the McDonald's.

So they are building a hotel expansion on the town beach, said Mariana. Because?

Prime real estate. Downtown, yet on the water. And apparently the price was right.

The two women stood up. The younger one took the beautiful one's hand and walked her toward the construction site. The guards leered at first but lowered their gaze when they recognized them. Luisa led her sister down a pathway between the construction and a ruin. They finally stopped at a broken wall.

Luisa blew the dust away to reveal carvings—the Nereids and seahorses of their childhood.

Muñeca's eyes darted between the wall and the broken glass. Was she expecting stained glass windows and billowing organza? What she saw were slumping roofs, hanging vines, swallow nests.

Sitting on the carved scallop shell at the feet of the Nereid, a kitten gnawed on a lizard's carcass.

Mariana's face aged, aged, aged. Incredulity, surprise, outrage.

She shouted. This is not Adrián Landeros's house. His house is next to Hotel Belmar. *That way.* She pointed to our neighborhood.

I gazed at her and pointed to the construction site. *That* was Hotel Belmar. Then I pointed to the ruin. *This* is his house.

Her milky lips trembled.

She reached into her pocket. She said, I found this last night.

She handed me a sheet of ruled paper ripped from a schoolchild's notebook. Yellowed, written in faded pencil.

> Queridas Mariana y Luisa:
>   We take care of the ocean. We sing for the nereids and the animals. I hid our shellphones with the Virgen de Placeres in Adrián's house. Remember: only we and Fernanda can sing into our shells. Keep the secret.
>   Alonso

Mariana took my hand. She said, Do you think Adrián can still—? She craned her neck left and right.

I tried to think of something to say.

She said, Let's go to the beach, sí? Get our feet wet.

She ran toward the ocean. Formerly the Malecón curved toward the city, following Olas Altas Bay. Now the removal of Adrián Landeros's house would allow the resort to grow toward the ocean. The billboard said it best: "Make Way for Fun."

She ran down the stone steps to the beach, but before reaching the sand her knees plunged into water.

I explained. Mariana, linda, the tide is up.

The tide, at the wall?

But look.

I held her shoulders gingerly, turned her around. What a surprise I had for her.

There, in a niche on the seawall, in black marble and bronze, stood the homage to Padre. It was as tall as a man. I read out loud.

BY MEANS OF THIS PLAQUE
THE PORT AND CITY OF AYOTLAN HONORS ITS FOREMOST CITIZEN
REMIGIO SÁNCHEZ MORALES
WHO WITH LOYAL DEDICATION SPONSORED NUMEROUS PROJECTS
IN DEVELOPMENT AND TOURISM TO BENEFIT THE COMMUNITY OF AYOTLAN,
THE STATE OF SINALOA AND THE REPUBLIC OF MÉXICO.

CONFERRED BY
JOSÉ MANUEL MENARD, PRESIDENT OF THE CHAMBER OF COMMERCE
ADRIÁN LANDEROS RAMOS, HARBORMASTER OF AYOTLAN
MARIO CHÁVEZ LEY, MUNICIPAL PRESIDENT OF AYOTLAN AND
FEDERICO QUIROGA JONES, GOVERNOR OF THE STATE OF SINALOA.
AYOTLAN, SINALOA, MÉXICO.
FEBRUARY SECOND, NINETEEN HUNDRED AND NINETY.
"TOURISM IS IT!" REMIGIO SÁNCHEZ MORALES, 1930-1976

They were waiting for you to come back to inaugurate the plaque. But then Adrián caught pneumonia, so Menard expedited the ceremony. You should have seen Madre—the whole town celebrating Padre. They will move the plaque, on account of the erosion. It will go in the lobby once the hotel expansion is finished. It will be grand.

I exhaled freely. I had been taking shallow breaths for weeks. I turned to Mariana.

Her face was bathed in tears.

Twelve

I came home to the wrong house.

A house without Alonso cannot be mine. Where we talk through a veil of reticence. Instead of clear words and a strong voice, Madre produces a stutter and a line of spittle. Forced smiles are the only things Amalia, Luisa, and I have to face the intolerable pain.

A house of silence where music always reigned. A home of boisterous games and enthusiasm no more. Madre sits by the phone. I want to console her—but can't she see that a call from Alonso two months after his disappearance grows less likely each day?

Osvaldo updates us regularly on the police investigation. No news, he says most of the time. Quietly, trying to shelter Madre from more pain.

I feel anger. I did not hear of Alonso or of Madre's stroke *for a month*. When Luisa reached me in Prague, I could not suppress the idea that she had not deemed me indispensable. Yes, the concerts. She had to protect me—or keep me out of the way?

I feel remorse too. Everyone expects me to lift spirits, to lead the search and Madre's recovery. And what do I do all day? Lie curled up, half-naked in bed with a notebook and a pen. I scribble something on the G-clef stave. I cross out some notes. I hum a melody, my eyes barely open, shrouded by the mosquito net.

What else can I do? I contacted Osvaldo on my arrival, heard details of the search. Alonso left the restaurant one Saturday night. Then, the ocean may have swallowed him.

Helping Madre gives me the promise of an outcome. That, if success includes the sight of a wheelchair-bound forty-odd-year-old woman who looks and acts like a geriatric patient.

I sit in dusky nooks, a book or a guitar on my lap. The doves alight, looking for seeds. If the phone or the doorbell rings, I listen, hope for the joyous news.

This Tuesday there was a rapping at my door. I covered myself, waited for quiet to return. Instead, a breeze blew into my room. A ray of light hit my eyes.

You know it's almost noontime? Luisa touched my shoulder through the netting. Fernanda is in the courtyard.

I shut my eyelids. Some other day—tell her I'm not OK. I'll call her.

True you're not OK. And you won't get better staying in bed all day.

Go away.

I waited, but she came closer. She was parting the tulle.

I sat up and shouted, Leave me alone! I slapped in her direction, then opened my eyes. In the mirror my hair was wet and disorderly, my chest naked, my expression mean. Next to me stood a very tall person. My skin prickled.

It was Fernanda shaking her hand.

Ay, niña. Qué manita. She leaned forward to kiss me.

I covered myself with the sheet. I'm sorry, Fernanda. I didn't know it was you.

Nada, nada, linda. Now you know. Let me see you!

Oh, I'm awful dirty. Give me a minute to wash up?

Of course.

I waited a moment, but instead of leaving the room, she sat in the wicker chair next to my bed. It was piled with laundry—some folded, some crumpled, some spilling onto the floor. Fernanda's mane was pulled back from her face and tumbled down her back. She glowed. She took an ashtray with a swiveling top from her bag and lit a cigarette. Nobody's perfect, she said sheepishly. Don't tell doña Clavel.

I washed, dressed, combed my hair, followed by Fernanda's gaze. My skin burned.

She asked about Madre and Alonso, showed concern. She bantered. Three other people disappeared on July 14—the same night as Alonso, right? A couple of activists from her biology program. Also Juliana, Belisa's cousin. Would there be a connection?

What could I say to that? I know nothing about my uncle, much less about other people.

45

Fernanda was settled in Ayotlan. She had a project with some beasts at the beach.

Want to take a look?

Sure.

She stopped her cigarette, closed the ashtray, and tucked it into her bag. She stood up and held out her hand. ¿Vamos? Her palm seemed smooth and warm.

I looked at my clock. I sat on the bed and reached for my notebook.

Some other day.

Luisa tells me you've been busy.

Quite.

She leaned over and kissed my cheek. Call me when you're free.

I nodded, glanced at my pillow.

You're a lot prettier standing up, you know?

Thirteen

In Jacinto's hands, the job of butchering a sea turtle seemed straightforward.

The slaughterhouse consisted of a few bright, surprisingly clean rooms, their floors strewn with fresh sawdust. The turtle lay belly up on the cement table. When Jacinto's machete pried the porcelain-like dome open, Luisa and I took a step back. The room was well ventilated, yet my breathing was labored. That the turtle had stopped suffering hardly made the watching bearable.

I went over yesterday's conversation with Fernanda, tried to pinpoint the argument that persuaded me, of all people, to visit this place. I knew I had to do something. I just could not sit on the bench, could not find the music. Meanwhile Fernanda called every day, serenaded me. You remind me of my boss, she said. La Mar is a little sick, but we are healing her.

Eventually I relented.

Glad you decided to come, bonita, she said as we got in her car. Done enough hand-wringing?

And then, We begin with the slaughterhouse.

How could she do this to me?

Jacinto pointed his knife at the center of the turtle's body. They die when we section this part here. They can't defend themselves belly up, he explained. So if they're in a hurry, some compañeros skip the killing and go straight to butchering. But I'm glad you told me you were coming. I had a chance to kill it before you all showed up.

Thanks, Fernanda said. My friends may not want to hear the turtle complain.

Gee, Fernanda, Luisa chuckled. That was thoughtful.

Luisa's eyes were wide, probably taking notes on the color of the gushing blood.

Jacinto cut deeper. You guys are brave. Some people get sick.

That might be me, I said. I'll wait outside. Something cold to drink?

Nice. See you at Cantina Cholita? Women are allowed now.

Let's go, I told Luisa.

You get ahead, she said and took out her notebook and pencil.

I crossed the street, sat near the entrance of Cantina Cholita, and fanned myself weakly. How out of place is a silk fan at a slaughterhouse?

On the water, several boats waited for a wave to hurl them onto the beach. A few refrigerator trucks were parked on the sand, their drivers sitting in cool cabins as fishermen loaded their catch by the wheelbarrow full.

Jacinto was a different person when he showed up at the cantina with Fernanda and Luisa: wet hair, fragrant of soap. A blue-and-purple morral bag hung from his shoulder and across his chest, reminiscent of his Mayan ancestors.

I pointed across the street. Didn't you guys have the entire beach for your boats?

Jacinto nodded. We moved. Some guy Menard paid us a load of cash. He said he wanted his hotel to look good, gave us each something. I got a new outboard engine. We call him the Godfather.

And you moved what—a hundred yards down?

Jacinto smiled. He didn't specify how far we had to go.

We laughed.

He placed a plastic bag on the table.

For you, girls.

I opened the package and had to control a sudden arching. Inside was a second plastic bag with something dark, moist, heart-shaped.

Amalia can make a good stew with that, Jacinto said. It's the best meat. That turtle was a champ. Not big—they don't come as they used to. But still fleshy.

He handed me a small paper bag. There is also something from Belisa.

In the bag was a rose-colored jar. I opened it.

Fernanda took a sniff. Roses. The perfume you wore yesterday?

Aunty is milling the rice for the face powder. It will be ready in two or three days.

Jacinto, Fernanda said. You know it will be illegal to catch turtles soon?

Everyone is talking about the new law. I'm sorry you had to watch me; I thought you had come to buy some meat.

Luisa told Fernanda, I explained about the Seris as we were walking over.

Thanks, Luisa. But I do eat caguama.

I thought turtles were sacred for your people!

It's not so simple. The Comcáac—that is our name—we eat green turtle at communal feasts once or twice a year. But we don't fish for commerce. And we never kill Leatherback. She's our Grandmother.

I know we need to take care of them, said Jacinto. Any idiot can see we'll run out sooner or later. But one has to pay the bills. And where do I find a job? At hotels it's always "come by next week." And Belisa is terrified of restaurants. On account of her cousin Juliana.

Across the street the fishermen were still loading the trucks.

Other business options?

What am I supposed to do—open the neighborhood's fifth estanquillo? There is one señora on every corner selling sweets and beer. No one buys much else.

El pinche dinero, said Fernanda.

I took a whiff of my perfume. This is lovely, Jacinto. My friends loved the jars it came in.

He smiled. Uncle Manolo likes to blow glass. Did you see the ones with animals? He makes shells and mermaids. Pale pink, like a shallow bay.

Could they make more? Fernanda asked.

Jacinto smiled. Belisa's mom dreams of going big.

Madre loves the polvos de arroz. And my madrina Luz used to wear the gardenia perfume, all of it. Was it from Belisa's mom?

How do you know what doña Luz wore? Luisa asked.

Fernanda and I used to sample during parties.

We smiled at each other.

Luisa gazed at us. She asked, Do you also have mother-of-pearl cream?

Sure. That's from the oyster farm.

You have an oyster farm too?

My padrino does. I harvest the oysters and run his stand when the fishing slows down. Belisa scrapes the shells for her cream.

Would she and her mom be interested in setting up a factory? Maybe with others?

Jacinto scratched his arm. There's the comadre she shares the pots and pans with. And the friends on the hills harvest the aloe vera and make the jojoba oils.

I shook my head. But how do you find more customers?

We sell to our acquaintances, Jacinto said. But other people are not going to buy a cream in an old Tupperware. They're going to want a pretty label and such.

Your uncle wouldn't make more jars for a business? asked Fernanda.

Jacinto laughed. You should see his setup. He can make a few a week. How does he get a real glass blower's equipment? Picture us walking into the Banco de México for a loan. Not even if I get a manicure.

I nodded. They wouldn't give my mother credit now, the way things are.

There are other financing organizations, said Fernanda. Not banks or the government. Would you meet with folks from México City? They want to help replace the sea turtle industry with something good for communities.

Fernanda took out a business card.

Who are they? I asked.

Your friend called me yesterday, the one you gave Belisa's cream to for Christmas. It's a nonprofit called BioTerra. They give low-interest loans to business cooperatives. And they train in marketing and distribution, to get rid of the middlemen.

She copied the numbers on a piece of paper and gave Jacinto the card. He placed it on the crimson package on the center of the table.

Thanks, Fer. We'll let you know if we talk to them.

He looked at the plastic bag, then at us. So that's why you came by!

I said, This might be the last time I ever see turtle meat.

For all of us, Fernanda said.

The sun was setting. Under the business card the turtle heart palpitated in the pink light.

Fourteen

svaldo, mira nomás, your head! Luisa rubbed his fuzz.

The sisters and Osvaldo sat on a park bench having ice cream, waiting for the breezes to pick up. Twelve weeks since she had returned to Ayotlan, Muñeca had regained a flair for simple pleasures: taking shelter under an almond tree in Plazuela Salado, watching kids splash at the fountain, licking lemon syrup from a wafer.

The three went over old jokes, reminisced about the roaming serenades they used to offer neighbors and friends. They had all been there. Luisa. Fernanda. Alonso and Karina. Osva, next to Mariana. Loving her.

Now six years later, sitting on that park bench, Osvaldo took Mariana's hand, and she pulled free. He gazed at her hand as she wiped her lips, then settled on her thigh.

Mariana focused on the road, watched every passing car, every pedestrian.

Luisa brought them back.

You said you had new information—a body?

How could Luisa talk like this?

Let me give you some context. Comandante Riquelme's team is sifting through a strip of beach twenty-two kilometers north of here. They recently found a number of bodies.

On Padre's terrenos del mar? Why there?

Osvaldo's mind flew to the ghastly sight at the morgue, the young bodies, four from that night, others from an earlier date, others more recent. Naked. Damaged.

We are thinking of one body. A young, tall male, with long fingernails on the left hand.

Where is he? Muñeca straightened as though off to the morgue.

This is a mummified body. The dry climate preserved it, but the skin is so damaged that it is not identifiable. It pains me so much to tell you this.

Mariana quivered, and Osvaldo struggled to keep the calm tone. Could he enfold her in his arms?

She stood up. I need to see.

Luisa stood too.

You said you would show us pictures. You want to see them, Mariana?

The young women gazed at him. The frown, the stance, the hand on a hip reminded Osvaldo of doña Clavel. No more high school girls, no more anyone's sweethearts.

He produced the photos. The sand, the dunes, bleached cacti, charred grasses. On the Sánchez Celis family's Terrenos del Mar lay the remains of a human being, curled into a fetal position, the arms stretched backward, the wrists bound together. The neck, so bent it seemed broken. Shreds for clothes. Long fingernails on the left hand. A shattered conch shell a few inches away.

Mariana leafed through the photos. She did not want to see the grimace, the burned-out hide. Would it shatter like a buñuelo when touched, or was it hard like a drum?

The last photograph was taken from a distance to include the blue sea. Only then could one see that these were color photographs.

Mariana shook her head, pushed them away. That is not him. He disappeared after work. He was wearing formal clothes.

Osvaldo said, Don't let that fool you.

Looters? Luisa asked. No face, no fingerprints, no belongings. How do we know?

There is DNA testing. It compares genetic characteristics only close relatives share. The problem is, it's not in the Police Department's budget.

We can pay, Mariana said. Anything to have this over with. Should we bring samples?

They have yours and mine and Madre's from our hairbrushes, Luisa said quietly. I got yours the day after you arrived.

The indignation in Mariana's eyes.

I'm sorry, Mariana. We were all so upset. Osvaldo thought the DNA—we thought it best to have information as soon as possible.

How did he die? This—person. Do they know?
Single bullet. Assault rifle. On the nape.

Assault. Morgue. A slaughterhouse. A crimson heart. A charred hide.

A siren wailed, loud, unbearable. From behind the almond trees an old red Impala approached, spewing a lament and black smoke. The driver seemed deaf.

A bloody procession followed.

A rusty VW Beetle.

A scarlet station wagon.

A crimson Ford Galaxy.

A red pickup truck with flames painted on its front fenders.

The siren howled. It howled more.

Mariana covered her ears, pressed her eyes closed. She saw a man in a business suit walk down the street carrying a guitar case. He disappeared around a corner.

She opened her eyes, stood up. What are we doing here? Let Osvaldo do his work.

She touched his arm. Her eyes met his for an instant. Then she turned and walked away.

Luisa kissed Osvaldo and followed her sister. A few paces away, she turned back and waved.

Osvaldo watched them walk away. Not far from here, on the backrest of another bench, were the words he had carved long ago.

> Mar. Aria. Mariana, mar y aire, song of sea and wind.
> Mariana: Sea woman. Osvaldo. 1984.

A few days ago, he had asked her if she would go and listen to some music with him. Alonso and Grupo Amanecer had started a movement—Huapango rhythms, a little jazzed up. Everything acoustic. The gringos called it Bossa Mex—they always have to find a label.

She said she would think about it, maybe some other day.

But Osvaldo did not dare ask again. Would she want to hear something of Alonso's, as though in celebration?
With him?

Fifteen

Careyes had been twelve miles of sandy paradise crowned by Adrián's mansion and the stately Hotel Belmar. Then the Belmar fell and the towers of Hotel Careyes grew and surrounded Adrián's house like sentinels. Now Menard had acquired Adrián's land, was building the central wing, and was poised to fully harvest the beauty his resort promised.

What would Alonso say about that?

North of Ayotlan, Boca de Cachoras remained. Luisa and I ventured there in the evenings seeking healthy waters to swim our daily laps, let the ocean cleanse us. It felt like sheer luck that Padre had acquired that tract of land outside Ayotlan. There the mirrorlike waters sustained me with cool buoyancy. I could swim, concentrate on my movements, nothing else.

We parked the car and climbed the dune. Tiny lizards flitted among the grasses. When the dune became steep, I pulled on the green manes for balance. On the summit we looked on the garland of bays: pearl and turquoise and gold. So many bays they got lost in the distance. When we rushed down, the hot sand crackled between my toes.

We dropped our bags and kept walking. On the intertidal slope we stepped on cool, hard sand. Then creamy sand.

We stopped for a moment to greet the crabs in the pools. An octopus slinked under a rock.

We went in. We floated.

Luisa swam from point to point of the rock-lined bay. Instead, I swam in a slow breaststroke toward the setting sun. Frigates and terns plunged around me, catching their evening meal. An osprey soared.

I enjoyed the sea, but was always vigilant. The jellyfish, the barracudas, the sting rays—I tried to block out the thought of the carnivore or the venomous swimming inches from me. Never touching, supremely able to hurt, yet choosing not to. Until when? I tried to focus on the surface and the birds overhead. Infinite, ancient—the sea was my constant. It would be here for millions of years, after I and my concerns were no more.

I hoped.

I swam, my head above water. So slow, I could never tire.

There were two other women. They, too, favored a leisurely pace and headed toward the sunset. They chatted and chuckled, slowing often to tread water, so close to one another I wondered if their feet were tangled. As I swam past them, one rested her forehead against her companion's cheek.

Hello, I said.

Good evening. They smiled at me, glanced at each other, and swam away.

I felt a shock of recognition. Those two were together. They trusted each other. They took pleasure in each other.

As I swam toward shore, I looked again. Could I put my feelings into words? The pressure in my chest, something dizzying and important and unnamed.

I reached the water's edge and waited for Luisa. I sat on the rocks, toweling my hair. Dusk settled over the tiny beach like a blanket.

There she was. I said, Luisín, did you—

But she spoke over me.

Hey, Mariana, did you see those tortilleras? What would Papá say if he saw them do their stuff on his beach?

Sixteen

As we headed to our car, we made out shadows roaming behind the dunes.

Mariana, Luisa whispered.

Ten soldiers in assault gear. More. We picked up the pace. We had almost reached the car when a voice barked.

¡Alto! ¡Ejército Nacional!

I slowed down.

Hands up!

Metal clanged against metal. I began to turn around.

I didn't say to show your pretty face.

The cool water, the gentle breeze, the smiles of two lovers, the calls of the birds—all gave way to fear and anger. I clenched my shoulders. Luisa muttered.

One of them paced behind us, spewing his hot breath on my shoulder.

We held our hands up.

Something metallic tapped my ankles. The barking voice said, Open your legs.

I shook. Water was dripping from my bikini.

A woman's laughter. I knew that voice!

Fernanda. ¡Eres tú!

Ya. Now don't be pouty. Put your arms down. Let me introduce you. Come on, girls! Being army doesn't make them bad guys.

I struck her on the arm.

You scared us shitless with your little joke.

Fernanda turned to the men. It worked, guys! Then to me: niña, your little piano hands can hit. I'll let you know if you leave a mark. Now come on.

You will tell me what you're doing here?

We are patrolling the beach.

Since when does the army hire biologists?

No, no. The army works for *us*. Armando—Sargento Bermúdez. Can you explain?

Sure, though you're boss, Dr. Lucero. We are protecting this beach.

From narcos?

He smiled with white, disorderly teeth.

That's our day job. Now we are freelancing for the turtles.

Fernanda nodded. We survey turtles for the National University, protect the nests. The moon and the warm breeze will make a good nesting night. The moms should be here any minute now. Want to help?

What do we do? Luisa asked.

I looked to the cove where the two women had been.

Shout "Mamá" if you see one. Also if you see two-legged coyotes.

Say what?

Coyote.

I glanced at the soldiers. But no violence?

We've never confronted poachers at this particular site.

But imagine, Fernanda said. The stories you get to tell your grandchildren.

Just for that, I'm staying, said Luisa.

The students in the group started a fire, took vegetables, meat, and tortillas out of a cooler. Everyone crouched around the food. I stood back, gazing toward the mangrove.

Fernanda called, You'll need food if you want to last the night, reina. Those mama beasts will give us plenty to do. Have a taco or two, and a good drink of water.

The sky was graying.

Fernanda came to me with a taco in her hand. The first is for you. Friends again?

I opened my hand. Fernanda's hand nestled itself into mine.

The night was breezy and bright with the full moon. It was also abuzz with mosquitoes, goopy with eggs and stinking of turtle.

One beached near me. It shone in the moonlight like an alien dressed in silver. I could hardly shout "Mamá."

Golfina, yelled Fernanda. Beginner's luck.

The turtle dug; the biologists measured her, counted and collected the eggs. They got dusting after dusting of sand. Students placed the eggs in coolers. Fernanda clutched a clipboard with a tiny light clamped on it. Everyone addressed her, Doctora Lucero.

The army men moved behind the dunes.

I was riveted; I learned to assist with measuring, counting, collecting. When a turtle came up, the scientists called ¡Golfina! like an endearing swear. Were they little sluts because their mates were unidentified? I soon realized *golfina* meant "olive ridley," the most common species. There were also some cries of ¡Prieta! Black turtle!

Then someone gleefully shouted ¡Carey! The gorgeous hawksbill was making a rare appearance. She was golden in the moonlight.

In my mind I was a little girl. I escorted a hatchling into the waves.

How long does a hawksbill take to reach reproductive age? I asked Fernanda.

Twenty, thirty years.

I saw one hatch about seventeen years ago.

Fernanda nodded. This is your Moosni Quipáacalc, nena. Look how big she got.

Wasn't that at Careyes? Luisa asked. Don't they always come back to the beach they were born on?

There are exceptions. Playa Careyes is busy now, so your little sister came here instead. Look how pretty are the jewels on her back.

The rainbow patterns glowed in the moonlight.

Fernanda measured the nest. These will be females.

How do you know?

The temperature in the nest decides. If it is cool, the hatchlings will be male. But add a few degrees and they'll be female. The mom creates a batch of boys or girls, depending on how deep or where she digs. Sometimes a nest is very deep. The bottom hatchlings might be male and the top female.

Don't they get mixed up at the hatchery?

We give them the same conditions they would have had in

the wild. We'll dig this nest in a sunny place, so you'll have a whole bunch of little nieces in sixty days.

The leathery eggs plopped gently into the bucket placed inside the nest. Fernanda came and went, making annotations. At one point she took out her pocketknife.

Here, so no one forgets this is your Quipáacalc. My dad did this for my Moosnípol sister back home.

She carved tiny letters on the carapace: MSC. Mariana Sánchez Celis.

You know your Quipáacalc, but your loved ones might need help recognizing her.

I crouched next to Fernanda as she worked her knife. At times her thigh grazed mine. Her skin was silk.

We stood up at the same time. I circled her neck, rested my head on her shoulder.

Fernanda hummed and stroked my hair. Quipáacalc will take you on her travels, she said.

Thus the lone migrant brought me to the world of the living. The mother covered her nest, then clumsily crawled back to the water. There were tears in her eyes.

Once home, she rushed to the depths with a graceful stroke of her fin. She scraped my thigh.

Fernanda held my hand.

¡Laúd, Doctora Lucero! a student shouted.

Moosnípol, Fernanda whispered, and bolted. I ran after her.

The student laughed. That leatherback is the size of Doctora Lucero's VW!

But once next to the turtle, Fernanda's head dropped. Just a large prieta, she told the erring student. Moosnáapa, not Moosnípol. She walked toward the dunes and dropped her clipboard on the sand.

We haven't seen a leatherback here in decades, a scientist told me. He whispered something in Fernanda's ear and took the record book after she nodded.

I sat next to her. She smoked with one hand and doodled snakelike figures in the sand with the other. She said, I've waited all my life to see her again.

She spoke as though referring to a loved one lost in the immensity.

I stroked her hair. The breeze picked up, and two slender clouds passed over the moon. Fernanda's smoke billowed toward them.

My knee bled from the hawksbill's scrape.

You need iodine.

Fernanda stood up, found the first-aid kit, cleaned the wound and bandaged it. She kissed my cheek and went back to work.

It was as if she had gone home and closed the door.

The sky blushed timidly. Fernanda read from her notes.

Eighty-six mothers, no disturbance—though I saw a couple trucks parked behind the dunes for a good hour, Sargento Bermúdez?

He nodded. They were probably waiting to see if we would leave.

Approximately 12,430 eggs. Not bad.

Twelve thousand eggs is not bad? Do you really need guns to protect them?

We'll be lucky if from this batch forty turtles come back to nest. Without our friend soldiers the coyotes would not leave a nest standing. Twenty years ago turtles came in by the thousands. The new law is the least we can do if we want any turtles at all.

Sargento Bermúdez grinned. When the hunting ban goes into effect, we'll be doing this patrolling as our regular job. No more moonlighting.

Hey, you'll sleep better, Luisa said.

And the income?

Fernanda chuckled. There will be plenty of problems you can help us with, Sargento. When have we been without, ¿pues?

Morning was breaking, and everyone stank. The students took coolers loaded with eggs to the hatchery. Fernanda, Luisa, and I stayed behind.

Shall we take a dip? We can clean up with sand.

Fernanda undid her braids and took off her shorts and tank top. She wore nothing underneath. From the front, her waist and hips hardly curved, giving the impression of extreme slenderness.

Yet no bone stuck out on her chest or collarbone. Behind her rump cascaded her black hair. One could hardly make out her nipples from the surrounding skin, it was so dark.

I glanced away.

Oh, Fernanda said. I forgot my bathing suit.

Aren't you afraid of men out here?

Who would touch la india Fernanda, friend of macho soldiers?

She scrubbed her head with sand, and we followed her example.

Don't forget your scalps and foreheads. A lot of muck gathers there.

Rubbing mud onto the bikini marks on my sides was a balm.

In the water, Fernanda and Luisa raced across the bay while I did handstands and somersaults. Luisa reached the end of the cove, panting. Fernanda trailed her underwater—a black dolphin with a train of black hair. She touched a rock, turned, and headed back. She touched my waist. Then she came out.

How can you stay underwater so long?

Fernanda shrugged, and her hand dropped from my side. The water covered my chest, but not hers.

Luisa swam laps across the bay, her arms arched like fins.

¡Moosnípol! Fernanda called. A good swimmer like my sister.

Shall we swim out to sea? I asked.

When we turn back, we'll be facing dawn, Quipáacalc. Your return.

We swam breaststroke, our heads above water. The soreness in my joints began to ease.

So I am hawksbill and Luisa is leatherback. Like you?

Leatherback are our kin. The one my dad carved with my name was this huge sister Moosnípol. She might be in Japan now. That's how far she travels.

And you swim like one. Thanks for slowing down, though. I yawned.

Tired Quipáacalc! How long have you been up—twenty-four hours?

She looked out to sea. Your sister is probably gorging on jellyfish now.

Visions of a hawksbill racing in waters teeming with jellyfish filled my mind. Far from resisting it, I relished the image. On the surface the water was a mirror. I blew some bubbles.

They are your kin?

She nodded. Moosnípol is grandmother to us Comcáac. She built the earth with sand from the ocean bottom. She brings us news from far.

I nodded, and my chin dipped. I licked the salt on my lips.

You know the ocean better than anyone. Is there anything here you're afraid of?

How would it help? Just relax and move. Breathe.

It seemed easy in the calm waters. Her long arms stretched under the surface, parted, and drew a large circle.

She grazed my side.

I'm in your way, I said. But neither one of us changed course.

I was five years old when I saw Moosnípol. She is the last anyone has seen in Punta Chueca. Talk about endangered.

But that's where the analogy ends. The Comcáac have been around forever. The Spaniards couldn't wipe you guys out.

Nor the Mexicans. We know to stay afloat. That's why they sent me to school in Ayotlan.

Your parents sent you here as a kid—to help your people?

The elders asked, and my folks couldn't say no. They wanted me and others to learn the Mexican ways to get the Comcáac ahead. A Moosni Cooyam learns fast, they said. I became a migrant because I was good at languages. Some job for a ten-year-old.

I'm sure they're proud of your PhD now. What a recognition for your people's knowledge of the natural world. I blinked a few times. What other kinds of Moosni are you?

My limbs felt warm in the water, the strain gone. Would I stay afloat if I stopped for a moment?

Moosnáapa, of course. Big like a green turtle monster.

She slowed her pace to match mine.

I pinched her cheek. And just as ugly.

But sometimes, just sometimes, I must be a golfina.

A Moosni Otác?

Aha. A common, unassuming little slut.

She turned to me, and our mouths met. Her tongue was salty. She licked my lips.

I opened my eyes wide; my arms stopped. I dipped. I swallowed. I struggled back up and broke into a cough. Panic fluttered in my chest.

Fernanda reached under my arms. She pulled my chest out of the water and floated on her back. She rested my nape on her chest and turned my chin to one side. She held me below the rib cage, exposing my breasts. I struggled.

Breathe, Quipáacalc. I'll take you home.

Fernanda swam toward shore, my safety raft. Her hair floated about my flanks, enthralling me.

The sun dressed the bay in violet.

Buen día, whispered Fernanda, kissing the crown of my head. Buen día.

Luisa waited on shore, sitting on her haunches.

I stumbled out of the water as she walked away from us.

Seventeen

esert. I know I heard the word *desert.*

I wheeled myself down the corridor, inspecting the begonias, expunging a weed or two.

Osvaldo and my daughters chatted and sipped lemonade under the limonaria tree. They watched me mill about in the wheelchair, heading off the hibiscus. They celebrated my new mobility; the girls joked about my arm muscles. Yes, the rehab is paying off, I said. Then the conversation sagged. So I went on to pick some low-hanging mangoes and guavas, placing them into the bag I hung from my armrest.

When I reached the limonaria, I heard the word *desert* again. Desert, in Ayotlan? And this muttering? It was Alonso, I knew. There he was in their controlled voices. In Mariana's stroking the dove as if it were a doll.

I came closer. They did not see me.

. . . same place where the others were found.

I got closer yet. Osvaldo looked up.

Doña Clavel, your garden is truly gorgeous.

Gracias, Mijo. I finally can do something useful.

You can do a lot, Madre, Mariana said. Luisa nodded. They smiled.

I got busy again, wandered toward the service area. Only when I reached the other side did the whispering resume. I turned to approach them from behind. Mariana fed the doves rice from her hand; Osvaldo watched her, his eyes soft. Luisa watched them.

I hid behind the limonaria foliage.

. . . the other ones. At the nape, assault rifle.

My skin prickled.

How do we know it is Comandante Riquelme? Mariana's hand shook.

His wife provided identification. She's devastated.

Mariana pressed a fist. Then she opened it, dropping the seeds. Camelia picked on them.

I let go of the wheel handle. My knuckles ached.

Regrettably, we've lost the only official we trusted, Osvaldo said.

Is it a warning?

Mariana dropped the rest of the seeds at her feet. The doves pecked, but they could not keep up with the cascade, so they ambled away.

Any news about the first body?

Don't forget there are four bodies, Osvaldo said. The case is not complete if we do not understand who they are and what happened to all of them.

Luisa let out a huff, and the doves flew off to the limonaria. Can we afford DNA for four? We don't even have an ID for left-handed-fingernails.

I cringed.

Osvaldo stared at his hands. We've got a problem there too.

Mariana dusted off her lap, bit her lower lip. Her mouth looked raw.

Let it out, Luisa said.

About your DNA samples. The lab people have some questions.

Mariana stirred on the bench. They make us wait weeks, now they have questions. What about answering ours?

They won't tell me anything clear, Mariana. All I know is they want to perform another study. They say they will take care of the costs. They just want accurate results.

Luisa smirked. Is there a mutation in our genes?

Mariana stood up among a flurry of black-and-white feathers. So what if we're mutants or apes? What matters is finding Alonso.

She paced along the corridor. I concealed myself as best I could.

Mariana was almost shouting now. We submitted the samples months ago. How long after Alonso went missing? She covered her face. Her shoulders heaved.

Osvaldo walked toward her. I'm so sorry, Mariana. Even when procedures are straightforward, they take time. The Police

Department is understaffed. The lab is overwhelmed. A lot of people are looking—

He placed his hand between Mariana's shoulder blades, cupped her elbow with his other hand.

Sit down, Nena. Let's try to be calm.

Nena. The endearment Osvaldo had used for Mariana during their adolescent relationship brought warm memories. He was the only one who could comfort her now.

Mariana shook him off and walked toward her bedroom. The door slammed.

Minutes later, Osvaldo stood up. Luisa folded her arm with his and walked him to the door.

You'll keep us informed—whatever it is? Her voice was soft.

Who's taking Comandante Riquelme's place?

Someone from here. Menard says México City cops are not trustworthy.

And what does he have to do with this case? What did the local cops accomplish before Riquelme took over—besides asking us to be patient?

Above them, a cloud of moths swarmed the lamp.

I picked up some clothes in the laundry room, Juana on my shoulder. The doves seemed so attached to me lately. As I walked out, Madre was sitting in the dusky corridor. She looked so small.

Mija, is everything OK?

Sí, Madre. Osvaldo was talking to us about the investigation. I placed my hand on her shoulder. Nothing to report, unfortunately.

Oh, child. We've got to be patient. You'll see. When we least expect it, Alonso will be opening that door. We'll embrace him, and this nightmare will be over.

I smiled tenderly. Madre's words brought back the times when Alonso uttered sweet melodies, when I accompanied him at the piano. When Madre was the pillar of our family, when Luisa colored our world, when Amalia was sunny and open. So much more than months had passed.

I leaned over to kiss her.

Are you going out with Osvaldo tonight?

I stopped before my lips reached her face. Juana flew off.

You've been following that story too?

My sharp tone surprised me.

She shook her head. I'm busy with my own things. I feel better, even if I can't walk.

I'm glad, Madre. But listen. I am not going out with Osvaldo. Don't worry about me.

I went to my room.

I crossed my daughter's threshold. ¿Se puede saber?—what keeps you so busy that you can't keep Osvaldo company, thank him for all he does? And must you have these animals in your room?

Mariana glared at me silently. No matter; I knew where to find answers to my questions. Since she was little I could gaze down her body, read her intentions as though tattooed on her. Tease apart the story of an afternoon of homework from the truth of playing hooky with the boyfriend.

Camelia. Mariana picked up the dove, made her coo. Osvaldo is not helping us in order to get something from me. He's Alonso's friend, a friend of all of us. And if you need to know, I am working at the beach tonight.

Yes. Those were the plans written on her arms. On her shoulders.

To my regret, I saw more. Her panting chest told me. The blush on her neck. Her fleeting eyes. There was more than work in my daughter's plans.

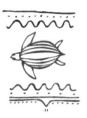

Eighteen

ave you considered coloring your hair, Fernanda?
We stopped painting and turned to look at Madre sitting in the middle of Alonso's room.

You would not pass as blonde, mind you. But a chestnut shade would make a difference. You—you could control the greasy look.

Mariana dropped her paintbrush, and it clattered on the tiles. ¡Por favor!

Cállate, I said to Mariana. Don't shout at Madre.

Amalia ran out. Fernanda shrugged. She was the only calm person in the room.

Mariana had decided to reorganize Alonso's room, and I was glad. Anything to take her out of the dark room where she read all day and stared at empty corners. Away from nights chasing sea turtles and who knows what else. Cleaning cleared the mind. What I did not anticipate was Fernanda joining the party. Even less did I expect Madre to poke around. And now this teasing? What had Fernanda done, other than look the way she did?

I could almost understand Madre. I liked Fernanda all right, but I was weary of seeing Mariana and her always together, as though joined at the hip. Why could Mariana not open the piano and practice?

Amalia came back with a scrubbing brush and a pail with water. Mariana and I wrested them from her. We busied ourselves with the cleanup.

Fernanda continued to paint and Madre to chatter.

You're a smart girl. It is not your fault your people decided to clamp down over there, what's the name of the island you come from?

¡Madre! Now even I hissed. Fernanda glanced at me with a small smile.

I come from Punta Chueca on the Sonoran coast, señora. But we do own a little island. Have you heard of Isla Tiburón?

I chuckled. Isn't it the largest in México?

Twelve hundred square kilometers. We take care of the animals and plants there.

Good for you, Madre said. You can't be blamed if your people stay primitive. Pretending nothing is amiss with their life has not done them any good. They seem to finally recognize that. Didn't they send you over at—how old were you?

Eleven.

You learned Spanish well.

Fernanda knows a few things besides Spanish, viejita. In fact, she is the best-educated person here. Unless you are hiding a PhD diploma in your armoire.

Felicidades. You are learned, now you can get ahead, get along with people.

Mariana scrubbed the floor forcefully.

And all that begins with my hair?

Could Fernanda be taunting Madre? Was she enjoying the confrontation? There she was, innocently glancing at her braids. They fell, woven with turquoise and opal beads, to her waist.

Does it look dirty?

Mariana stood up. She gently took one of the braids and brought it to her nose.

I love the perfume. Is it rosemary?

Madre held forth. Some things we cannot change. Like me, I do not deny I am somewhat dark. Not like you, of course. Tú eres india pura. Let me tell you my story. My father married the best woman in the world. Except that joining her, he took a step down the ladder. Because Madre was a mestiza.

And, as we know, I said with a singsong, Español y mestiza da castiza. ¡Española no! It was the story she had droned into us since childhood.

How would we tell ourselves apart without our handy nomenclature?

And what did these racist terms have to do with my family? I looked down at myself, and at Madre: coffee with a drop of milk. And at Mariana: pure cream.

Madre went on. My daughters are fair as can be. And Mariana is even blonde. That is how marriage can improve families.

Me, fair? Now, that was a departure from the script.

Do you have a boyfriend, Fernanda?

No, señora. Free as a swallow. She winked at Mariana. She was pure chocolate, what Mariana drank for breakfast: spicy cocoa with cinnamon, no milk. Every morning, she touched her lips to the dark, frothy liquid. I saw Mariana and Fernanda swimming in a cove. My sister drinking from those dark lips. Being pulled out of the water, naked and half-drowned, by a woman as tall as a man.

Mariana smiled at her. A heat rose from my belly.

Madre resumed her lesson. Have you wondered why the rich are prettier? Rich men have a choice of women. They want healthy, fair.

And they can buy them, I said. Perdón. I meant, marry them.

Is that why well-to-do people are often fair? Now my genetics lessons at university are making sense.

Not only the men pick. I am satisfied with the decisions I made with my marriage. Thanks to Remigio, may God have him in His Glory, things turned out well for my daughters. He used to exercise on his stationary bike in his shorts. The sweat rolling down his legs looked like milk, he was so white. Like you, Mariana. You do remember that?

Not really.

Maybe you could perm your hair.

A perm? I can't believe I haven't thought that, señora. And these braids are—nacas? She pulled on one. These Comcáac ribbons have to go?

¡Madre! Will you let us work?

Mariana is right. I disengaged the wheelchair break. The paint fumes can't be good for you. And your radionovela is about to start. Why don't I take you there?

She pushed my hand away and reengaged the brake. Girls, I don't understand the haste with changing Alonso's room. He won't recognize it. And that hay color?

I'm sure he would—he will approve. It's sunny.

Like Mariana's hair, I said.

And Amalia's, said Fernanda. Let me compare. She took Mariana by the shoulders and walked her toward Nana, put their heads together. Same color. I'll bet if you wrap braids around your head like Amalia, you'll look like Michelangelo's Delphic Sibyl.

Yes, I think my hair is now long enough.

Mariana pulled her bangs from her face, revealing a high forehead and long, straight eyebrows. She looked like a ballerina.

Madre seemed to simmer.

Come to think of it, I said to Amalia, you too must have looked like the Sybil when you were young. I can't believe you've never shown me your kid pictures. I'll show you the Delphica, and you show me yourself at ten or twelve?

Nana's eyes darted from Mariana to me, to Madre.

I don't know if I have pictures. I'll look—all done here.

And she was gone.

I wheeled Madre to the table with the phone, the chime, the radio.

How old was Amalia when she started working with us? I can't believe I don't know how old she is.

Oh, I don't remember.

There it was, the handy faulty memory.

Is it true she was a little girl? Alonso says they used to play with her rag doll together.

Of course not. How would a little girl work as a maid?

Madre gripped the wheelchair's armrest.

I agree. Children's only obligation is to study and respect their elders, right?

I found Fernanda sitting on her haunches under the ficus outside my house, some twenty feet away from the entrance door. She stood up when she saw me. She was polishing something between her hands.

I am so sorry, querida. My mother can be a brute.

Don't worry, buki. I'm used to it. It's just a matter of saying the truth.

I looked up at the street. Cars passed slowly by.

Look buki, I made this for you.

She offered me a carved wooden spiral.

So beautiful! Is it ironwood? Did you just make it?

One of my many talents.

The bracelet was adorned with two sea turtles facing each other. I pointed at the smaller one.

¿Quipáacalc?

And here comes Moosnípol to meet her. Try it on.

It seemed loose on my wrist.

No. It goes between your elbow and your shoulder.

She eased it up my arm.

Thank you, dear.

I rose on tiptoes to kiss her. She found my lips.

A large SUV passed slowly by. The headlights were off.

Nineteen

Mariana walked toward the water, the rising sun on her shoulders. As her little feet plowed through the sand, she felt a rugged surface. She sang into her conch shell: it's a sea star.

A star indeed, Alonso sang back. He pointed at the water. And your hawksbill, he said. Look how far she's gotten. It is a good day.

With her hand cradled in his, they walked back toward their tent. Through the wisdom of dreams she knew Luisa was still sleeping. Beyond the tent stood a small bentwood arch decorated with crimson blooms. Next to it sat a beautiful girl.

Mariana shifted in her bed, and her hand dug under her pillow. She cherished the cool sheets and the dream ushering her back to childhood. The breeze, the sand, Alonso. A faint whirring underlining the waves' rhythm reminded her of chicharras, those tree-dwelling beetles who announce the clouds loading up a storm.

Careyes Beach—a strange place for chicharras.

The girl by the arbor crouched with her feet tucked under her body, singing gentle sounds. Her black hair cascaded down her back. Mariana's heart caught a flutter when their eyes met. Her cheekbones were decorated with two wavy lines the color of sand, crowned with green and blue dots like freckles.

We will do your faces, she said, and reached for a scallop shell containing powders in all shades of sea and sand. Then we can sing to Moosnípol.

Alonso knelt and offered his face to her paintbrushes. Then it was Mariana's turn. When the three children's faces were adorned with the blue of the waves and the white of the sands, they looked under the ocotillo arbor.

There she was—Moosnípol. Her carapace was marked with seven parallel edges, the lute strings she is named after—now enhanced with gypsum powder. Two small letters were carved on her side: FL. Fernanda Lucero.

Ihapa iya ihapa, Fernanda sang. A lullaby for the slowest animal on earth. She repeated the verses with short pauses, looking into Mariana's and Alonso's eyes.

They tried repeating the song.

Ihapa iya ihapa.

Fernanda repeated, listened. With a few more iterations she was satisfied with her pupils' singing, and the song's meaning gradually opened up to Mariana. Moosnípol, the fragile one, brought sand up from the depths. The gracious one built our earth and is now back, needing our assistance.

Mariana sang along. She offers herself to our celebration.

We give her shelter.

Fernanda bathed her with water from a gourd. We will keep her company these four days.

Until she returns home, Mariana repeated. Where we all will meet again.

The dream brought Alonso to Mariana. A joyful place where nothing was lost.

Four days of singing next to Moosnípol passed, Fernanda's melodies floating under the arbor. Alonso pointed at the leather-back's dorsal lines, as if noting the melody on a tablature. The arbor's branches were tangled with pungent limonaria. Flowers fluttered, landing on the children's hair and the turtle's back.

Then Alonso, Mariana, and Fernanda flanked Moosnípol on her return to the depths. Fernanda spat at the letters carved on her carapace.

Fernanda called, Remember your friend: Fernanda Lucero. My fortune goes with you.

See you when you come back! Alonso and Mariana called into their seashells.

Laced with the chirping of the chicharras, the song brought the children and the buzzing of the insects to the courtyard in their home.

Under the limonaria, the children built an arbor as small as their hands to commemorate Moosnípol. Mariana placed her conch shell where the turtle would be. Ihapa iya ihapa, they sang. Camelia alighted on Mariana's shoulder, Juana on Fernanda's. Little Luisa crouched next. Mariana pulled her close and stroked her hair.

In her bedroom, the adult Mariana shuddered under a cool draft.

In the courtyard, the child Mariana looked up. Her mother stood before her, blocking the sun: beautiful, frightful. Camelia flew off.

What muck did you paint on your face? Madre demanded and wiped the blue and green and white makeup off her daughter. Mariana touched her face, then looked at her fingers. The smear was a cloudy sea. But in Clavel's fingers the makeup turned to tar. She touched her face in distress, staining it dark.

Juana took flight. Luisa wept.

The pain of Moosnípol shows on the face of those who hurt her, Fernanda said with a tinge of sorrow as she looked up to Clavel. Then she smiled at Mariana. Don't worry; blue is the ocean. Our home.

She traced the waves on Mariana's cheeks.

At the kitchen door, Amalia nodded. Luisa ran to her.

Clavel saw her black hands and wailed, piercing the song of the chicharras.

In her bed, Mariana dipped her head under the pillow.

In the courtyard, Clavel left in a rage. Alonso touched Mariana's and Fernanda's shoulders. He pointed to the limonaria tree. The girls climbed up and soon swayed on a branch, looking down on the house surrounding them. They giggled as Camelia and Juana alighted on their heads. The girls rubbed noses. A dark nose. A pale one.

Here, Mariana giggled in her sleep.

There, Alonso sat in a wicker chair next to the limonaria. He played the song they had sung on the beach. The girls hummed. The doves cooed; the chicharras whirred.

Amalia and Luisa disappeared into the kitchen as Clavel returned, demanding Mariana's whereabouts. She lifted her hand menacingly, stained a tarry black. Her hair waved and writhed and lurched as though moved by muscles.

The children pitied her. On the tree, the girls looked up at the clouds sailing past. They held hands, dark and pale. Mariana brought her seashell to her mouth: todo claro, she whispered. It is true: ihapa iya ihapa.

Alonso answered. All clear here too. Ihapa iya ihapa.

Time was true on the limonaria tree.

But the song changed and turned shrill, drowning the voices and the doves' cooing. It grew louder, locking a tremulous E. Then the E grated, turned sharper, and soon it was an F. Now the F was bursting into an F sharp.

There, the trees smoldered in white light. The noise pierced. Black-and-white feathers strewn about the branches.

I opened my eyes and lifted my head from under the pillow. There was a damp spot where my head had rested. As I sat up in bed, sweat trickled between my breasts.

I pressed my temples. The head-splitting noise from my dream lingered as I walked to the door. I opened it, and the noise became unbearable. A wild light blinded me. I had never seen such glaring light in the corridors. The foliage had always kept them shady and cool. But now the courtyard was littered with branches. A bird's nest, broken eggs. Black-and-white feathers.

¡Camelia, Juana!

On the limonaria, two men straddled branches, wielding chainsaws.

I bolted to my room, threw some clothes on, ran back out. My shouts startled them.

Please cut only one branch. This is a very old tree, and it can't take many changes. We'll prune a different branch next year.

Señorita, we are not pruning, the older worker said, a puzzled look on his face. La patrona said to cut the tree down.

Hold it there. Please don't do anything until I talk to my mother.

In her room, Madre was placing a glass with water on the little altar next to her bed. She crossed herself for San Antonio, then scowled at me.

Niña, you need to learn to knock on doors. What's the matter now?

The limonaria, Madre.

Oh. How long before it's gone?

Gone? Why would you kill it?

Mijita, that tree only makes debris. It doesn't give fruit. Amalia is too busy to have to sweep all that every morning.

Please, Madre. I can sweep.

Madre turned back toward the altar.

Did you know limonarias only grow in spinsters' houses? Remember your tía Laura? With her accident came the hard times.

I know the story. Tía Laura won three titles of Queen of Carnival on consecutive years. Then a fire during the third carnival disfigured her, and the fiancé left her. Laura's sorrow, Grandma's pneumonia, then Grandpa's cancer, or something. All dead within a year. It was amazing that Madre and Alonso survived. There was little evidence of Laura's passage through life beyond the photos on Madre's wall: Carnaval 1962, Carnaval 1963, Carnaval 1964. The hand-painted fan she bequeathed Madre and, recently, me. Why did Madre favor me and not Luisa? And what does tía Laura have to do with the tree?

That is when I met your father.

I sat on her bed. It must have been tough times.

My father was about to lose the house. Laura waited months for Raúl, and we began to fear he might not come back. In her hospital bed, Laura told Madre to cut the tree. The same night it came down, Remigio requested my hand.

Had you two been going out for a long time? You must have been very young.

I was sixteen. We had met at some dances. He helped Padre keep our home.

That was the happy ending. A girl marries and saves the family. I asked, And the limonaria came back after Grandma cut it?

It is a weed.

Now you want me to follow in your footsteps. In which ways exactly?

Madre smiled. I'm talking about the tree and how the family fared. You'll see how nice the yard will look. I'll plant something easy to care for, cool and shady. A ficus, or a royal palm. You'll love it.

Madre, I know you have a history with that tree. But I don't see how it affects you now, whereas its loss will hurt the rest of us. It's mine and Luisa's, and Alonso's. I'll sweep.

She stretched her neck. You forget the fundamentals. This is your home; everything in it belongs to you, your sister, and your uncle. But as long as I'm around, I make the decisions. Why don't you go get clean? It's almost noontime. Give me room.

She turned back to the altar.

We are talking about Alonso. Don't you care?

Niña, my concern is for the ones here. You.

She poked at my chest, then pointed at the door.

Your sister. And me.

Her thumbnail scratched a white mark onto her flesh.

I don't understand. If this concerns me, why can't you honor my wish?

Don't cry, niña. She pointed at a box of tissues on her dresser. It's time you and your sister thought about your futures. You know Osvaldo—

I looked up at her. I stood up and walked out.

Señores, your work is done. We will leave the tree as it is.

The workers sat on their haunches and smoked under the diminished limonaria shade. They stood up. One stomped his cigarette with his boot.

Cutting the tree down is a day's work, miss.

What fee did you agree on with my mother?

Madre followed me into my room, her hair wild like the Medusa in the dream.

You are neglecting your future.

I moved about as casually as I could. I packed my tote bag with a towel, a water bottle, and a binder full of pamphlets.

Are you going to spend time with esa muchacha again—what is her name?

Fernanda.

Oh, yes. Like the Catholic king.

We have a meeting this afternoon, then work at the beach.

I spread sunscreen on my shoulders. I took a sundress the color of a lobster. Madre watched while I dropped my sleeping clothes and stood stark naked in front of her. I pulled the bikini on, then the dress. As I leaned over to adjust my sandal, Madre peeked inside my clothes.

Let me remind you. A respectable woman stays home until she marries. Or she ignores that at her family's peril.

Oh? A woman has so much power she can destroy a family?

If she cannot respect her home, she leaves.

I thought you said this was my house. Then—

Madre swiveled her wheelchair and rolled away. She is a master in the art of ending conversations.

Twenty

A beautiful place of disappearing beaches, of nameless bodies; a mother's insensitivity. Some destroy trees; others kill innocent animals to survive. In this very place, some were hopeful—or blind—enough to try to heal us.

Belisa, Jacinto, Fernanda, Luisa, and I stood on Olas Altas Street under a giant ficus. Facing Adrián's ruin, we admired what remained—the basalt and limestone facade bathed under a thick layer of dust.

Luisa blew at the wall and showered us in dust. Here is the Nereid.

There she was, the heroin of the stories we had told as kids. More blowing revealed the seahorses pulling her scallop-shell chariot. Belisa and Jacinto joined in. Soon a procession of mermaids, lobsters, octopuses, and serpents woven with seaweed garlands appeared before us. Behind the ruin a tangle of construction equipment made a deafening noise. And farther behind, the ocean roared.

It's a miracle the facade remains, Luisa said.

And Jacinto: I hope they don't bulldoze the building materials out to sea.

If you build your business here, you should use the designs. But can you really buy it?

Fernanda paced the sidewalk holding a ledger. The sponsors have signed off on the loan.

She traced a path between the cornice, the sign of Olas Altas street, and the tree under which we stood. Over her Comcáac skirt she wore a T-shirt reading "Salva Playa Careyes."

What was there to save—the facade of a ruin? I passed my hand behind my back and clutched my other arm by the elbow. A self-hug, or my own little straitjacket.

Belisa giggled. I never dreamed I could buy a place like this.

It would be the co-op's, Jacinto reminded her. But, can we really turn a mansion into a factory? Is it legal?

I admired my friends' courage. The law protecting turtles was about to obliterate their livelihood. They owned little more than the clothes on their backs. And here they were, building a business on a shoestring, with credit from people they hardly knew. For months they had worked with us—Fernanda insisted on consulting with Luisa and me—to make cosmetics from natural ingredients, harvested delicately. They had persuaded several hotels to use their products as a draw for a new clientele—one aware that their choices could make or break the beauty they came to enjoy. And they had the audacity to build their factory on what remained of Adrián's property!

I clutched my arm tighter, made it tingle.

Who says it has to be a sweatshop? Fernanda asked. It can be a clean, welcoming workplace to create beautiful things.

Luisa nodded. These designs can be more than decorations. They say your products are traditional, natural. You should replicate the pattern in your label.

The scallop and the seahorse. The baroque columns. The old home, I said. As if naming them could bring them back.

Have you thought of a brand name?

Yes, Jacinto said. And no, Belisa said. They laughed.

Belisa's eyes were wide. We've been honest from day one. Mamá and I know about creams and perfumes. Jacinto gets the buyers.

We work hard, said Jacinto. We won't disappoint you.

It's not for us, said Fernanda. This is your business.

It's certainly our work, but the investment?

That's the BioTerra people. Mariana, thank you for connecting us with them.

Did they raise the money they promised?

Fernanda took a document from her ledger. They've got half the funds in hand, most of the rest pledged. Could you guys help with some fundraising? A concert?

I pressed my arm behind my back. I haven't played for months.

Fernanda shook her head. She gave Belisa a document. The place is yours if you want it. BioTerra approved the loan. Now it's up to you.

Jacinto and Belisa beamed. And a name?

I freed my arm for a moment, pointed at the street sign. You could use that.

¡Olas Altas!

Adrián might like to see his house restored. At least this part can look like before.

A car parked next to us. A chauffeur got out and opened the door, and Adrián walked out.

Padrino, finally! I kissed his cheek. We heard you haven't been well.

Oh, hi, dears, he said in a gravelly voice. I almost didn't recognize you.

He bent under a coughing fit. His chauffeur offered a silk handkerchief.

I'm sorry about your house. What happened?

I turned to Belisa, Fernanda, and Jacinto to introduce them, but they had stepped back, looked toward the street as though waiting for a bus.

Ay, Mija. Adrián shook his head. I had to move. You come visit soon? Bring your mother.

He patted my cheek. Now I have to talk to those hooligans. They're trying to sell off what remains of the house.

Luisa feigned surprise. Was it not going to be part of the hotel?

They promised they'd keep the facade and build something harmonious behind it, like an office suite. You can't throw it down even if it's yours. Historic buildings law.

Only the front was historic?

They got permission to rebuild the back, all the way to the sea. He smiled with some effort. That hotel is going to be something. Twenty stories, joining the two towers. The largest tourist complex in Ayotlan, a worthy successor to the Belmar.

I clamped my arm tighter.

I thought you cannot demolish historic buildings in the downtown area.

It must have been approved overnight, Luisa said.

Adrián scowled, took a leather binder from the driver. Everything is here?

What happens now with the front of the house?

The hotel people couldn't harmonize front and back. So the government made them put it on the market. Whoever buys it must rebuild, but keeping the structure and style intact.

The chauffeur checked his watch. Mr. Landeros, your meeting—

Adrián held my arm and shook it. And now a bunch of pelagatos want to buy it.

My friends receded farther under the tree. Amazing how Adrián would not notice them, or recognize Fernanda.

A white Suburban parked next to us, two of its wheels climbing the sidewalk. From it jumped Chepo Menard wearing a wrinkled linen suit. He rushed toward the hotel, but stopped when he saw Adrián. He slapped his back.

Ready, compadre?

Adrián coughed.

Menard scanned Luisa and me. And you must be—

Sánchez's daughters, Adrián said.

Luisa shook Menard's hand. We saw each other last year, at my father's plaque dedication.

Certainly. And this is the Muñeca? Haven't seen you since you were this big. About the ceremony for your father. Now that you are all together, we can organize it.

I smelled the alcohol on his breath. I pried my hand from his, clutched my arm behind my back again. We're not all together yet.

Any news of Alonso? Adrián asked.

The new detective is getting his bearings, Luisa said.

Menard rubbed his nose. Your uncle will be here in no time. He looked at his watch, then at Adrián. Let's get that thing going.

Adrián peered at the ruin. Did you hear they want to start some—factory here?

Menard sighed. That was not the board's intention.

Do you understand what that means for my home?

Menard shook his head. Turned into a sweatshop. Those losers think they can manage. They should go manage the shack they crawled out of. He glared at Fernanda, Jacinto, and Belisa, who recoiled farther. Then he took Adrián by the arm.

Adrián fanned himself. They have no right to cheapen my— He coughed.

We shook Menard's hand and kissed Adrián. They left.

My friends came out from under the fronds.

Belisa was ashen. That is the guy my cousin Juliana was working for, she said.

Are you sure?

Fernanda paced the sidewalk.

Let's focus, guys. The BioTerra people need an itemized budget.

Supplies, salaries for three months. We've got a week. We need an administrator. A designer. We need money.

I have a few ideas for the designs, Luisa said. And I can help with paperwork.

Will you? Belisa and Jacinto asked, their voices high like children's.

I freed my arms, and they unfurled like banners. I stretched my hands before me.

I could give a concert, with some friends and teachers.

My fingers fluttered.

Osvaldo might want to play.

And Alonso.

Twenty-One

The things I have to do for Madre. Sitting in an alcoholic cloud in the back seat of Menard's car while Madre enjoyed the views of the Malecón like a tourist. We watched the diver climb to the top of the cliff, stand on the edge and wait for the right wave to swallow him without letting the rocks shred him to pieces. The sun was about to set—he better hurry, I thought.

Madre clutched her handkerchief. She said, I always fear they will fall into a shallow.

And Menard, you don't get used to it after all these years?

I know. But tell me about your project. You will expand the hotel now that you have Adrián's land?

The diver stood on tiptoe on the platform, opened his arms into a perfect T, and let gravity pull him into the roaring water. Madre yelped.

Menard said, Inward twist. Perfect posture. The plan is for the third tower in the center, and to grow the first two. Twenty stories. The pool will be so big you won't distinguish it from the ocean. A cabaret, tennis courts, a club for young people. You will love it, Mariana.

We approached the side of the construction site where the retaining wall was more visible.

I said, Is that to keep the building from sinking into the water?

He chuckled.

There was Careyes Restaurant with the crowd of demonstrators chanting "Salva Playa Careyes." Months ago, Alonso turned a key on that glass door and walked out of our lives. Could some of the demonstrators have seen him?

Madre said, Those people. Don't they have anything better to do?

And have you heard? The police broke up an orgy and found several of them dressed in leather straps and hitting each other.

¡Santo Dios! I saw it in the newspaper. I did not know it was them.

So disagreeable. Better focus on Adrián's land. It will give us the space we need for the project. Remigio would approve, you think? Although it would be much better if we had all of it.

He pointed toward the pink bay curving for miles and miles north of Punta Farayón.

Ah, Kilómetro 22, he said. What a beauty.

Did you know those lands belong to our family?

The lighthouse blinked.

Menard acted surprised. Would you sell them? I have had a few good years, and it is time to reinvest in Ayotlan. You know I will take care of our community, Remigio's legacy.

Madre beamed at me. Your father would be so proud.

The lighthouse blinked.

Madre, this is something we have to—

And your Juilliard is so costly.

You should discuss it, Clavel. I am sure Muñeca and Luisa will support your decision.

Don Chepo, it turns out those lands are on my—

Madre touched my arm, wiped her brow with her handkerchief.

I can show you a blueprint, so you see what we can do. By the way, the sculptor is done with Remigio's bust. You should see it, pure white marble.

I am so grateful. Have you thought how we will dedicate it?

With all honors, as we should. The Week of Mega Tourism: dinners, conferences, a ceremony at the theater. What do you say, Muñeca, will you play some tunes?

Without Alonso?

Mija. Think how Padre would love Ayotlan to honor him.

As we got home, Chepo held me by the arm.

Pérez, help Mrs. Sánchez into her home. Mariana, let me ask you something.

Madre waved at him as though a family member, let the driver drive her wheelchair, left me alone with my nausea. I waited for Menard to scoot aside and take the space Madre had left, but he stayed in the center of the seat. I leaned on the wall of the SUV. He expanded his arms.

Don Chepo, I don't think this is the best time for my family to discuss business.

I only ask you to think about it, Muñequita. It would be wonderful if you made the announcement at the theater. Imagine your father gazing at the touristic complex he always dreamed about. And your mother. Here, take this.

It was a piece of paper.

I know it is not easy to come up with certain words. So I took the liberty to suggest a few lines. You can say them as if they were yours. It will make the dedication of the bust so special.

I had nothing to say.

Your mother has improved miraculously. She hardly stutters now. And I don't lose hope she will walk again.

Of course. She's doing well.

But nothing guarantees a full recovery.

Right.

The doctor said the stroke had been caused by trauma?

His hand approached me. I tried to move away, but there was a wall behind me.

He touched Fernanda's bracelet.

What a nice little thing. So ethnic. Did you buy it at the market?

And then: I just worry for your mother. How terrible if she were to suffer more.

Twenty-Two

Esteemed ladies, gentlemen. We are gathered to honor a man who dedicated his life to our beautiful port.

A sight for a photo album: everyone congregating at the Diamela Rialta theater.

Microphone in hand, white tie and tails. Menard's baritone voice echoes on the tropical wood and the leather seats. Look around at the sparkling earlobes, the silk lapels, the patent leather. All of us, all of Ayotlan, wrapped in silk and velvet. Where else would we rather be?

Menard paces, marking the rhythm of his words. The austere stage, its black floor and Bordeaux velvet curtain, are graced with twelve marble columns adorned with lilies, gardenias, roses, all in white. In the center stands a taller column covered in purple satin, embroidered RSM—Remigio Sánchez Morales. No one works gold thread like Clavel. The intricacy. The delicacy. It must have cost her months of work, before falling ill. Luckily she was able to finish.

We take this opportunity to celebrate Remigio Sánchez Morales's stewardship of Ayotlan. Menard addresses us all, but first and foremost the family in the front row. Clavel, so dignified in her rose gown, her pink pearl choker. Were it not for the wheelchair, we would think her fully recovered. She holds hands with Luisa, who lights the space in her coral dress and necklace. A notebook on her lap, a pencil in her hand, she must be sketching the glorious scene. Next, Muñeca's aqua gown plays up her eyes of blue. No jewelry save a wooden band clasping her upper arm. A nice, humble touch. They even brought Amalia; they are so good that way. And Osvaldo. So ready. All Mariana has to do is take his hand. And there is an empty seat next to Clavel. They don't lose hope.

Menard continues.

Not too long ago, Ayotlan was little more than a fishing village. But Remigio understood that the way out required resiliency and focus.

Clavel nods and sits taller. We have so much for which to thank her husband.

The storm outside batters the roof—it is almost a hurricane. But in here, the cupola's fresco gives us sunny pastoral hills where cherubs, shepherds, and nymphs play harps and flutes.

Years ago, Tigrillo—what an apt nickname for our little tiger—understood that the sardines feeding us would eventually run out, so he led the fishing industry's transition to red snapper. And as the snapper diminished, he showed the way to shrimp. Finally, he reached his greatest achievement—large-scale tourism. He coaxed us to contribute our beach lands, turn sand into gains. The resorts have reproduced along the coast, creating a sustained flux of profit.

We clap wildly; Clavel too. And her daughters? Mariana seems pale; Luisa is busy with her notebook.

We now present this award to Remigio. We would love to bestow it on him personally, see his ample smile, hear his virile voice declare, Tourism—

Is it! we cheer.

Tourism *is* it. You surely remember. Sadly, illness took our Remigio too soon from us. So we call on his gracious wife, Clavel Celis Coulson de Sánchez, to accept his likeness in marble. She, too, deserves honors. She and Remigio never hesitated to protect orphans as their own children.

We know. There is dear Amalia, who one day wandered down the hills and into Remigio's and Clavel's arms. Look at her blonde braid circling her forehead, those blue eyes, that turquoise gown. She looks like family.

Please greet Madam Celis Coulson de Sánchez. Her lovely daughters, Mariana and Luisa Sánchez Celis, will accompany her.

What applause! Mariana pushes the wheelchair up the flower-lined ramp across the orchestra pit. But she stops before reaching the center, perhaps out of stage fright. Menard walks to them, takes the wheelchair, parks the family next to the column.

A veritable work of art, he says, as Clavel pulls the satin drape off the marble bust, a Roman Caesar. The talented artist Marco Antonio Trava has honored our leader's memory.

Clavel praises the bust, thanks her daughters. They have of

late taken the reins of the household, she says. Much as I had to when God summoned Remigio to His Kingdom.

Menard introduces Muñeca. Thanks to Remigio's support, Mariana is an artist of the highest caliber, an interpreter of mankind's best. Wise is the woman who tends to her temple.

We cannot wait for the piano to roll onto the stage, to hear her melodies. Art and beauty—what Remigio wanted for those girls. Certainly not pushing papers in some gray government office. They say she has been visiting fishermen at the market, at the slaughterhouse. Is it possible?

Menard hands her the microphone and a sheet of paper.

Fair as a sugarplum fairy. Even paler than we remember.

Dear friends. Her voice cracks a bit.

Speak up, Chepo calls. We chuckle.

Mariana looks around, catches her sister's eyes. Chepo paces behind them. He watches the paper in her hand.

There, she talks: I was young when my father passed away. And my memories of him are colored less by experience than by his legacy. He made sure my mother, Alonso, Luisa, and I had everything we needed.

Menard nods.

From him I learned the need to invest if we are to preserve the path to happiness. So others find it too.

Clavel smiles. Menard slows down.

My father died before he could repay his moral obligations.

What did she say? Menard stops.

My father was a prudent businessman, seeking to reduce debt. He taught me that capital grows by reducing obligations. She says, Same as we tap into our natural resources. We take a kilo of shrimp from the ocean, we fill our children's bellies. If we sell a ton, we profit. But what does our net leave on the ocean floor? How do we restore the sea that feeds us?

We look left and right.

Clavel's hand rises.

Sardine, snapper, shrimp. When a species of fish depleted, my father turned to a new one. Did the overfished species recover? What can we do not to lose another one? We build Hotel Careyes in downtown Ayotlan. Under its weight the sands slide, the beach disappears before our eyes. What can we do so the hawksbill turtles whose name and breeding grounds the hotel took can thrive elsewhere?

She says. Can't she see?

What is my job as my father's daughter?

Música, we say.

I have understood that I must try to rectify my father's few but important mistakes.

We gasp, we fan ourselves. The theater is stifling.

You know our family is going through difficult times. We are anxiously awaiting news of Alonso. He taught me to respect the beauty we are blessed with. Luisa and I want to honor him and our father by supporting the Ayotlan we love.

We look left and right.

Tonight we announce two projects with common goals. We will restore a building in downtown Ayotlan that housed some of our most cherished memories—the former home of our padrino, Adrián Landeros.

What a relief. We applaud our third patriarch. He stands under the limelight, leaning on his ebony cane. In his face is the question we all have.

Luisa raises her hand and the stage curtain parts. Mariana pushes the wheelchair to the side, and Luisa follows. They abandon Tigrillo's bust! Where is the piano?

On the Cinemascope screen is now a photo of Adrián's mansion: the stained glass windows, the trees in whimsical shapes. How beautiful it was.

How do we give these broken stones life? she says.

Now we see the Careyes construction site, a sign advertising its new wing. Next to the construction, Adrián's veranda with the limestone columns, the portico, and part of the garden.

Luisa and I wish to restore the front of the house to its original beauty, she says. A cooperative-run cosmetics factory will provide jobs for shareholders of a business that will make my father—and I am sure all of us—proud.

Our hands go to our hearts. We behold a picture of those gañanes that have been stirring up kerfuffles. They huddle together like a soccer team. Some wear embroidered huipiles, others T-shirts with that Salva Playa Careyes logo.

It is true!

Mariana says, These fishermen must relinquish their livelihood in the sea turtle industry. As you know, new legislation will ban hunting, trading, and consumption of sea turtles, leaving the fishermen jobless.

And our peace? Who will stop this shameful show? Some of us stand up.

With the support of the nonprofit bank BioTerra, they will create the employee-owned Olas Altas Natural Cosmetics.

More of us stand.

Housed in our Padrino's home and inspired by it, Olas Altas cosmetics will celebrate our unique town without depleting it. I know my father would support Olas Altas's efforts to improve Ayotlecos' well-being.

We walk up the aisles.

Finally she stops, peers beyond the spotlight. Can she only now be hearing the rustle of silk, the flustered voices? She walks to the edge of the stage, the spotlight following her. She shades her eyes. She sees some of us leave; the house is half empty.

Chepo takes the microphone from her hand.

Friends. We thank Mariana and Luisa, who will usher Ayotlan out of our antiquated ways. Spreading Remigio's wealth—and Ayotlan's. Right, Muñeca?

In the dark theater we hear Estúpida. Pendeja. Chinga—

Now, Menard continues, to crown this glorious evening in a way Remigio would appreciate. Please come by my humble home—su casa—for a surprise supper. The pozole you eat tonight will stay with you forever.

India lover, someone shouts in the dark.

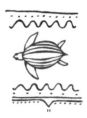

Twenty-Three

Fernanda knocked at my window at two in the morning.

I opened the door. Take off your shoes, I whispered. She walked in as though afraid of being heard—although the storm made that impossible. She followed me into the pitch-dark house, her hand on my shoulder. Like a blind person's guide, I walked her across the corridor and the drenched garden. We walked gingerly among the trees. At one point she grazed a branch, and a cascade of accumulated water soaked us.

On the opposite end of the courtyard we turned to the corridor lining the bedrooms. Under the roof again I handed Fernanda a towel. We dried our hair, arms, shoulders. Walking toward the front of the house, we passed the sewing room, the linen closet, my room and the bathroom I shared with Mariana, before we reached her room.

All this convolution just to avoid passing close to Madre.

At Mariana's door I turned to Fernanda. A few hours ago I would not have let her close to my sister. How could I have imagined that, just from spending time with her, Mariana would turn into one of *them*? I forced myself to declare—Mariana es tortillera. Why do people call them tortilla makers? And how could I broach this subject with my sister? God knows I had tried, just for her to imply I was jealous. And was it not true—did Mariana not travel and study while I stayed behind to take care of our mother? Did she not break all the rules and have everyone drool over her pretty face?

I shook. Fernanda waited.

I opened the door and stepped into the room.

Mariana lay in tangled sheets, the mosquito net turned into a haze by the night light. Her hair was matted. She was naked, terribly vulnerable. I shook—she *could die.*

She was awake when I went to let you in, I whispered. Touch her. She's been in and out of a delirium.

On her flushed cheek Fernanda's hand looked black. You think it's 103, 104? The concern in her eyes mirrored the one in my heart.

Mariana's head swayed. She hummed faintly.

She took two aspirin about two hours ago. No effect for an hour. Then she vomited. She had already thrown up the food at Menard's. Then the delirium started. She soaked through her clothes, then a nightgown. I couldn't dress her again. She got up and sleepwalked. I was terrified she would hurt herself.

You did the right thing calling me, Luisa. Thank you.

It felt good not to be alone.

Ihapa iya ihapa.

We looked over at her. I explained, Some singsong she has been going over lately.

Fernanda smiled. It's the serenade for Moosnípol. My nahual, the leatherback turtle.

I lowered my gaze.

Does that fan have a higher setting? Fernanda uncovered Mariana's feet and shoulders. Nothing else.

I aimed the fan at her, left the room and came back with a basin and some cloths.

Fernanda dripped water on Mariana's lips with a soaked handkerchief. Her tongue darted and licked. I sat crossed-legged on the center of the bed, stroking her arms with a towel. We worked hours before she began to cool off. I was so drowsy I could have lain down beside her.

Luisa, Fernanda said, and I startled. Let me understand. The food at Menard's made her ill. What did they feed you?

She picked strands of hair from Mariana's temples.

I gazed into Fernanda's eyes. Guess. Really, you should be able to.

I heard it was pozole. Wasn't it your dad's favorite? Doesn't Mariana like it too?

When it's made with pork.

Are we talking food poisoning? But then, how is it you're fine? I looked away.

Didn't you eat the same food? Was anyone else sickened?

Fernanda reached across, took my chin, made me look into her eyes. What was wrong with the food? What did they do to her?

She was not about to let me forget.

Just a few hours earlier, I had sat at the table of honor in Menard's garden surrounded by Madre, Mariana, Amalia, Adrián, Osvaldo. Across from me, one seat was empty. The place card read "Alonso Celis Coulson." Mariana had insisted.

Chepo's garden was garish, strewn with Greek goddess sculptures. He said, The artist is Marco Antonio Trava, the same who made Remigio's statue. Under the tent sat a hundred guests at tables dressed with starched tablecloths. They smiled, bejeweled, wrapped in silk, enjoying a good meal on Padre's behalf.

The menu was abundant. First came Padre's pozole, the spicy broth, the hominy, the shreds of meat. Each guest was presented with a plate of garnishes—shredded purple cabbage, pickled onions, cilantro leaves, crimson pepper, lemon wedges, silky arches of avocado.

Madre chatted with Menard and ate heartily. Her cheer reassured me. I complimented Menard's memory of Padre's favorite soup. He prodded us—Eat! Aren't you famously against waste? He stank with contempt.

Amalia stared at her soup, tasted it with caution. She put her spoon down and looked at Menard with—disgust? Sorrow? Mariana added pepper sauce as if to mask the flavor. The meat was odd—more muscular than any pork I had tasted. It was fishy. It felt heavy in my stomach.

The second course was huachinango zarandeado. A waiter brought to each table a platter of red snapper opened like a butterfly, sprinkled with spices and grilled. He prepared tacos with tortillas baked over a mesquite fire at the corner of the garden.

Ah. ¡Las tortilleras! Menard wandered toward the ladies clapping the dough into disks, picked up a steaming tortilla. He rolled it with sea salt and stuffed half into his mouth. What would we do without them? I don't care if they sleep with boys or girls. I *love* to eat their delicious—he paused, looked over at my sister—their tortillas. ¡Vivan las tortilleras!

The crowd chuckled, shifted in their seats. I was too mortified to look at my sister. Madre appeared oblivious to the insults.

But the worst was still to come. With dessert and cordials Menard took the microphone. He said, It has been a wonderful dinner, although we did not have the menu cards on time. Please forgive a small planning blunder in what I hope you all will remember as a special event.

As though on cue, menu cards were placed before each guest. With a flourish, one solicitous waiter brought the menu for me to read.

As I recounted this on my sister's bed, I saw in my mind the perfidious card. I retched.

What was it? Fernanda demanded.

I looked into her eyes. The meat in the soup was leatherback turtle.

Fernanda's hand rushed to cover my mouth, with horror in her face.

I wet Fernanda's fingers with my tears. We didn't know until they had cleared the plates, I said. On that crimson stained table, the notice of the crime was crumpled next to me.

It read, Delicioso pozole de Tortuga Laúd. The Seri—or Comcáac—people of Sonora call this delicacy Moosnípol, the fragile one.

Something wet ran down my neck.

How could one answer to such cruelty? To counter it, we had only kindness. Caring for the dear woman. Being with her.

Her fever had cooled. Soon there was little to do besides watch her. Luisa leaned on the headboard. Her head fell to her chest.

Why don't you lie down? I said. Her fever is practically gone. You should sleep too.

And tomorrow?

Madre takes her time with her bath and such. You can slip out before she leaves her room. Lie down now. Luisa patted the bed.

But there was no space for three, with Mariana outstretched like a sea star.

I stood up. I should get going.

No! Please stay. I—Mariana needs you.

Ay, little Moosni. Why don't you rest in your room? I will watch her.

I knew what I risked: having Luisa throw me out for pushing my perversions on her sister. What did the story she had just told mean, otherwise—the word *tortillera* thrown around as an insult. Her relations deriding women because they love other women.

But I could not do otherwise. I looked up at her fleetingly.

I'll keep an eye on her. Call you if anything happens.

And there was relief in Luisa's face!

I'll take you up on that. She stood up, stretched her limbs. At the door she hugged me.

Thank you.

She reached up and kissed my cheek. She closed the door behind her.

I turned around and reached the bed, drew the mosquito net open. I pulled the sheet away and looked. Just looked. The same beautiful body I had once pulled from the water at Boca de Cachoras. Nothing new—in my dreams I had seen and seen again that image, felt that softness. I had tasted every nook of the sweet skin. Counted one by one the freckles on her shoulders.

I took my clothes off and folded them on the chair. I climbed onto the bed and pulled up the sheet above us. It billowed with the breeze from the fan then floated down like an egret's wing before enveloping us in its cool. Mariana smiled.

I closed my eyes. Her breath tickled my shoulder.

I checked on her several times that night and found her in peaceful slumber. Once, as the church bells rang, she stirred. She looked at me. In her eyes was no fear, no rejection. Only joyous recognition.

We held each other, and slept.

Twenty-Four

The storm abates before daybreak. Osvaldo walks the Malecón awash with debris. The news he brings to the Sánchez Celis house is unambiguous. Finally, after seven anxious months. Everyone had tried to stay hopeful, yet ready for the worst.

Now they will find out how ready they really were.

This is an urgent errand, yet Osvaldo sits on a bench he just wiped with his handkerchief. He runs his fingers over the frayed manila envelope containing fourteen sheets of paper. They are so familiar. He has handled, flipped, pored over them for twenty hours. They are as heavy as Alonso's story. And Mariana's.

Yesterday, as he opened the certified envelope at the lunch table, Osvaldo knew he would have to keep its existence secret through the theater event and the dinner at Menard's. After Mariana's illness he knows it was the right thing to do.

He pulls out the four sheets containing the summary, a line of kinship clearer than any genealogy could draw. Over the years, Mariana's family has dwindled so that we can count its members with the fingers of one hand.

Page 1 says Subject ID #1191956, the mummified remains found on a desert beach 22 kilometers north from Ayotlan on August 22, 1989. This man shares his Y gene and mitochondrial DNA with Clavel Celis Coulson and Luisa Sánchez Celis, to whose samples his were compared. Absent other siblings to Clavel Celis Coulson, his name is confirmed: Alonso Celis Coulson.

What nobody wanted to hear. Alonso, Osvaldo's band leader, his friend: gone. Now they can mourn him. Refocus the criminal investigation.

If only there had been a different way to find out.

An oily stream on the pavement next to Osvaldo swept an

azalea petal into a storm drain. What if the paper were to slip from his hand and follow the flower to the ocean?

But he flips to page 2.

Subject ID #1211940: Clavel Celis Coulson. Kinship to Subject ID # 1191956: Sibling. The only known living person with his exact biological makeup.

Subject ID #03031963, Luisa Sánchez Celis. Daughter to Clavel Celis Coulson, niece to Subject ID #1191956.

And last.

Subject ID #07031956, Mariana Sánchez Celis, shares the Y chromosome with Luisa Sánchez Celis. But she does not share the mitochondrial DNA of Alonso Celis Coulson. She does not share it with Clavel. Nor with Luisa. Luisa and Mariana Sánchez Celis were fathered by Remigio Sánchez Morales. But they do not share a mother.

The stream next to Osvaldo's feet drags a drowning gecko. Osvaldo leans, dips his hand in the water, and manages to pull it out. But the terrified reptile flails and lets go of its tail. It plunges into the current and rushes toward the drainage. Osvaldo bolts to his feet, sticks his hand in the water again, feels for the little animal; he brings out a lump of rotting leaves. He wipes his hand on the side of the bench.

The awful news will bring closure now. But what about Mariana—can Osvaldo tell her that the person she calls Madre is not? Is it his business to reveal a secret that has allowed her to grow up safe and confident?

And who is her mother?

A weak sun peeks behind Nevería Hill, and Osvaldo knows he must complete this errand. He reaches the Sánchez Celis house, walks past its mahogany portal. The gray stone walls show no hint of the lush courtyard inside. The high windows are fortified with iron bars and louvered screens to let the breeze in and to protect the interior from outsiders' glances.

But there is a crack in one of Mariana's screens: a vertical oval with pinched sides like a parted mouth, through which the adolescents had held after-hours conversations years earlier. Osvaldo had seen Mariana's bare arches, touched her fingers through the crack. He once slipped a stack of Polaroids of a sixteen-year-old Mariana sleeping naked on a towel on one of their camping trips. Close-ups of her pink foot curled over its twin, the small of her back peppered with sand. How could such an attractive body seem so oblivious to its own eroticism?

Years ago, his finger followed the photos until they landed on Mariana's hand. Now he can use this crevice to prepare her for the chain of losses he will deal her. How will he call her? He could use the ascending blackbird's whistle he perfected to elude Clavel. Will Luisa be in the room? Osva is grateful for her support. He is also glad Mariana has found meaningful activity after pausing her music studies. Her work with the cosmetics cooperative, the sea turtle project, Luisa's and Fernanda's support, are all reasons to get out of bed every day. They will keep her busy until she determines her future. Will she return to the States? Hopefully she will hold off her decision until he comes back from Texas. It will not be a long trip—just four concerts. He will dedicate them to Alonso's memory and his family.

Osvaldo stands under the massive ficus shading Mariana's window, peeks through the crack, and waits for his eyes to adjust to the dark. A lump on the floor becomes crumpled towels. A rectangular shadow is the bedside table. On it, a pitcher holds an infusion.

The bed. Under the mosquito netting Mariana lies on her side, her back to him. Her hair cascades across her shoulders. Her rump is barely covered. Her foot dangles off the edge.

Osvaldo strokes the crevice. If only he could reach across the room, trace Mariana's silhouette.

He turns around. On the street a yellow dog sleeps beneath a parked car, two or three flies circling his ear.

He looks inside again, his lips pursed. His lungs fill, ready to whistle. But there is a sound; Mariana turns. She bares her belly. One breast. The other. Her legs separate for an instant, revealing her center. She tucks her hands between her knees and curls up, facing him.

Osvaldo's eyes ache. He will not blink.

An arm swings from behind Mariana and circles her body.

How did Luisa get so much sun? Just last night, she was the color of caramel. Now her arm is dark as the mahogany Osvaldo is spying through. The hand reaches around Mariana's torso. Mariana takes it and places it on her breast. She smiles.

Her lover. Mariana's lover sits up for a moment and kisses her neck, raining long, black hair over her smiling face. Then lies down again.

Fernanda has kissed Mariana.

Fernanda.

Osvaldo staggers away from the window, turns and crosses the street. He walks a block. The envelope slips from his hand and lands on the pavement. Like an ocean liner, he walks a few more paces before he manages to stop, turn around, retrace his steps. Pick up the documents.

Osvaldo walks back to the window as the church bells ring seven o'clock. He pushes the envelope through the crack. It claps as it hits the tiles. He will call Mariana and let her know where to find her story. Once he reaches Houston.

Twenty-Five

Tú
llegaste a mi sufrir
resurrección de luz
amor, pasión y vida.
Soy
aquel dolor de ser
por ti vuelvo a nacer
soy polvo enamorado.

You
Arrived in my suffering
A resurrection of light,
Love, passion, life.
I am
That distant pain of being
For you I am reborn
I am dust in love.

osé José's melancholy voice woke Clavel to a new day of pain. For the three minutes of the song she let her tears flow, safe in the intimacy of her bedroom.

But soon the seven o'clock bells rang over at San Carlos, announcing Amalia's knock on her door. She dried her eyes, pushed the last sob away, and turned off the radio.

Buenos días, señora. Would you like your bath now?

Give me a hand. And silence, please.

Amalia helped her into the wheelchair, avoiding eye contact. In the bathroom she eased her out of her nightgown and into a special seat in the bathtub filled with warm, aromatic water. She left her alone.

Clavel massaged her legs with a sea sponge. She exercised them as the nurse had instructed. The progress was remarkable. She took care of herself, never gave in to despair, learned again to sit straight and to use as little assistance as possible.

Self-control was the bedrock of her character. In the presence of others she was always composed, never invited pity. Life had provided excellent training. She was barely thirteen the afternoon her parents called Laura and her to their bedroom. They sat on the edge of the bed and clasped the two girls' hands.

Mijitas, we have nothing, their father announced over doña Felicia's sobs. We are poor.

Clavel tried to picture what this would mean. Would she and Laura walk the market stalls, barefoot like the children there, extending upturned palms?

Laura burst into a tearful fit, and Madre pulled her to her breast.

Clavel handed them tissues and fanned her older sister. She said, I can transfer to Escuela Pacífico, if it helps.

Leaving Colegio México, the school run by the Sacred Heart nuns, meant losing friends, comfort, and the education that would turn her into a woman of charm and delicacy. But the cheerless, swarming Escuela Federal del Pacífico was free.

And I can sell my lace.

As they ministered to Laura, her disconsolate parents thanked her, marveling at her dry eyes.

Days later, when Clavel came home from her first day at the Federal School, she found Laura changing out of the Colegio México uniform with their mother's assistance. Both Laura and doña Felicia turned red, but Clavel stood taller.

We each do what we can, she said. Doña Felicia and Laura smiled, abashed and thankful. And thus Clavel discovered the meaning of her sacrifice.

The loofah, please.

We do what we can.

Amalia walked in and offered to scrub her back, and Clavel covered her breasts.

Leave the loofah on the table.

Amalia obeyed and left.

Clavel counted on herself, as many counted on her. She supported her parents when Laura's fiancé abandoned her, taking comfort in easing the family's poverty. That is how a life is made.

She hummed the José José song.

> *Tú*
> *llegaste a mi sufrir*
> *resurrección de luz*
> *amor, pasión y vida.*

> *I am*
> *That distant pain of being*
> *For you I am reborn*
> *I am dust in love*

Laura had been dead for almost thirty years. Was she floating in the universe as dust in love? Clavel wiped off a tear. Why would she cry now? She did not cry the day Laura stopped breathing, nor when Madre joined her in the cemetery, a few months later. She held on. She found her baby brother a wet nurse. She married a man she hardly knew. She did not even cry weeks after the wedding when Padre, too, passed away. Perhaps it was cancer—there was little money for doctors.

Relatives, neighbors, Padre's associates, even the cleaning staff they had recently fired—all rushed to offer help for the orphan caring for her orphaned brother. But Clavel sent them away with a polite *I can manage*. And manage she did. While the other girls gossiped, flirted, danced, Clavel arranged funerals. Flesh and bones caring for dust in love.

Resurrección de luz, amor, pasión y vida. She washed the tears in the gardenia water.

I did not call you, she said. Her eyes were closed, but she felt Amalia's presence.

Disculpe la molestia, señora.

Clavel did not show resentment of her sister's privileges or her husband's cold ways. She pressed her lips into a line and sustained her glance at what lay before her, an incarnation of the saying "la que se enoja pierde"—she who loses her temper loses the fight. She had no confidants and did not seek them. Her personal life was buried treasure.

She lifted her left knee with both hands, then let go. Stay up, she commanded, only to watch in frustration as the knee slowly sank again. She looked into the mirror and saw clenched lips and naked eyes, a sallow face. She looked away. She avoided looking at herself until she had the rice powder, kohl, and rouge in hand, the tools to create the person of calm dignity that she was.

Her self-control was so ingrained it might be harmful. Perhaps, the doctor suggested, her composure had exacerbated her collapse the night Alonso disappeared.

She held on to the bar bolted to the wall and untied her underwear with her other hand. She had designed it to undo from the sides without having to pull through her legs. She lathered her genital area with a washcloth. She would do anything to prevent anyone from seeing, much less ministering to, her delicate parts. That was her promise to herself and, save for the few weeks she had been severely disabled, she had always kept it.

She reached for the two-piece bathing suit on the table next to the tub and slipped one of the pieces under her bottom. She dedicated vigorous effort to securing it. Then she pulled the bathtub cork by a long chain.

Amalia walked in and leaned over. Clavel locked her arms around her neck, and Amalia picked her up, then set her in the wheelchair lined with a plush towel.

Clavel took the hand mirror. The blank slate that was her face awaited her brushes.

The church bells rang seven times. The eighth beat was a gentle slap.

I sat up and saw a yellow rectangle on the floor. Fernanda lay peacefully in the tangled sheets. Prieta linda. I parted her hair, tucked it behind her ear, and kissed her mouth. I stretched my limbs. The cool breeze dancing in my room delighted my body. It was a miracle how much better I felt after rejecting the despicable food and sweating the fever away. I rejoiced at finding Fernanda next to me—hiding our feelings no more. She and Luisa set their differences aside. Fernanda held me. We held each other. Now there was nothing between us but love.

I walked a few steps. It was an envelope on the floor.

Fernanda opened her eyes. How did that fall in?

I knew how. The sender was a lab in México City. Osvaldo's name and address were typewritten on the envelope.

I held the papers tightly.

Need some privacy, bonita?

I did not look up. She kissed me, then walked toward the door. I think she said, Call me.

Don't worry about Madre, I said.

I'll be quiet as a mouse.

I held a yellow square in my hands. I read.

Subject ID #1191956. That is what this paper calls a human being. DNA does not lie. It was Alonso found on the beach, shot from the back. Faceless, naked, seared by the sun. My Alonso.

The floor undulated. The room darkened.

I threw clothes on, ran out. There was no Fernanda in the hallway.

I rushed to Luisa's room.

Arms intertwined, we walk into Madre's room.

She sits surrounded by billows of talcum powder, her dressing gown parted over the cream lace of her camisole. Her wet hair falls in white coils over her shoulders. She covers her face with the hand mirror.

She says, I'm not ready. Wait outside.

Dazed, we sit on the small brocade bench in the corridor, with the warmth of our bodies as consolation. In the mirror before us, Luisa resembles Madre more than ever. How quickly can a person age?

Madre summons us finally. She sits erect, her chignon flawless, her face pale and composed. Black eyebrows arch above her eyes deepened with kohl. With the pink pearls around her neck and her starched linen blouse, she looks noble, strong. She has had all these months to prepare. Is she ready?

Can she ever be?

My daughters came in, holding an envelope. They leaned and hugged me.

Madre, Luisa whispered. Alonso passed away. They sobbed quietly.

My hand rushed to meet my mouth. But I stopped it midway and stretched it toward Mariana. She offered me her own hand.

I pushed it aside, pointed at the envelope.

My daughters sat on the bed sobbing while I read the first page. I put the paper on my lap and held my temples on my fingertips, closed my eyes.

We will honor him with a beautiful funeral. It will bring us peace.

They sobbed.

Don't cry.

While I waited for them to compose themselves, I flipped the papers in my hands. Page 2 had my name, my relation to my adoptive son. But, as these papers clarified, Alonso was and would always be my baby brother. My orphan companion.

I pushed down a tide of sorrow growing in my chest.

Page 3 was Luisa, her relationship to Alonso told by a unique chain of proteins dictating how her body and her personality were built. Dear Luisa, so sexless and loyal. Feíta, like me. My ally and companion. There she was, putting her sorrow aside for me.

The dread came with the last page. I looked at the lovely Mariana whose character I had drawn from the void. She was page 4: a person as intimately related to Remigio as was Luisa. A tiny letter Y, its uplifted arms binding the sisters as closely as they now held hands. And to that common shaft, their father.

But the intimacy depicted in this little family album broke with the words mitochondrial DNA. For no feature related Mariana to Alonso.

She was not related to the subject of the study.

My sobs taper now. Something lifeless and powerful has entered our home. But Madre acts. She holds something behind her back.

Madre. Can I see the papers? I only read the first page—

She is so pale.

I know what is at stake. There is no need to add to her pain now. She must rest.

Let me see those papers, Mariana says.

Madre tightens her grip.

Madre, please.

We struggle. She is so strong.

We insist. I pry the papers away.

She shouts, There are things you don't understand! Everything I've done is for you!

We rush to Mariana's room. Amalia follows us, embraces us.

Nanita, Mariana says. Let us for a moment.

We lock the door behind us.

I ran to Madre's room, something clawing at my throat. I could hear nothing. Luisa ran after me. I pounded the locked door. Clavel! I yelled. What did you do? Who am I? The words bounced on the walls. How could you keep this from me?

Amalia rushed to me. I pushed her away.

Mother! Tell me, twenty-three years ago: How did you get a baby? Who was the mother?

Amalia placed her hands on my shoulders.

I turned in a rage. How did she? What was your part in this? Where is my mother?

Amalia's reached for her braids. She pulled at them slowly, but so strongly, I was scared she might rip them from her scalp.

I held her wrists. Don't, Nana! I'm sorry if I hurt you. But tell me what you know.

Nana stopped crying and tried to speak. And then the door opened. Madre looked up at Amalia. Nana folded her hands and turned her gaze down.

In that transformation was Madre's power, a power I had known all my life and never seen.

Come, Mariana, Luisa, Madre said and gestured toward her

room. This is a family matter. She jingled the sapphires and opals in her rings as she snapped her hand closed toward her.

Luisa followed and offered me her hand.

I stood in the threshold. I looked to Madre and Luisa in the room, then to Amalia in the hallway. She nodded. In her eyes was something so hers. Something I had always known but never named. *Surrender.* She was sending me away.

I have to talk to you, Amalia.

Yes, dear. But first go to Madre.

You are part of this family. I need to hear what you know of these documents and their—I need to discuss my history with you.

Amalia glanced at Madre, waiting beyond the threshold.

I sat on the hallway bench where Luisa and I had waited.

If you can't go into that room, then we can talk out here.

Luisa sighed, pushed Madre's wheelchair next to the bench in the hallway, and sat next to me. I held my hand out to Amalia and made space for her. Amalia clasped my hand but did not sit. She did not get closer. Our arms were a hanging bridge over an abyss.

Madre sat up, her eyebrows forming taut arches.

Mariana dear. Adopting you was a moral imperative. Your father's will—

I know. It mentioned several children Padre had had with other women. What I want to know is why he treated me differently from the rest, why he raised me here. Why you passed as my mother. Did she die? Where is she?

Amalia tried to pull her hand away.

Madre trained her eyes at her. You must understand, she told me. She talked cogently, profusely. She talked of her Christian obligation to assist a helpless child.

You would have grown up a beggar. You would have led the life of her who brought you to this world in a moment of folly. A terrible mistake. You would have been that person—miserable.

I watched her excuses grow, *keep that person away.*

When Madre exhausted her arguments, I turned to Amalia. Shocked Amalia. Despairing Amalia. The tears in her eyes made them bluer.

Nanita. Tú dime. ¿Quién es mi madre?

She let my hands go. Tears streamed down her cheek.

Yo.

She turned around and walked down the corridor.

I got up, but Madre clutched my arm. Her gnarled hands clawed. I heard garble. I gazed down the corridor where Amalia had fled.

Madre shouted. You were lucky to have me for a mother. To have all this!

I closed my eyes. I saw Amalia in her room holding the portraits of two quinceañeras. I saw her holding me in the water, teaching me to trust. Combing my hair, feeding me the most savory bits from her plate.

Madre exploded. No piano. Your hands would have scrubbed floors. That is what *she* would have taught you.

I walked.

A growl: Don't forget, Mariana. *I let* you stay here. And I let *her* stay with *you.*

Then a supplication: With Alonso. With Luisa. You, my children.

I walked.

A plea: ¡Hija! I just lost a son—and now you?

I turned and saw her head droop sideways. Two tears drew dark lines on white powder from her eyes to her jaw.

I ran.

Twenty-Six

Camelia and Juana flutter to their food bowl. Empty. Their birdbath, dry. They walk out of the kitchen, fly onto the limonaria. They coo, they preen each other's feathers. They fly, circle the courtyard. They circle the gallery. They enter Mariana's room. Juana alights on Mariana's trembling fingers. Camelia joins. She takes off again. Juana follows.

The doves fly down the corridor. At Madre's closed door they alight on a lump. It is Luisa crouching, her head hiding between her knees. The doves cross the courtyard, fly into Amalia's room. She sits in a chair. When has she *sat* before? Camelia alights on Amalia's braid. She coos.

Juana sits on Amalia's shoulder. She coos.

In Amalia's hands there is no food. Just a square: hard, flat, shiny. It has black figures. Juana approaches Amalia's face, drinks from her tears.

They fly, sit on Clavel's window shutter. They glimpse a formless figure through the glass.

They fly; they roost on Alonso's guitar.

Twenty-Seven

She held up two pictures in a single frame. Why don't you put them here, Mamá? The wooden rectangle seemed tiny on that vast wall.

How can I, Mijita? I was elated. And disturbed. How could I put that picture on that wall? How could she call me Mamá? What was I doing in Alonso's room? I scanned the tall windows, the polished frames, the hand-painted floor tiles, the brocade couch, the art deco lampshade. This was the only luxurious room in the south side of the mansion, the part battered by the sun and left to the staff. Years ago, Alonso had renovated it and turned it into his studio.

How can you? Luisa smiled. With a hammer and a nail.

We froze as we heard the wheelchair roll past the door outside. Then the sound receded, and we relaxed.

What am I doing here, Mariana?

María. Me llamo María.

I relished my daughter's name—the one I had given her. The same as my baby sister's. She had reclaimed it in a mad dash to the Civil Registry, brushing off my pleas to be mindful, to pause and reflect. Here was the dear girl in a frenzy of activity, reorganizing house and family. She had not stopped in the days since the terrible news of Alonso. She made phone calls. Prodded detectives. Found Osvaldo in Houston. Planned honors and memorials. She found time for her work with the cosmetics co-op, and for Fernanda. She called me Mamá imprudently. The before—the days she had spent in bed seemed so remote. My beautiful, strong girl was back.

María, I said, and I couldn't help but smile. All these delicate things. What if I break something? I wiped a night table with my rag.

They laughed. Luisa took my rag and led me to the sofa. How many years have you cared for these trinkets? Change is good sometimes. You'll be comfier here.

And we'll be closer, said María. I'm taking your old room.

The maid's room? I was incredulous. Why would you want that?

You've been alone too long. My place is with you.

And your career in the States?

She shook her head. My work is here. I'll keep playing music, don't worry.

And Madre? What will she do all alone?

No es mi madre. María held the picture stiffly in both hands.

She's not alone, said Luisa. We are here. She has Patricia, and now Mrs. Guzmán.

I don't understand why you want to leave the north side. This side is hot. You hear the noise from the street. Why would you want to live in the maid's room?

There are no more maid's rooms.

We'll fix it all, said Luisa. We'll plant trees outside. While they grow, we'll use awnings. Things already look better here. You can add any decorations you want. I'll go see if the workers are ready to move the furniture.

She walked out.

María, I said. The dear girl smiled, and so did I. What mortifies me is la movedera.

What's wrong with moving furniture? She kneeled on the rug facing me. She held my hands. Tell me. Please, Mamá? Such a sweet word.

I looked around. It was all a strange land. Mijita. What will they say when they hear the maid is moving in with the family? Don't you see all this is going to hurt Madre?

Clavel, she corrected me.

Doña Clavel. I corrected her. But I also fell to the temptation of stripping her of her title. In this house *madre* commanded more respect, more authority than *doña* or *señora*. She was the mother, the center of this world. And I was helping my daughter deprive her of that dignity.

Isn't this bound to trouble your family?

She shook her head.

You are my family.

The wheelchair rolled down the hallway. We waited.

All I want for you is your rightful place, the respect you deserve. I lost my uncle the day I got you back. I want you to have his room. You've worked a lifetime. Please understand.

She smoothed my hair.

You lost your uncle. But you heard her—she lost two children in one day.

Now you repeat the lie? She *stole* a child.

This started with your father, María. She pulled me toward the couch.

He raped you, didn't he?

I searched her eyes. I hoped she would deny it.

I did not know what was happening. I don't know if he would have helped me. I was frightened. I had nowhere to go.

And then Clavel swoops down and snatches me like a rag doll. And has you stay, to do the work, and help her tell the lie?

And if not? Maybe she is right—this way you had me. Who was the one who held you and brushed your hair and told you stories? The one you talked to about music? It was a cruel secret, but what would the truth have cost?

We heard a knock on the front door and a car idling in the street. The wheelchair rolled toward the door. Patricia opened it and said something. She and the taxi driver grunted as they helped Clavel into the car. The front door slammed.

It's the first time since the stroke she goes out without you or Luisa.

I shrugged.

Her hands enveloped mine. Perdónala, Mari.

I lifted my chin. In my mind I saw Clavel make the same gesture.

Twenty-Eight

Mariana, amor. Luisa? I rang the chime.

I sat in the corridor, rested my hand on the inlaid wood table with the chime and a vase of white orchids. Luisa came and started arranging my pillows, then Mariana arrived. She stood, resting her hands on the backrest of the Louis XV armchair. She gazed at me, and I glanced away.

Her hair was braided and pulled back tightly around her face. She was flaunting.

Hijas, I just spoke to Monseñor Arredondo. The funeral will be this Friday at the cathedral. He was kind enough to accommodate us on short notice.

Luisa looked at her feet.

Please bring the phone over. We need to place a notice. Select the casket. Oak is probably—

It's all done, Mariana said. We will have a memorial service at Teatro Diamela Rialta. Luisa will show her portraits of Alonso and the family. Osvaldo will play with Alonso's Grupo Amanecer. I will too.

My smile froze. We will have a Mass.

I looked to Luisa. My only daughter, I could now say. The one who supported me in the worst times. The one who begged me not to send her to the orphanage. Of course I would not. She did not need to be pretty or talented. All she had to do was be with me.

Tell her, Luisa. Explain.

And she spoke. Alonso was not religious, she said. The art and the music will honor him.

I rushed my hand to my throat. Do you—

Luisa nodded. It will be at the theater, Madre. As he would want.

I gasped. I trained my eyes on the blonde's forehead. The instigator. Who did she think she was, that daughter of a—

I extended my hand. The bishop will send Alonso to his Father in heaven. Bring me the phone. I snapped my fingers onto my upturned palm.

Alonso will go where he wanted, she said.

Madre held on, but under her makeup she seemed gray. Her eyes hid something small and terrified that I could not name. On the table her fingers twitched. I feared. Another stroke would kill her.

We will have a Mass!

She reached for the chime. Who can she call now? She shifted uncomfortably in her chair, as though accommodating something large in her stomach, a cancer.

And the burial? she asked.

We will scatter his ashes on los terrenos del mar.

Her mouth was a gaping hole.

I placed my hand on Madre's shoulder. We'll build a walkway for your wheelchair. It will be a beautiful service. Alonso will always be there, in the place he loved so much.

Madre pushed my hand away.

My sister looked up at the clock. She said I have things to do. Mrs. Guzmán is waiting in the dining room. She will work evenings. And Patricia will do days, as usual.

And we are looking for a third person, Madre.

I went to arrange her coverlet on her lap. So you're always—

Covered? So you don't have to bother with me? She almost slapped my hand.

We prepared the room next to yours for Mrs. Guzmán.

Your room, Mariana?

My name is María.

Clavel flinched at the sound of the name she had stolen from me.

I have work to do, I said. See you in the morning.

It is six o'clock in the evening. You are not spending the night at that beach again?

Yes, again.

Niña, have some sense. Don't you see what is at stake?

I see it more clearly than ever. We have always risked the same. Heart.

She brought her hand to her throat. Luisa drew closer to her.

Why get in harm's way after all we've seen? You heard the police. They suspect those invertidos from the music school Alonso used to run around with. You want them in a ceremony? And that friend of yours, that—

Clavel swung her hand downward as if tossing something away.

Her name is Fernanda.

That one. Those—people—don't check their impulses. If their passion calls for murder, murder it is. Don't you see?

I will not discuss Fernanda with you.

¿Invertidos? Luisa said with surprise.

This is serious. There is news all the time on *El Heraldo del Pacífico* of one or another of them turning out on the surf, right where Alonso was found.

Have some sense, Luisa said. Now gays kill each other, since the day Menard bought that newspaper?

Those murders took place on the same beach. What was Alonso doing there? An awful mistake. Someone thought wrong of him, and now he is gone.

She seemed about to weep. Something welled up in my chest.

Those terrenos are cursed. Who knows what deals your father got them through. Sell them, children. I hear Menard made you an offer. You'll never get one quite like it.

That sounds familiar too. Luisa shook her head.

I have always respected your sense, Luisa. You can tell decent people apart from—

Her hand swung downward again.

And now when our lives are at stake—

About the lands, I said. Luisa can do what she wants with her part. But I am not selling mine. Alonso will rest there always.

Clavel slapped the table and made the orchids quiver in their crystal. I must talk to the bishop. Bring me the telephone! When is enough going to be enough?

I faced the woman I had called Madre for twenty-three years and said, When I can do no more.

The front door opened, then slammed.

Madre looked up at me. I thought of the children in the orphanage, begging to be received in a family's home. I remembered myself as a child, begging my mother not to send me there.

We heard footsteps up the corridor. Amalia was pulling a long cord. She placed the telephone between the orchids and the chime.

Aquí tiene, doña Clavel.

Twenty-Nine

almost tripped on Jacinto as I rushed out of the house. He stood up from the stoop, stumbled, stood up again.

Hey. I didn't hear you knock. I wiped my face with my arm.

Look what I've got.

He handed me a box labeled "Olas Altas" and, on the side, "Fragile."

The samples?

They are exactly as we wanted them.

I sat on the stoop with the box on my lap and tried to pry it open with my keys.

Jacinto leaned over. I have something to tell you.

Sure. Let's go inside. Are you thirsty?

No, no, no, no. I'll walk you—you are going to Fernanda's?

He took the box from my hands, tucked it under his arm. He held my elbow and started. Fernanda's house was behind the hill, some twenty blocks away. We walked up Rebaje Street, leaving the ocean behind. As we climbed Nevería Hill, we crossed the Las Brisas neighborhood. There every house was a fortress topped with surveillance cameras. At the gates stood guards armed with guns. They glued their eyes on us. The static of their walkie-talkies followed us.

What's up? I asked. Is it your friend at the restaurant again?

Jacinto's glance hushed me. We walked in silence until we left Las Brisas behind. Just yesterday, he had told Luisa and me that a friend who worked at Careyes Restaurant had seen men carrying scores of guns in. So Menard collects guns, I said. What does that have to do with Alonso? The men mentioned Alonso by name and laughed. They joked about the weight of some fish when tied up. I was disturbed, but what could we read into that? I called a private detective from México City. He asked the friend's name, but Jacinto won't give it to me.

We panted as we walked up the hill. Then we turned a corner and lost the breeze and the ocean views. The houses on this side were much more modest, with no guards or fences. The aroma of frying onions and peppers flew out windows. People walked to errands, children jumped rope or played soccer. Couldn't things stay this way? Couldn't Jacinto just say, today we focus on our work?

He tightened his grip on my elbow.

My friend heard Menard discussing some lands he calls Kilómetro 22 with some Omar guy who totes an AK-47 and a spear gun.

You think he is the killer?

Well, we can't prove it. But my friend heard things.

He spoke in a hurry as if he had to say this once and never again. He said, There is a passageway between the kitchen and Menard's office. Menard uses it to leave the restaurant when trouble comes through the front door. This morning, the door was ajar when my friend was prepping. Menard said, We'll get Kilómetro 22. Level the obstacles just like before. And the Omar guy said, Like at Mr. Landeros's? Isn't Kilómetro 22 where your uncle was found? The lands they've been using as a dumping ground—aren't they yours?

I was dizzy. Were they really talking about Alonso? And who was now in their crosshairs?

Jacinto, I need your friend's name. The detective needs to verify the information.

He walked faster. Look. I'm happy to talk to detectives from México City. But my friend made me swear I would not give his name.

I hung my head. This is as good as nothing. If the detective can't—

Jacinto huffed. You do remember Juliana used to work at that restaurant?

Who?

Juliana, Belisa's cousin. We are all trying to stay alive here. You understand?

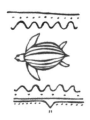

Thirty

Welcome to my palace.

Fernanda stood barefoot in her fuchsia skirt and embroidered blouse. She rested one hand on the door handle and extended the other to my cheek. I took a step back.

She brought her hand down, and her smile.

I stepped in. Her house was so small. First there was a kitchen with a pine table, two chairs, and a small couch. Beautiful shelves organized pots, plates, tools. A door opened to a bedroom; behind that was a patio. Each of the rooms had a large, wide-open window pouring sunlight onto marigolds, roses, begonias, lilies, all yellow. They were in pots, on tables, on shelves, on the floor. It was as if Fernanda had gone to the nursery and carried back the sun in planters.

She closed the door.

Make yourself at home, Mari. Oh, I love your name.

I set the box on the table and kicked my sandals off, pushed Fernanda behind the window casing. Our chests, our bellies, our hips met. Our thighs, our feet. My hands traveled up and down her back in a hurry to enjoy her beauty.

We kissed. I tasted the salt of the ocean, just like the first time. Her mouth curled into a smile. Mine too. There were so many reasons to smile when we were together.

I thought you were mad at me, she said.

Of course not, silly. I was just worried someone would see us.

Eventually they will.

I sighed. She turned, took an ironwood jar from the table.

This is for you.

It was tall, dark, beautifully carved. On its side swam Quipáacalc between the waves. On the ocean sands el caracol rosado—Strombus Alatus—brought messages to and from loved ones. I turned the jar. Quipáacalc swam and swam as if time did not exist. I looked up at Fernanda, my eyes stinging.

I made it for you a month ago. But now I realize it belongs to Alonso.

Fernanda offered me the "tour of the manor." We sat in folding chairs on the little patio next to the well, under the laundry billowing on the line, and she smoked. She pointed at a little bush among a profusion of plants.

It is my limonaria. I got a cutting from your tree. See how well it's growing?

In her bedroom she showed me the walls of science books above her bed. She had built the shelves out of thick parota wood, carved with sea motifs.

Moonsípol travels the great Pacific, rushing to meet Quipáacalc.

I turned to her. I pulled her strap off her shoulder, careful not to touch yet. I leaned toward her throat. I parted my lips and kissed the quivering hollow, tasting her sweetness with the tip of my tongue. Fernanda braced herself on my hips, as if afraid of falling. She leaned her head back and shivered in my arms. Her hair hung low on her hips, caressing my hands as I held her by the waist.

I pushed back and drew a deep breath. I gazed into her eyes. I placed a knee on the bed and brought my love down with me.

An hour later we lay, our legs entwined, my lips still on her shoulder, her hand on my waist, watching the dusk climb the walls. We had loved each other, and it had been so very sweet. The closer I got to Fernanda, the stronger I felt. But a little distance between us—even of centimeters—brought back all my misgivings. Fernanda thought we were free, but couldn't she see my class did not forgive? I closed my eyes, buried my face in her locks. I did not want more pain.

But soon it was time to go, and I remembered the box I had left on her kitchen table.

We were busy, I said. We chuckled.

Don't tell—

Jacinto just brought the samples to go with the budget proposal.

I cut the adhesive tape sealing the box. In a bundle of tissue paper lay twelve jars made of glass the color of pearls. I took one. Its tapered, cylindrical shape had a spiraling pattern.

Fernanda brought it to her ear. Strombus Alatus, she said.

The linen label read "Olas Altas. Polvos de Arroz." And below, "Porcelana." I opened it. Inside, a small sponge lay on a circle of waxed paper. Everything Belisa, Jacinto, Luisa, and we had been toiling to accomplish.

Fernanda cupped my hand with the jar, brought them to her face. Gorgeous.

It has Madre's—I mean Clavel's—jasmine fragrance.

I thought back to the time before this week, before the person who had called herself my mother had hurt me so. Somehow the hateful feeling felt muted.

I looked closer. There is a mistake. This is tan, not porcelana.

Fernanda giggled. It's hardly any darker.

I looked at her quizzically.

I suggested a small change for porcelana. Belisa decided to try it.

I checked a mild annoyance. We said we would keep the original formulas.

Well, I thought you could present doña Clavel with a box of her polvos de arroz. It's a very slight change; perhaps she will like this color better, closer to her beautiful sienna.

Fernanda sat on the couch and reached for my hand.

You changed it for—why would you worry about her?

She reminds me of folks back in Punta Chueca. So many people carry the disdain they suffer on their skin. It's a wound that doesn't heal.

My arm was gray and cold as I held Fernanda's warm hand.

But you wouldn't know that, would you? Being so blanca. She traced the tiara of braids above my forehead. I love your new hairstyle, mi reina.

I'm not sure what I would not know. My tone was harder than I had intended.

Fernanda shifted position, cradled my head on her chest.

Sabes, querida. Moosnípol comes back to Punta Chueca every now and then. She brings a little grain of sand from the bottom of the ocean.

She stroked my cheek lightly. Her voice was low and dreamy.

She climbs up the beach and leaves a broad, broad path: la calle. We follow her, build an arbor, give her water. She teaches us.

As I rested my head on her chest, Fernanda's heart beat in my ear.

Last time, Moosnípol said—skin is kin.

I waited for Fernanda's explanation.

Color doesn't mean a thing to some people. They are fair, innocent. Good things come their way; it is all so natural. They have friends, teachers dote on them. They marry, get good jobs. They are not afraid.

Fernanda's black eyes were deep and almond shaped, like Moosnípol's.

They never suffer on account of their looks. And they don't understand why others do.

She paused. Her breathing was so slow I thought she might fall asleep.

I looked down at my expensive sandals, my linen dress. I thought of the mansion where I lived. I compared those things to the hand-made garments Fernanda wore. Her house, smaller than any room in my own home. Was I one of those innocent-blind ones?

How many times had Clavel told Luisa that girls like them—and she always included herself—had to be cleaner, more gracious than everyone else? Es que tú y yo somos feítas, she said. I had hated my mother—and back then she had been—for calling Luisa ugly, for sowing poison in her mind. I felt lucky not carrying the wounds she inflicted on my sister's skin.

But why would Clavel think that way? Suffering, Fernanda had called it. I looked at my pink feet. I thought of Amalia, so blonde; of my father, so fair; of Clavel, so dark. Who had she been before stealing a baby? And why would she do that? I saw a sixteen-year-old girl forced into becoming a woman. An orphan taking care of her orphaned brother. She had given everything for her family. What did she get in return?

I looked up. Fernanda opened her knowing eyes. I placed the sponge in the jar and screwed its top in place. I wrapped it, put it in the box.

Thanks, Fernanda. Perhaps she will accept.

Your gift.

Part Two

A Prayer for the Elders

1968

Thirty-One

The day I became a woman started like any other Tuesday. I was twenty years old and had been married four. I had become an expert in running a house and taking care of a child. And then that one morning, I discovered it had all been a rehearsal.

I drank black coffee at seven o'clock. I bathed and picked a turquoise blue sheath dress from the wardrobe. I brushed my hair until it shimmered, pulled it into a chignon on my nape. I clipped the cameo brooch at my heart and dabbed Miss Dior on my wrists. Then I called Amalia and Alonso. The little boy was ready with his polished booties and his miniature guayabera. I opened my black umbrella, and we set off under the August sun.

I walked briskly under my moving shade, tall on my high-heeled pumps. I scanned the sidewalks for potholes and the occasional rotting fruit to keep my ankles safe. Alonso ran to keep up. I pulled him by the hand.

Vamos, nene. You don't want to miss playtime.

Behind us, Amalia carried a pair of market bags, her face turned toward the waves. Tú también, I said. If we're late to the orphanage, I won't make my next appointment. And Dr. Colunga takes ages to reschedule.

Sí, señora.

The cathedral rang nine thirty as we climbed Rebaje Street. We stopped at Caramelos y Puros Coppel.

Three kilos of jamoncillos, pecan and almond, I said.

As the young woman packed the candy in tissue-lined boxes, I arranged some stray hairs back into my chignon at the humidor glass.

The store door opened, and a gust of wind followed Cristina

Manzanero. She wore a straw hat and round sunglasses. Her long pigtails tumbled to her midriff. She walked to the periodicals display. Some magazines were local, some imported, a few in full color. But they all had on their cover a photo of those British rock and rollers in gaudy shirts. Cristina picked one and walked toward the counter.

Nice dress, Clavel, she said and pressed her cheek to mine. You coming to the beach on Saturday? She aired herself with the magazine, and her silver bracelets jingled. The whole Colegio México gang will be there. She jiggled her toes in her flat sandals.

Cristina—you know I have a family.

Come on. You can have fun too. And Alonso—don't you like the beach, cutie? She cupped my boy's chin. His eyes grew even bigger.

Alonso's gaze grew something soft in me. Cooling my feet on the wet sand.

I shook my head.

Cristina sighed. If you change your mind, we'll be at Careyes.

¡Careyes! Alonso ventured. But a glance from me stopped the nonsense.

We left the store, in my hand one of the candy boxes strung with multicolored twine. I led my little entourage toward the orphanage, the umbrella shading the turquoise sheath and the cameo brooch and the steep shoes. How long had it been since I'd gone to the beach? What would it be like to have a husband I could enjoy things with? Or no husband at all? To be cared for, like everyone else?

Higher on Rebaje Street, we stopped at the mirador on Nevería Hill. Alonso pointed at the rocks below: The town is a dragon, Mamá.

Yes, indeed. On the slope at our feet the houses clung to the rocks as if they could slip into the ocean. The rocks and houses and foliage tapered to a curving peninsula where the water foamed. That was the dragon's tail. Across the bay, the three islands: Deer, Wolves, Birds. Did they really have those animals?

Alonso pointed toward the pink, curved belly.

Yes, that is Careyes Beach, I said.

¿Vamos? His eyes were large, four years old.

I opened my mouth to speak.

The cathedral bells rang ten o'clock, and my voice didn't carry. Alonso said again, ¿Vamos?

I yanked the little hand. Stop nagging.
He looked down, and his bangs shadowed his face. We walked on.
As soon as we veered around the hill, the breezes would die.

Thirty-Two

Ants crawling on a pineapple rind were not as relentless. The children crowded me with outstretched arms, hooting their delight at a break in their joyless succession of rote lessons, fistfights, and chicken broth.

I held the box of caramels out to the boys—the girls sat in a separate courtyard, altering the clothes Amalia had distributed among them. Alonso held out one jamoncillo at a time, watched it instantly snatched away.

You are so kind, doña Clavel. Mother Asunción smiled with her long teeth. Some children even call you Mamá! And Alonso is not jealous, of course.

Doña Clavel. After four years it still sounded new.

Alonso nodded. I live in the house. We have Amalia, and jamoncillos.

They are santos inocentes, the nun said. Please take no offense.

I brushed my brother's bangs away from his face. As my hand receded, the hair spilled back like a silken curtain the color of the candy.

Not at all. What would I want more than being a mother?

The nun sighed. It is a matter of time. God will answer our prayers.

I studied the nun's profile and wondered at the word *our*. How long would "we" have to wait for God's answer? I was not a zealot, but I paid my dues. In my house the floors were scrubbed daily, rugs and curtains washed every change of season. At lunchtime I greeted Remigio with the consommé, the fresh tortillas, and a good guiso. After his nap came a second shower and a fresh shirt ironed with lavender. When I was not attending to him or my brother, I responded to many needs: wheelchairs for the cripples, charity dinners. And above all, the orphanage. Could anyone find fault in my ways?

Having doled out the sweets, Alonso joined a game of choc-olateado. Two boys raced around a circle of intertwined arms, vying to break through the fortification and exclude the slower child. It had been one of my favorite games.

The only thing lacking in my home shone in the eyes of those children: a life to cultivate, someone absolutely mine. For this I endured my share of pain.

Enough pouting, niña—Remigio's voice came to me from last night. Now turn over. You liked it before, didn't you?

Now the simple act of walking was painful. But I knew: the hours I spent pressed under that man, his contempt and my compliance, would surely translate into the joy of growing a child. My validation as the destitute daughter of an ancient family. Remigio might not be faithful, but he was loyal. He had gained contacts through us. As long as I did my part, he would not deny me the dignity as Clavel Celis Coulson de Sánchez. But for that I needed a child. From my body, and with my husband's skin.

We sat in the Patio de los Naranjos next to the chapel, under trees loaded with immaculate blossoms.

Those candies are all the children want, the nun continued. But so many things are hard to come by here at the orphanage. Thanks to you, we will place a rush order for uniform fabrics. Keeping the children clothed is a struggle.

Is that why some wear street clothes? I leaned on the iron armrest. Instead of orange blossoms, I smelled disinfectant from the floor a novice was mopping.

Some of our benefactors favor specific children.

Indeed, two or three of the boys would not look out of place in our neighborhood: their play clothes were tasteful, in good condition. They had chestnut hair and fair skin, whereas the uniformed children had black hair and hooked noses.

All but one. The boy who had turned down Alonso's candy—he was now leaning on the far pillar with his pale, deep frown. He stood there, not a wrinkle on his stiff uniform pants, as if he never sat down. He did not play either—he did not like those girly games, he had said.

We welcome any assistance. We only wish the support were as abundant as the children Ayotlan brings to our door.

The nun trained her yellow smile at that boy, then at me.

Was she hinting at the rumor that some wealthy men filled the orphanage's coffers, *and* its cradles? Did they prefer to acknowledge their offspring through dress, if not by name?

It would be fair for those who burden you with obligations to support you in kind, I said.

The boy was closer now. His hair stood on his head like a scrubbing brush. Behind him, the sun pushed through a cloud and blinded me. Why was Remigio so enthusiastic about my support of this institution, while nothing else I did called his attention? Then there were the casas chicas he was said to keep. Had those women succeeded in producing the children I had failed to give him?

And where were those houses?

The Colonia Nueva Esperanza, it must be.

The ride Remigio gave me to the seamstress's a year ago came to mind. I was going to try on a chiffon gown for my first Rotary Ball as a married woman. As I directed him behind the hill to Leticia's house, he began grumbling that her place was farther than I had made him believe. As we turned into her street, a ball made out of rags landed on the Galaxy's hood. Then a boy climbed the car to retrieve it. I saw the dusty handprints on the windshield and braced myself for Remigio's rage. He pressed the steering wheel as if his fists could bend it. He watched the boy take the ball, climb off the car, and wave at us. The other boys snickered.

How rude, I said. Do you know him?

Remigio glared at me. He threw the car into reverse so swiftly I hit my shoulder on the dashboard.

Where are we going? Leticia is waiting for me. I need that gown—

He slammed the brakes and turned to me. Why can't you make your own clothes?

The whites of his eyes were crimson. Do I have to remind you what your mortgage costs?

I never returned to Leticia's. I borrowed Luz's dress for the Rotary Ball and had to smile at people's comments of It suits you better than Luz, dear!

Thus the issue of clothing joined that of the mortgage as Remigio's way of reminding me *you may be the lady with the big house, but I am the man. I pay your bills. And I write the rules.*

But what if the rage came from a different place? What if the product of his night outings had sat that day on the car hood, and now here, enjoying my candies and gifts?

I see you would prefer to clothe them equally, I told the nun. It must be hard to teach them they are all children of the Lord when some get more than others.

She laid her clammy hand on my arm. The children take the lives we offer them.

So you do well unto others, et cetera. ¿Haz el bien sin ver a quién?

We each do what we can.

And the wives? What would stop the nun from thinking I found it convenient to ignore my husband's sins? I pulled my arm free. The nun stirred, and a smell of overripe melons wafted from her habit.

A few paces away, the uniformed boy looked on as though recognizing me.

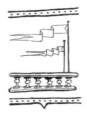

Thirty-Three

Carreritas, Alonso squealed. We now walked toward the ocean and the fresh air.

Below the mirador our house resembled a large box with a rectangular cutout of palm trees and bromeliads in its center. Four solid stone walls, four corridors, four wings of rooms, all perfectly contained. As if nothing had ever happened.

Alonso pointed at the doves in the courtyard. Camelia and Juana, Mamá.

I smiled. That is them, all right. I gave his hand a gentle pull, and we continued our walk. On the Malecón he and Amalia skipped ahead, their hands forming a link: cream and vanilla. Blonde braids circled Amalia's head like an indigent princess's tiara. A pretty child; was she twelve now? In that huge uniform she looked like a scarecrow in a tent.

Where did you say you were from, Amalia?

Concordia, señora. Behind those hills.

And your family, are they Mexican?

Just as I finished the question, I remembered having asked it before.

Concordia seemed to be one of those French intervention towns. When referring to the disgraceful invasion of México by France, Sinaloenses proudly described their men in valiant combat. The upstream towns were the birthplace of brave fighters ready to sacrifice before relinquishing their independence. But at night, mothers sent the invaders welcome gifts in the form of their teenage daughters. If a señor is going to occupy you anyway, why don't you choose a white one, they seemed to say. Blond kids are happier. Generations later, girls like Amalia were the sunny result of those nighttime visits.

Twelve o'clock, the bells rang. The umbrella shaded me to the knees, but my calves and feet peeked into the sun with every stride.

Walking outside at noontime?

From death, I heard Madre's reprimand loud and clear. Death was the dwelling of my entire family but Alonso and me. To visit them, I had to leaf the calendar four years back. Why had I been spared—because Alonso needed me?

The light receded, and I entered my childhood bedroom.

At the full-length mirror, Madre rubbed my cheek with a sponge.

Try Carmela's mother-of-pearl cream, dear. She promises quick results.

Madre coughed her dry little cough. Every night she stroked me with special creams. I relished the attention, thinking the dark would one day fall away like grime from a scoured pot.

Sometimes Madre was nervous; then she rubbed harder, and I turned crimson.

But Carmela said to take no sun, she said, rubbing my arms and shoulders. No sun at all if you want to be lighter and stay that way.

Now, under the umbrella, my arm was the brown it had always been. My mother had married a fair man. But she had been victorious only with Laura and Alonso. Why did Padre not marry a criolla woman? All their children would have been fair.

And I would not be.

How differently the mirror treated Laura, bringing Madre's blessings. She stroked Laura's hair, patted her face continually. The mirror did not lie. It was Laura's friend and my mocking foe.

The chasm between Laura and me widened prior to her third coronation as queen of the Carnival. Covered in sequins, her gown was the heaviest anyone had seen in town. To finish it, Leticia moved her atelier into our bedroom. She worked so closely with her that she seemed to stitch the sequins onto her precious body.

The evening of the coronation, I helped Laura out of the drying helmet, freed her hair from the rollers, and watched the stylist perfect the golden coils with the curling iron.

It would be so easy to touch the iron to Laura's scalp. Would she feel something?

Carrying Alonso, Madre talked of Laura's recent engagement to Raúl Medina, a man cut to her measure: handsome, eager to bend his knee before her.

That night, her beauty at its peak, Laura had nothing to expect but the adoration of the best man in Ayotlan and everyone's jealousy. The ball went as expected. My sister danced some but mostly sat on the dais and presided over the merriment. Under the stars the penthouse terrace of Belmar Hotel brightened the bay with searchlights. Blue and silver banners fluttered as though reaching out to touch Laura. Everyone marveled at the depiction of Botticelli's *Birth of Venus* in her dress, at the goddess's uncanny resemblance to her. Indeed, Leticia had said, her model had been Laura herself. Raúl sat next to her throne, almost as beautiful, as if he, too, had a scallop shell to escort her apotheosis on the waves.

From where I sat with my parents I saw a man circling the terrace. He seemed to inspect, to count and measure everything with his gaze: how many brandy bottles, the ladies' diamonds, the width of my shoulders. Then he stood at our table. Mister Celis, he said. Sánchez, he introduced himself, as if he had no first name. He asked me for a dance, and I looked to Papá for permission, hoping he would acquit me.

Instead, he tapped under my elbow, pushing my hand onto the man's.

We danced to "Perfidia," and I said something about Agustín Lara's boleros. He grunted, his mouth reeking of old pineapples. His fingers poked into the small of my back. Something hot rose to my chest. I squeezed his arm. No one saw.

When I sat again, my parents were deep in conversation with Adrián and Luz Landeros. So poised were the compadres, so lovely doña Luz's gown—a flapper dress in orange that seemed to catch flames.

On the corner of the terrace the castillo's fireworks wheel expelled spirals of yellow, golden, orange, scarlet—the small rockets spun the wheel, raining sparks on the velvet night, into the ocean below. I lost myself in the light of the spinning rockets, the torches, the candlelight, the stars. Five stories below, the waves roared, foamed, glittered. It filled my hunger.

The wind picked up, and the banners danced. A hundred horns struck up a mambo, and the dance floor filled with frenzy. Even Luz and Adrián stood to dance. The spinning fire and the dancers entranced me; feet in high heels and tuxedoed legs pounded and kicked; manes caught the breeze and the light; lips stretched in ecstatic grins. The fireworks wheel sparked and spun its spirals of fire until a rocket burned through its bonds and escaped. The projectile flew at floor level among rapturous feet. Dancing its own dance, the buscapiés bounced against chairs and tables. It strayed at tremendous speed; it tripped on the dais. It did not stop until it landed on the well formed on Laura's lap.

The sequins exploded; the flames climbed up her torso.

Laura leaped. She howled. She was a human torch.

Raúl and others lunged. They risked their lives to stop the flames.

To touch her.

But they could not save the beauty of her arms and shoulders.

They were perfect, like ivory. Not fat, not bony, not a freckle. For weeks, Madre walked the corridors, coughing, droning her refrain, tears drenching her reddened cheeks. As if repeating these facts would restore for us the future the fire had stolen. Those arms and the disfigured face Madre could not bring herself to mention were the marks of a cast-off muse. Her life's purpose gone, she spent months in a tent built with sheets and pillows on a hospital bed, refusing to eat, wilting toward the grave.

Now, at age twenty, I remember, will remember all my life, the lovely sight of Laura engulfed in her own fire, her curls lighting up the night.

Thirty-Four

Laura's absence was felt in the house as acutely as earlier her presence. Before the accident, the young men who gave their all to save her had strolled past the house hoping to catch a glimpse of her. Our elegant but dilapidated home had been the site of homages to our family, its heiress, Alonso and me. Evenings, Laura sat in her wicker chair on the open entrance corridor and smiled lazily at those who greeted her, at times whispering an absentminded adiós. I rocked the baby during Madre's breaks from breastfeeding.

After the accident, the same men who prolonged Laura's life began taking a side street. Who could bear the sight of her face and arms—a sea of scars?

They needn't have worried.

A few days after the trauma specialist sentenced her to life without a face, Raúl announced a short trip to the capital to restock his business. Laura waited.

She had been waiting for months when word arrived of Raúl's marriage to a woman "as beautiful as Laura had been."

She would not live much longer. Infection, the doctor explained.

Heartbreak, we knew.

Heartbreaks seek company, and mine was just in the making. Laura's accident was only the latest in a string of misfortunes. After many financial disasters Padre was being forced to relinquish our home.

One desolate evening, I tried to follow Madre to her bedroom. I need to nurse the baby in peace, she said between coughs, and locked her door behind her. I went looking for Padre in his library. A bulb hanging from the ceiling barely lit the corridor flanking the garden. The trees exhaled their perfume. Next to the wicker sofa lay a heap of branches. Madre had just had the limonaria tree cut. Those trees are barren, she had said; no girl can find a husband with them.

I picked up one of the branches and breathed into a white flower. I walked toward the end of the corridor—the library door was ajar. I was about to push it open when I heard a grunt, smelled a scent of rotten fruit. It was Sánchez.

I clasped the doorknob; if they looked in my direction, they would see me.

The man spoke in a businessman's cadence. Perhaps he would make Padre a proposal. Any money to pay the hospital bills. A nanny so Madre could rest. I held the flower on the crook of my neck, as though a newborn kitten.

I hear you're a man of modest resources, Padre said.

Mr. Celis, I am an even-keeled man. I work more than anyone. I owe nothing.

To pay a mortgage, you need cash, not words.

The word *mortgage* sounded like mortaja—shroud.

There was a clacking of buckles.

I have here the registry of monthly payments as the bank assigned them.

He stood next to Padre as if he had permission. He laid a ledger on the desk.

This is the date of your default. The amount due, with interest and penalties.

I waited for Padre to throw him out. The man went on in choppy sentences: Cancel repossession. Children stay home. Yours. Practical purposes.

Could this stranger really help us stay where we belonged? I restrained the urge to storm in, beg Padre to accept. I waited for him to offer whatever it was the man wanted—shares in something? A piece of land we might still own?

Padre looked at the man through a sliver above his spectacles. How will you pay?

Ask around. I say, I will do this, and it is done. My fortunes are growing. The bank has approved the transaction—pending your consent, naturally.

I held the wilted flower at my chest.

Listen, don Armando. Compared to Raúl Medina, I may be nothing. But there is a problem. Your older daughter is incapacitated. Do you have someone else to turn to?

My father did not answer.

I clutched my belly, and the petals slid to the floor. I was the payment. This body. Laura was unable, and I would have to do. Sixteen years old and turning into a woman in a heart's beat. I almost smiled. *I had value. I was the only thing my family had.*

How much?

In my mind I stood Raúl Medina next to this Sánchez and Laura next to me. The ugly did not only do without the pleasures of the mirror, the love of a mother and a boyfriend, the jealousy of others. Being ugly was lesser, but still a currency. It paid for safety. Not love, not admiration. Nevertheless, it paid.

I tried to lean on the door, but it flung open. Padre faced me, ashen.

I knew the script. I pronounced my lines.

Sí, Papá. Acepto.

Remigio Sánchez Morales stood next to Padre. His frown carved an eave across his forehead. He tightened his gray teeth.

The pungent perfume of the flowers at my feet rose to my face—strong and ruthless like that man. I could bear his heirs. My world was small, but I would shape it.

Acepto, I said, and I became a woman.

Four years later, I clicked my heels on the Malecón, quick and strong. I looked down at the blue silk dress I had stitched. Amalia and my brother reminded me of our mansion—my posthumous gift to my parents; more than Laura had ever given them. Remigio might fool around. But he had one home and one wife. He would have one legitimate family.

I glanced at my flat abdomen.

Hurry up, children. I will not be late to Dr. Colunga's.

Thirty-Five

Click-click, click-click. La señora's heels marked the pace. Like a flag, her black umbrella showed the way. Her spine was so straight it was as if she had a sword tied along her back. I chuckled.

What's funny? asked Alonso.

I pointed away. Those pigeons, fighting for the corn the lady is giving them. They have more than they can eat.

¡Qué mensas!

My little boy whispered, Amalia. Tell Mamá we go to the beach.

I laughed. *You* tell Madre to take us. I gently pulled on his earlobe. Escuincle.

Oh, you don't know the way? I'll show you, he said, pointing at the immensity.

I smiled to my little boy. You guide me.

For an instant the cramps I had had all day eased. If only that little hand had guided me as I made my way to his house two years ago. I walked from the mountains, a ten-year-old and flat-footed. I walked alone for ten days, a shoebox for my luggage.

As I arrived in Ayotlan I rested for a moment on a house's stoop and drew strength from the ocean in front of me. I would cool off at the water, but first I had to go find my new home. Above all, get something to eat and drink—I had had my last bolillo the night before. I pulled out the paper my mother had written for me. I read the address—Aquiles Serdán 64. I folded it carefully and placed it next to my María. She took up most of the space on my underwear. I stroked the yellow yarn braids woven around her head. Like yours, my mother had said when she'd made it.

I stood up and staggered a bit, asking directions here and there. The screech of peppers and tomatoes wafted from kitchen windows, so delicious. The sun was hot on my back, but I saw only dark, like a tunnel. I knocked at Aquiles Serdán Street 64, then pressed myself against the wall while I waited. Finally, someone ushered me down a corridor, onto a terrace.

It was like a castle. There were big chairs with blue pillows the size of flour sacks, but so soft. And fruit trees inside the house, flower trees, flowers everywhere. The heart of the palace was a bush with white flowers. I was told to wait there while the patrones finished their meal.

A little boy ran out of the dining room and waved at me. A señora's voice summoned him back.

It had to be a dream. All around me were shiny lamps, candlesticks, vases. Was it gold? The furniture shone, its pillows cool and blue and impossibly smooth. I squatted under the bush, its shade fragrant of lemon, loaded with white flowers with a yellow finger in the center. But it could not be limonero. This was the season for unripe fruit, and this tree had none. Lemonade would be nice now. I had drank my last drink at the river in the haze of dawn. Then, as I approached the city, the river had disappeared under a road.

Hola, the little voice brought me back.

I sprung from under the bush. I brushed twigs and blooms off my hair. The little boy squatted next to me, licking a lollipop. He pulled on my arm, and I squatted back down. He held out his candy. ¿Quieres?

I smiled. What's your name?

Alonso. ¿Y tú?

I said Amalia, and he stuck the lollipop into my mouth. I gagged.

The señora's voice rang out. Alonso jumped to his feet and shrieked as he ran around a screen folded like an accordion. It was painted with flowers and birds and children with helmet-like hair. Alonso took the corner so close to the screen I thought it might topple.

I licked the lollipop he gave me and looked around, found the elbow of the bush where I could hide the candy. But I finished it before the señora appeared.

Then my work started. The beach would have to wait. Clean, clean, all the time. Start with my own room, which was so dark it needed a lightbulb during the day.

Alonso and I made friends. Part of my job was to look after him, and that was the best. Once, he asked about my doll.

Her name is María, like my little sister. I took care of her.

When we have a baby, I'll help too. When do you see María?

I shook my head, pointed at the ceiling. She is playing with the little angels now.

One year earlier, my family had held my newborn sister for two weeks when she got a nasty bout of vomiting. Madre borrowed money for formula and medicine, but the mollera receded on the baby's head, forming a tiny bowl. One afternoon, Madre fell asleep next to her. When she woke up, the baby was cold. The white box we buried her in was a bit bigger than the shoebox where I kept my belongings.

So she is with Madre, said Alonso. And Daddy. My other daddy. Now I have Papá Remigio, and Clavel. He squeezed my hand. They all play together?

Sure.

After all, doña Clavel told me the first day, If people ask, I am your madrina. You will learn to be part of this family.

When we came back from Dr. Colunga's, doña Clavel asked me to fix dinner for fourteen guests. I spent the afternoon on the mole poblano. I roasted the seeds and nuts on the comal, sixteen kinds of chiles, garlic and onion, chocolate, vanilla, cloves, and cinnamon. I ground everything on the metate, fried it, added the stock. That was easy compared to stirring the huge, simmering pot for an hour. I scraped the bottom with a spoon as long as my arm to thicken the mix without lumping. And I had to keep my gala uniform clean—that black thing with the white apron. My abdomen cramped. I dabbed my forehead with a kitchen towel.

Doña Clavel walked in, dressed all in black lace. Her hair was pulled back so tightly that it sharpened her eyes. She gleamed.

I stirred with two hands. I prayed for no additions to my chores before the guests came knocking on the door.

Mister Sánchez needs toilet paper in the bathroom.

¿Cómo, señora? I always make sure there is paper in the cabinet next to the—'xcuse me.

La señora paced on her high-heeled sandals, clickety-clack. Aired herself with her lace fan. She said, It is called the toilet.

The toilet.

The toilet, Alonso added.

La señora fanned herself. It's not a bad word, you know. How do you people go up there, on the hills?

Actually—

She shut her fan with a clap. And you'll get to speak correctly, won't you, dear? Just like you've learned to cook and clean, and keep yourself clean.

Sí, señora. But I know I put the twelve rolls in yesterday.

Doña Clavel chuckled. Now, you don't expect el señor to lean over and get something from the cabinet?

My face was hot.

She checked the clock. The Manzanero family will be here at eight. Is the silver polished?

Sí, señora.

The table? Set. The flowers? In their vases. The champagne bottles? In the ice buckets. It was like a lotería game. The checklist was long, and the kitchen was stifling. Doña Clavel walked out to the corridor. From a drawer in the console she took a mother-of-pearl box and a brush with long bristles. She dusted herself. Her neck, her chest, her bare arms. When she came back into the kitchen, she was like a pretty ghost, her big eyes rimmed in black.

You'll go and place the toilet paper on the rod where it should be. Then come and greet the guests. You'll do me that favor, dear?

Sí, señora. I stopped the fire and walked out of the kitchen.

Sí, señora. The two words that kept a roof over my head.

But first I rushed to my bedroom. I could not remember if I had latched the door—I had to on account of the rats. Two years ago, I was given this shell of a room next to the laundry, "for the time being." I would not have minded if I had been sent home right then. But my parents had been so glad to place me with a good family. That first day, I scrubbed the walls and window screens, mopped the floor. I hid stains on the walls with flowers I made from the tissue paper that often fell in shreds from gifts to Alonso. My María slept on the cot, in the dress and bonnet I had made from an old bed sheet I'd found on the lid of the wastebasket next to my room.

Sometimes things appeared there, always during the other maids' day off. First was a greeting card with a pretty picture, and the greeting page was torn. I threw it away. On another day I found a painting in a frame. It was carefully placed on the lid of the trash bin. The painting was beautiful; printed at the bottom was *Rafaello. Madonna della Tempi.* I used a blue paper flower to cover a gash between the Madonna's hands and the baby Jesus. I propped it against my mirror.

The gifts had to be from doña Clavel. Maybe she liked me—weren't we girls? I was twelve, she was about twenty. The other maids were much older—and el señor the oldest of all. Alonso was a child. It was a kind of family.

I knew what family was. Mine was up in the sierra, but it was always in my head. My sister Dionisia's laughter as we played quemados through the woods. The sweet breath of baby María as she napped in my arms during her short visit. The flavor of Madre's soup, spicy with peppers and greens, heavy with white corn from Papá's milpa. The smile they sent me away with. Later, after I walked the first few paces toward Ayotlan and turned around for the last wave, the heaves I spied in Madre's shoulders.

My family was far, but it was in the letters and photographs I kept in my shoebox. Padre's skinny cheeks. Our house's thatch roof. And the details that came on the notes Padre dictated to the town typist: The price of corn is going down; We'll pay the seed loans with this year's harvest; Thanks for the presents—we bought milk.

Doña Clavel was good. She looked at me when one of her guests mentioned my braids or my cooking. In public, I called her madrina.

The other servants—Carmela and Dora—were nice but odd. They often interrupted their conversations as I walked into the kitchen, said a loud hello with a stiff smile. They waited for me to leave before going on with their chitchat. Afternoons, between lunch and dinner, their shut bedroom door muffled gossip and laughter. You don't want to hear, they told me once I knocked on their door. We talk about men and partos. Go play, it's what kids do. We're keeping you innocent.

Then there was don Remigio—examining my chest, my behind. His huge hands squeezed papers, forks. He once bent his reading glasses shapeless. When he was done, he pulled out a couple of glass shards from his palm, dabbed the blood with the napkin, and kept eating his soup.

Every time he walked behind me I shuddered. And now I had to go to his bathroom and give him toilet paper.

I wrapped a length of twine around a nail on my door to tie it shut. Then I walked down the corridor past the dining room and the living room. In the courtyard the tiled paths were outlined with citronella torches. Everything was lit, except the corridor leading to the bedrooms. A strip of light peaked under the master bedroom door. How was I going to do this?

I knocked. When I heard footsteps, I hustled quietly down the corridor to the bathroom door. That way, as el señor opened the bedroom door, I could slip into the bathroom. I would place the toilet paper on its rod and be out before he knew it.

I opened the armoire, but the handle gave way. It had been loose for several days, and now it was dangling from my hand! The screws fell on the floor. Ping, ping. Clumsy, clumsy. Now el señor was next to me, the light of the dressing table glaring down my face and the porcelain handle in my guilty hand.

Are you sneaking around?

I picked up the screws, wondering how much of my chest he could see.

Señor, you called about the toilet paper? I'm sorry about the handle. I'll fix it first thing tomorrow morning.

Go ahead.

He was watching me.

I don't have all night.

I stuck my hand into the armoire, got one roll of paper, slipped between don Remigio's unmoving body and the washbasin. I placed the roll of paper in its cradle.

His shadow grew.

Gracias, señor. La señora needs me downstairs. For the mole.

As I tried to slip past, I wondered what I had to thank him for.

He did not clear my path. He grinned like a boy. An old, taunting boy.

I walked sideways past him, a hip and a shoulder first. Then he clamped his fingers on my rump. I tried to wriggle away, but he dug his fingernails in. I waited, fighting the tears.

He squeezed harder. I grimaced.

He grinned all the way to his gray molars. He watched my eyes fill, then spill.

He let go.

He pointed at the drops on my apron.

She's going to tell you off. Filthy.

I rushed away, a claw as sharp as don Remigio's pulling my innards into a knot.

My belly gave in after the guests were gone. It must be my moon again, I thought. How long had it been since last time? The pain grew more debilitating by the minute. The other maids were out. After dinner I just had to wait sitting on a small stool in a far corner of the living room. Finally, don Remigio signaled his wife toward their bedroom. She stood up and walked with him following her, hungry. The lock clacked into place.

I stood up. I slipped a few music albums into their sleeves and onto the shelf; placed the yarn in doña Clavel's knitting basket. I took the ashtray, the empty whiskey bottle and glass to the kitchen. There I boiled some herbs and carried them in small pots to my room. I was breaking a fever.

I closed my door and curled up like a kitten in my cot, panting, stroking my aching belly. It was small but bloated. Strange: I had always been skinny. My arms and legs were bony. Could it be a tapeworm?

A cramp made me gasp. I closed my eyes and took tiny sips of air.

I was used to taking care of myself. After all, I had been a criada since my tenth year. Criada—the strange word went on like a light. Criada, given to strangers to raise, to earn her keep. Doña Clavel was my madrina and would nurture me in return for my labor. Would I be cultivated like a lady, or like my father's milpa? Was I criada, like the neighbor's piglets in the criadero? My parents had hoped for the best.

The claw wrenched my guts. I did what Madre would—wrapped rags steeped in arnica around my forehead, back, and abdomen; drank linden and spearmint; kept as calm as possible. Perhaps I fell asleep.

A wicked cramp jolted me out of bed and made me squat with my head and shoulders on the cot. Then another cramp. And another. A cold sweat ran down my back. I found a pail and put it between my legs because I could no longer walk to the outhouse. The pain came in waves, deeper, more relentless.

What did I eat, for the love of God? It's going to kill me, it's killing me, virgencita, let it out.

Now.

A huge pebble forced itself out of me—a round, bloody, whitish ball. I thought I saw a face, the face of all my sins. I pushed and pushed and made out a filthy little body; it writhed. I pushed; I pulled desperately with my hands until the thing came out.

It was a baby.

How do I hide it? Where can I dump it?

It was choking. I wiped away an awful drool around its mouth. I slid two fingers in and wiped there too. It whimpered. Then the little chest puffed up, and it screamed.

Did Madre know this would happen when she sent me here?

I covered the wail with my hand—what if it got to los señores? It clamped itself to my palm; it sucked so hard it hurt. I sat on the bloody cot, looked up to the Madonna on the wall. I pulled on the tripe tying us together and gave it the chichi. It sucked in a rage until my teat was raw. I pulled away, put the thing at my other breast, lay on my side, and was finally comfortable.

I looked.

Una niña. Pobre.

I covered myself, and it, and fell asleep.

New pains woke me. Another one?

But it was just the itacate. I may be a dumb head, but I had seen the sow eat the piglets' luggage up in the sierra. The itacate was what fed the crías inside the mother. It was still dark out; I had time to get rid of it.

I took the gardening scissors and cut the rope. Emptied out the shoe box. Lined it with my apron and other rags, put the little thing in. Put the box in the chest of drawers. Left a crack open to let her breathe but make sure the rats wouldn't get in. Run, cut some old sheets. Come back, clean that mess.

I now had a new patrona. I did everything she commanded. In the hours before daylight I toiled to keep her fed and dry and quiet. I lay down, looked at her.

Just like María before she got cold.

But this one came from me.

When I closed my eyes, the roosters were crowing.

Thirty-Six

I lay the folded sheet on the dresser. I would not need it—el señor had promised una casa con todo. You won't have to work, he said this morning. Just take care of the baby and attend to me when I visit. Get ready; you are leaving today.

Would he give me an allowance? Would the baby call him Papá?

What would doña Clavel say?

I looked around my room. On the cot, my doll lay next to the Madonna della Tempi and the decorations I had made with Alonso. My clothes, folded in little piles: the street dress and shoes I would change into in time to leave; underwear; my rebozo; the baby's diapers, blankets, spit rags, a bonnet—all made from a flannel sheet in pale yellow with large orange flowers I had found on the garbage can lid. I folded my two uniforms, the gala one and the everyday one—so oversized no one had noticed a baby hidden in its folds. Not even I.

My parents did not know the first thing about this move. They did not know that their twelve-year-old daughter had carried a baby without an idea of what she was doing. Había dado a luz: I had gifted a baby to the light. My own María. I had come out of a night of pain and terror, but the baby in my arms quickly erased the fear and shame. No time for that when a small one needed food and protection day and night.

The fear made me forget that other night months earlier. The Christmas night I had awoken with don Remigio on top of me. His hand tight over my mouth, flooding me with his smell of rotten pineapples. He clipped my arms across my chest. His knee splayed my legs. He broke me open, forced something huge into me, once and again.

Like the bulls and the horses. I should have known.

Now I was shaking like a puppy.

On the sheet I was folding a stain the color of sepia and the size of a melon had been joined by one larger and darker, the one formed during María's arrival. I had scrubbed both with little success. I would have to leave the sheet here. I did not own it. And I did not need to be reminded of who I had turned into, or how.

For that I had the other maids. When I appeared with the baby, Dora dragged me into her room. You're not a little girl anymore. Now you have your own little girl.

She sat me on her saggy bed and took the baby. She and Carmela sat on the other bed, arguing over whose turn it was to rock her.

You are so lucky. Of course, he had to choose you. Look how blonde you are.

Dora poked my braid with her fingernail. I batted her hand away.

Carmela kissed the fuzz on María's crown. Look at this peach. I could eat her up.

They offered all manner of advice on running a casa chica for don Remigio.

With this jewel you're set. They say he never dumps his women. He makes a mess, but then he takes care of it. He's a gentleman.

Now all you'll need is to run the house, and every now and then—

Carmela smiled, leaned back on the bed, splayed her arms and legs. Her thighs rolled and quivered.

The bedspread was the color of blood.

I took María. I said, I have to go. She is hungry.

You're embarrassed? Now it wouldn't be the first time you show your teaties?

They laughed.

I walked out, feeding the baby on my way to our room, looking left and right. The strangeness on my body was gone. Perhaps it was true—I would be living in my own home, devoted to the baby. And don Remigio had a family—he could not possibly visit often.

But I had thought I would never have to endure another night like that Christmas. Ever since then, I had been careful to bolt my room every night.

I cupped my baby's head, pulled her tighter to my breast.

Couldn't things stay as they were? Would doña Clavel not want to keep me? I imagined her, stopping to admire my polished silver. She would remember the times a guest had remarked that I was practically one of the family. She would say—we *need you, Amalia. Stay.*

She was my madrina, after all.

When I asked, Dora laughed.

How do you expect the señora to feed you while you carry on showing off her husband's baby under her own roof? Although I suppose don Remigio wouldn't mind sparing himself the commuting and the expense of one more casa chica.

I never mentioned it again. I worked and waited for the señores to decide. I tried to clean quickly while la señora went out. I kept the baby in her box with me as I did my chores. I prayed she would be quiet. That doña Clavel would not look.

But just yesterday, she had, and how. I was mopping her bedroom when María started whimpering. Before I could wipe my hands to pick her up, la señora rushed into the room as if she had been waiting behind the door. She took her from the box and rocked her.

I'll take care of her. Carry on.

Her voice was creamy. She looked down on the baby like a zopilote on a cactus.

Dreams. What good were they?

I placed the sheets on the dresser and surveyed my room. It would be easy to carry my things in a large box and the baby in the little one.

I widened the crack in the drawer. At one week, María was beginning to stretch her cardboard cradle. She was a good sleeper. I picked her up and swaddled her like a tamarind pod. I kissed her lips, took in her sweet breath. I placed her in the box, slid the drawer almost shut, and rushed away. My breasts were heavy. She would be hungry soon.

I found a good box in the storage room and rushed back to mine. At my door I heard a humming. Doña Clavel was holding María!

La señora's eyes were soft. She paced the room, swayed back and forth. When she saw me, she scowled.

Señora, I'm sorry. I'll be leaving soon. I'm just—

Quiet. Pass me one of those diapers, will you?

On my cot a mountain of baby clothing covered my belongings: shirts, onesies, bibs, blankets, a stack of diapers. Everything was the color of roses or lilies. Under the new clothes my doll's braids dangled from the side of the bed. I took a diaper from the pile and unfolded it. From my hand tumbled folds and folds of gauze, pure like the clouds. My doll fell to the floor.

Doña Clavel paced carefully. María slept, her head propped between la señora's cheek and her cupped hand. The patrona tiptoed with difficulty, her feet straining to surpass the incline of her shoes to avoid the clicking noise. She placed the diaper on her shoulder and the baby on it. María puckered her lips.

I picked up the rag doll and, my hands folded behind my back, retreated to a corner while doña Clavel said her goodbyes. A tingle crawled from deep in my chest to my nipples. I had to feed the baby and leave.

Doña Clavel's eyelids seemed heavy.

We need to talk about your duties, she whispered. It was hard to hear her.

I tried to say something.

You'll change her diapers, bathe her, wash her things. Keep her comfortable. Don't worry, I'll hire someone else for cooking and cleaning.

Señora, and don Remigio? He said I—

She opened her eyes and spoke loudly. We are bringing the baby to her bassinet.

María squirmed.

Don't stand there like a statue, niña. Bring those things.

She walked out with María in her arms.

I stood there, alone. Then I took a pile of diapers and rushed after my daughter.

Fill one of the biberones I brought this morning, will you? Put exactly four spoons of the formula, then add boiled water to the line on the top. It has to be boiled for a good while, but make sure you cool it off first. It's important to keep everything sterile.

The instructions ebbed and flowed.

My breasts were bursting. Since doña Clavel started helping with the baby, I'd had a hard time keeping myself dry. La señora insisted on doing all of the feeding herself.

Es más higiénico, she said.

Then I learned I could squeeze the milk out. I kept it in a cup in the icebox and prepared the bottles with it. Then I fed the cats the right amount of powder. The switch was easy ever since Dora and Carmela moved out.

It could not be wrong. María was thriving.

Ay Amalia, how can those poor girls manage with a baby—far from their families, working all day, and taking care of a creature of God?

Sitting in the pink armchair with the curlicues, doña Clavel held María wrapped like a bolt of lace. She tried to insert the plastic bottle in her mouth, but María was not having it. Alonso rubbed the baby's feet and improvised a lullaby.

La señora smiled. A child must live where it can be cared for.

She offered her the rubber nipple. María squirmed. Alonso asked, We're not giving her away? This is our baby.

Of course not, dear.

The whimpers punctuated the conversation.

So many families pray to be blessed with a child. There is no better place for her than a proper home, where she'll grow up healthy and educated, not on the street. Those girls have only to thank the Lord.

How la señora talked.

The baby wriggled. Her little feet kicked. Alonso could no longer touch her, so frantic was her little dance.

Doña Clavel looked up at me, a smile etched on her face.

The street. That's something this baby will not have to face.

My chest pushed against my uniform. Pressed against the straps of my apron. Why did doña Clavel keep calling María "this baby"? What other baby was there?

La señora looked up at me.

Excuse me?

Sí, señora. Gracias.

Of course. How could I forget?

La señora smiled at María.
And she broke out into a wail.

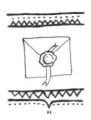

Thirty-Seven

Por fin. Finally, God deigned look down on my solitude, my need to restore my family. This gift came to me unsoiled. Free from assaults, from the orphanage's squalor. Born where she belonged. I could forget Amalia's transgressions. Protecting her was a small price to pay.

This baby belonged with us, and no one would question that. For confirmation one need only look into Remigio's eyes. I was not stupid. I knew what he did two or three times a week when he went out for "tragos with his compadres." I knew Tigrillo inside out, that boy from the Playa Sur slum who, at eight years, had swept offices to support his mother; who had sharpened a butter knife into a blade to defend himself from the street crazies. The youth who escaped derision using his fists in a boxing ring. The man who entered our community by buying a bad mortgage and a good wife. A tiger in business, a tiger in bed. Everyone in Ayotlan knew that the obstacle to conceiving a child was not in him. And me? I had endured his savagery four years—and still the disagreeable blood came every month. I was honest. I was not afraid of the truth.

But now everything was resolved. This baby was mine, Remigio's glance told me when he found me cradling it in my arms. When no questions came in weeks, I knew they would never come. And I knew what to do. I stayed several months on maternity retreat. Decent women do not show themselves in public all disfigured, I told my friends over the phone. Remember? All our mothers did the same. And Dr. Colunga prescribed bed rest. He's worried about eclampsia. No, no, no. You'll see us soon enough. When the baby comes.

It was a pleasant, introspective time, with only the family at home. The day I welcomed the preciously clad baby in my bedroom, I had just sent Dora and Carmela to good jobs in

Guadalajara. I waved at them as they stood on the second-class train car, holding their severance envelopes. This I topped off with gifts from my jewelry box: on Dora's ears shone the pearl earrings Padre had given me on my First Communion; on Carmela's chest, the matching crucifix. More would come, I said, if they stayed away. It pained me to part with some of my heritage. But it was the right thing to do.

One evening after work, Remigio found me talking on the phone at my desk. Alonso played marbles at my feet, and the baby slept.

What are you up to now?

The baptism.

He turned toward the bassinet.

We'll call her Mariana Eugenia, after your mother. Mariana Eugenia Sánchez Celis. My voice silkened to enunciate Celis, my family name.

It's not María anymore? Alonso asked. Then I'll just call her Mari.

You will call her Mariana, I instructed.

Remigio looked from the baby to me, then back to the baby.

I dripped hot wax on an envelope, pressed the family seal onto it. My neck crawled under Remigio's gaze. I steadied myself by wielding the seal as though a gavel. I handed him a stack of rose-colored envelopes.

Give your compadres these. And remember—the baby was born two weeks ago. August 15. She is a large, healthy baby, like her father.

Remigio took the envelopes in his hand, and I felt larger than ever.

And. I will mention this just once. Outside this house you do as you please. But here—I waved the seal in a circular motion, pointing at the walls with the family portraits: Laura as Queen of Carnival; my mother's melancholy face; my father, who threw both his daughters into the tiger's den. They all nodded.

In this house you do not touch anyone but me. Is that clear?

Remigio looked up at me as if at someone new, then down again.

And with that we turned an accident of lust into a miracle of justice. Free from controversy, from the pain of labor and childbirth, and through the art and will of one woman alone, Mariana Eugenia Sánchez Celis was born. She was robust and fair. She had a name and a family. She was a lucky, lucky child.

Thirty-Eight

Two years later came Luisa, and our family was complete. Two lovely girls; an uncle young enough to be their brother; an attentive mother raising them healthy and proper; a father who kept his promise of financial stability. A lovely home. I had countless reasons to be proud. All we had to do was keep that balance.

And Adrián and Luz. They indulged my children, showered Remigio and me with appreciation. That evening we played cards on the terrace of their lovely home. We admired the shining bay, the towering cliffs, the white dunes. To the side of the house, the beautiful Hotel Belmar gifted us its orchestra music.

Mariana is behind the peacock, Luisa chirped and bolted toward the topiary tree, her dark hair flying wild. I looked up. There was no cloud in the sky.

Luisa. Shade, sweetheart—

She is lovely, Luz said, touching my knee.

And loud. They bother los señores. I glanced at the table where Adrián and Remigio smoked.

Luz held her side a little. She took a slow breath, shook her head. As long as they have their brandy and cigars, they won't be bothered. And your children are a joy. They know beauty when they touch it.

Indeed. There was Alonso telling stories, pointing at the garland of fantastical figures carved on the limestone balustrade. The Nereid was born from this shell, he said. Her hair is woven with sea stars, you see? They light her way.

Does the scallop shell fly, or does it glide on the water? asked Mariana.

Where is her *home*? Luisa asked.

Here. Alonso pointed at the house, the garden, the beach, the ocean beyond.

This was indeed the home of beauty. It whispered in my ear: welcome. The trees rustled. The alabaster floor clicked under well-shod feet; the mahogany furniture nestled us in comfort. All the objects in this house pronounced three words—*it is true.* There really are places that stand for your ideals.

Next door, the Belmar Hotel presented us with danzón after danzón, bolero after bolero. Laura had met her destiny there. A reminder of genteel times and of immense sorrow, the hotel moored me to a past that was so mine.

The Landeros house was breeze and light. Every room looked to the ocean through a wall of windows as high as a cathedral's, opening onto the vast terrace. The billowing organza hangings breathed like lungs, bringing the outdoors in, the indoors out.

Soon the guests would come and dinner would begin, then dancing. I would be surrounded by the society poverty had almost robbed me of. I would sit with Luz, Adrián, and the other elders and watch my former schoolmates dance with fiancés or young husbands, their adult lives barely beginning. That some had just married had done little to bridge the gap between me and them. They had no use for me: rather than a role model, they saw me as their mothers' peer. When my sister and my parents died, they took my youth with them.

But I had my children, and the Landeroses. They held me where I belonged.

One of Remigio's associates joined us. There was something attractive in Chepo Menard's build. He was stronger than the others. He tried to hide his coarseness.

Luz and I sat in a love seat some twelve feet from the men.

This was the fourth house built in this town, over two hundred years ago, Adrián explained. It has always been in my family.

We are fortunate, Luz said. She touched her side and checked a grimace.

I took her hand and felt her brittle skin roll over frail bones.

I wish we had children to give the home to.
My heart took a plunge.

Thanks for the lands, buddy. Menard addressed Remigio, but his eyes were on Adrián. He was no friend of his—no "buddy." And Adrián always avoided any mention of business at his gatherings.

Remigio said, I sold Chepo some of my Careyes. Finally, someone will give that desert some use.

Adrián, Luz, and I looked beyond the garden. Every few seconds, the lighthouse showed a pink expanse, its grasses combed by the wind. That was the desert?

Menard said, And finally some pendejo gave you twenty times what you paid, cabrón.

A gust blew the curtains toward the terrace, then whipped them into the living room.

Adrián sat up. I thought you had sold him the beaches north of town.

He got some of that too.

You should give me all.

Now don't be greedy. When you're done building your ten hotels, come back, and I might have more.

Menard smirked. *Fourteen* hotels. One here—his thumb pointed over his shoulder to the beach behind him. The rest north of town. As many as you will give me space for.

Remigio raised his glass to me. Those terrenos up north? They are my life insurance.

Why would this tower of strength worry about insurance? He seemed thinner. His appetite was often upset. The sores in his mouth never went away. But that did not stop him from chasing after who knows what in the middle of the night. How much longer did he have?

He went on. Adrián has some lands you might want. ¿Verdad, compadre?

I felt my face burn. Adrián said nothing.

Remigio leaned toward Adrián. You want progress—let it in. Tourism is it. The gringos come looking for a place to drop their dollars. Trouble is, this town doesn't have enough beds. The pinches pensiones won't do.

Adrián pointed to his right. Pensiones? El Belmar es un señor hotel. The service, the banquets.

The Sunday dances, Luz said. The hundred-member orchestra.

The wind picked up, and the curtains rolled like waves.

And the botanical garden. It is a center for Ayotlan culture. Luz sounded hurried.

Menard looked over to me. Isn't that where you met your wife?

My name is Clavel. I stood up and walked toward the house. I said, All I remember is my sister being burned.

I batted at the curtains as I went in.

When I returned from the powder room, I felt calmer.

Remigio had a hand on Adrián's back. Don't be a fool, he said.

For all I knew Adrián could rise to throw Remigio out, and my family with him. I would not protest.

Chepo was leaning on Adrián's backrest. Those are the winds blowing these days. Hop on board or miss the boat. But then don't complain if it drowns you in its wake.

Adrián sat firmly. What kind of building do you have in mind?

A twelve-story hotel, Menard said. I've been buying some lands and just added Remigio's beaches to get something of suitable size.

There are not many empty lots downtown. What did you get?

Menard jerked his head toward the Belmar.

Adrián craned his neck. You bought Fernández out?

The lighthouse pierced the darkness.

You replace a four-story building with a tower three times taller. Adrián's words were a warning. It will choke the downtown and the bay.

Luz clutched my hand. Hers was ice.

Menard pushed his chair back. We'll build a hotel with comfortable rooms, the kind Americans want. TVs. A large swimming pool, restaurants, a discotheque.

I'm sick of danzón and boleros, Remigio sputtered. I knew they were his favorites.

Cheap food, lots of liquor. We'll make a profit finally.

Adrián groaned. You can't build on the beach. Coastal lands are federal property.

He is leasing for twenty years from the federal government. He can build on the beach as long as he provides public access.

Mayor Chávez approved diverting the road behind the hotel, added Menard. My budget includes the diversion, so the town won't incur expense.

Show him the blueprints.

Menard opened the papers like an inept magician. Luz's hand twitched when a coffee cup toppled on the Belgian tablecloth.

The maid worked fast, but everyone could see that the lace was ruined.

The men pored over the blueprint. I imagined the construction like a cancer of mortar choking, then toppling the Belmar.

Adrián's voice shook. My property—you are counting it as part of your project?

Luz covered her mouth.

The hotel will consist of three connected towers. I have the land for the left tower, Remigio's terrenos, and the right, here, where the Belmar is. So I just need the center tower. It will have a second discotheque, restaurant, parking lot. Another set of rooms.

I wrapped the alpaca shawl around Luz.

Menard's smile was almost innocent.

The hotel will bring so much cash in, I'm prepared to give you two million—well above this house's worth. Think of it as a token of friendship.

Adrián stared at the space between Chepo's eyebrows. He said, My house is not for sale.

Menard snorted. With two million you could build a better one anywhere you want. Make me a counteroffer.

I will: I propose a shorter building south of my property, but across from the Malecón. Or use the lands outside town. Not here. The Hotel Belmar, my house, the Malecón at the ocean. They are part of Ayotlan's history.

It was a plea.

That coffin might be fashionable for five years. Then it will fall apart.

That is why I'm planning a chain of hotels. By the time people get bored of one, we will have the next running, then we can sell the old one. And so on.

Disposable hotels.

Well, if you see it that way.

You'll have to take your project elsewhere.

Menard stood up, dropped his napkin into his brandy glass. Is that your last word? Where's the door?

Adrián stood up and led Menard by the elbow. As they walked away, he asked, Now your plans for downtown are off, where do you think you'll build?

Luz stood beside me. We tried to hear the answer. She gazed at the dunes until the lighthouse abandoned us.

We are not selling, Luz said when Adrián and Remigio came back.

Adrián sat in the love seat I had shared with Luz. I unclenched her hands, helped her sit next to Adrián. Will he call off the project?

Standing behind the loveseat, Remigio shook his head at me.

Adrián's voice was both firm and defeated. The plan stands, with or without my land. Nice neighbors, Did he say? You won't be bored, with discotheques all around.

I asked, He will not reconsider?

Chepo is giving *me* time to reconsider. I might yet come around, he said? He doesn't want his architects to fall out of schedule. Two million if I call back tomorrow. The next day the offer is one million. The day after that the deal is off.

There is no deal, said Luz.

Of course not, Adrián said, smiling bitterly. Before he left he discussed another transaction. We have to talk about your commission, he told Remigio. Or did I misunderstand, compadre?

No one said a word on the ride home.

I leaned on the door of our black Ford and watched Remigio turn the key in the ignition, smile with satisfaction at the engine's roar. On the back seat, Luisa rested her head on Mariana's lap; Mariana rested hers on Alonso's shoulder. He looked out the window.

Remigio gripped the leather-lined steering wheel and glanced at his silver cufflinks. He had left the white gold ones at home.

His clothes were impeccable as usual, the tailored evening suit and starched shirt, the polished shoes. But I knew every item in his pockets was modest, even cheap. His wallet carried very little cash. His documents—even his driver's license—were locked in a dresser in our bedroom. One never knew where exhaustion might hit. And who might be next to him, prying into his pockets.

At home Remigio unlocked the mahogany door. Luisa slept in Alonso's arms; Mariana hung next to him. I ushered my children into my home.

Alonso looked at Remigio. I'm not tired. You and I can—

No, Alonso, I said.

Clavel, I am not a kid anymore. I am fully—

I glared at him. Go to bed.

He turned around and walked to the bedrooms. Mariana followed.

Remigio took a padlock from a niche on the side of the entrance corridor. Then he walked back out and closed the door between us. Good night, I heard him say.

From the inside, I heard him turn the padlock's bolts and pins into place.

I brought my face close to the door. When are you coming home?

I heard Remigio's shoes slap the sidewalk. He had dragged his feet here—he dragged his feet everywhere nowadays—but now he practically ran.

I turned around and walked toward my room. What could I hope for—that on his return Remigio would not deride my outrage? That, just as of late, he collapsed, too tired to assault me?

How much longer now?

Thirty-Nine

Remigio was fond of riding with his friends on a horse-drawn carriage, followed by a second carriage laden with tubas, clarinets, and the outsized tamboras whose blasts he liked to credit with his smooth digestion. The midnight processions made the neighbors pull their pillows over their heads. Drunks! But on the street, small multitudes often followed him. He called the trumpeters to play "Alma Llanera" straight into his ears, welcoming the noise, the outlandishness. In Ayotlan, Tigrillo was king of parades, rey de la bacanal.

So today: the followers were disorderly, some drunk, some just curious hangers-on. The crowd grew with each turn onto a new street. This time, however, the moon and streetlights did not add romance and mystery. Instead, the sun exposed scarred pavement and filthy corners. I, too, was a novelty, following my husband's procession for the first and last time. It was a trip that would end at his grave.

No one was prepared for the death of a strong man in his early fifties. But now it had come to pass, no one wanted to miss his funeral. It began at the door of our home and handed out ruckus in all neighborhoods. Following the horse-drawn hearse drowning in a sea of carnations and cempasúchitl, the tambora bestowed its deafening music from three arañas. Then came the two-door, air-conditioned, silent Galaxy. Black, double-black like patent leather, polished and airtight. Next to me, Alonso struggled to stay composed in his suit and tie. Draped in white lace, the girls periodically informed me of new pilgrims joining the procession. Some came by car, some on foot, some in arañas.

And I? I clutched my handkerchief and stared at the driver's nape.

The entierro passed the cathedral, progressed around the central plaza, squeezed down Rebaje Street. At the ocean it took its place before Adrián Landeros's house. It was bathed in dust, sandwiched left and right by demolition machinery. Next to it stood the pile of rubble that had until recently been the Belmar Hotel.

The band played "El Sauce y la Palma." When the song ended, the musicians yelled ¡Compadre!, as instructed in his will and executed by Adrián himself, who now walked out of his house in tuxedo, white tie, and top hat. His attire belied the churning heat and, though black, the funereal occasion. He stepped onto the carriage next to his friend and readied himself to see him off to his last dwelling. A friend to the end.

The procession dragged through gritty streets and stopped at the market, where the marchantas treated everyone to asado a la plaza and tamarind drinks, refusing to take a dime.

Pos how could I charge, mister? It's Tigrillo in that box. To his health and good rest, ¡sí señor!

Some mourners waved at me through the window. My eyes felt like frosted glass.

We skirted Nevería Hill and reached the neighborhood Nueva Esperanza, its dusty slopes and potholes. Nueva Esperanza children were sometimes on the news during the flood season. Without proper drainage, flashfloods often swept away a critter or two, later to appear entangled with frigate nests in the mangroves.

The procession stopped in front of a dun-colored house. The band serenaded.

Siempre recordaré
aquellos ojos verdes.

Curtains rustled, the door opened, and a woman with thick ankles and a graceful neck hauled three children, her red hands straightening collars and buttoning Sunday clothes. My mouth went lax as I riveted my eyes on the oldest child. He was tall as a man, though scrawny.

Quihubo, Candelaria. Remigio sends his regards, Adrián's voice faintly carried through the closed window.

Luisa giggled. Adrián looks like Miss Ana just scolded him at school.

The woman with the thick ankles said something.

Candelaria has green eyes, Luisa said. Like in the song: Siempre recordaré—

I shushed her. Outside, the children added more flowers to the yellow tide on the coffin. The woman stole a quick glance at us. My heart pounded in my ears.

Dignidad ante la adversidad, hija.

My mother was back from the past. She taught me plenty about dignity. A legitimate wife, she was fond of saying, does not worry about what her husband does with other women. As long as he respects you and provides as God commands. You are the wife. If he spends the night out, he lets you sleep. Remember: las otras—the others—are chapels. You are the cathedral.

My life had given me plenty of adversity to turn into a cathedral of dignity. Remigio's illness had been the gossips' topic for a year: he had been weak and angry and sometimes incoherent, yet Dr. Colunga waved off my questions. What do you need to know? He is wearing out.

Luisa pointed. Are those daisies?

They're carnations, Mariana said. Haven't you learned the flowers at school?

Carnations are claveles, Luisa said. Madre, they put you on Papá!

Shut your mouth.

With some variations, the scene of serenade, woman, children, and flowers played at two other neighborhoods. I strangled my handkerchief and stared ahead.

I could kill him anew. Instead, I did not shed a tear. I did not complain. What my heart held was only mine. This procession—this day—would pass.

My heels echoed in the corridor. The children had run in before me, eager to peel off the funereal attire. They were probably relaxing in Amalia's room, or in the tree. I took this opportunity to see my family's home. This square of stone, these four lines of rooms surrounding four corridors with a courtyard in the center were finally, truly mine, a place to usher my children into adulthood. Where, I thought with nervous satisfaction, I would enjoy a freedom I'd never had.

But none would come easily. Sitting in a rocking chair in the gallery, I leaned back and looked up. Blackened with tar against the humidity, the beams buttressing the roof were in varying stages of disrepair. After two centuries of hurricanes and neglect, some were clearly rotting. I now understood why Amalia had arranged the furniture in this way, placing planters to catch the water leaking from above.

I drank the hibiscus water she had left for me on the side table. I was not one to shy from the truth. And this not only dripped from the ceiling's beams but crawled up the walls, where the peeling paint revealed the shifting tastes of many refurbishing projects, none undertaken in my lifetime. Splotches in aqua, rose, maroon. How much sunnier the house would look with a lick of fresh paint. I closed my eyes and drew a deep breath, seeking the aroma of flowers other than carnations and cempasúchitl. Instead, I took in another offense. Amalia must have used too much water in the laundry again. When would she learn to be careful with the sewage pipes?

Could I fix this house? Remigio worked hard all his life but had never truly brought financial comfort. We had to repay my father's obligations, he was fond of saying. No Catholic school for the children meant rubbing shoulders with servants at the public school—and with who knows how many half-siblings. Remigio denied me any luxury. You want curtains? There, your sewing machine. Fabrics? Take it from the household allowance. There were the drapes I had sewn, sheltering the gallery. The fabric was light and translucent, resembling organza, my attempt to imitate Luz's airy curtains that so elegantly diffused the light in her home. I toiled to produce the decent lifestyle I had been born into. I sent my children out well groomed and behaved. My guests saw good taste, simple elegance. I belonged in Ayotlan's society by right of birth, no matter Remigio's coarseness or his vulgar hunger for wealth. Now I could ask whomever I liked to my home.

But how could I hold on to it? Wouldn't Menard be glad to buy it!

I could move into a smaller, modern place. I could sell my lace embroidery—a good occupation for a well-born widow.

A pang of sadness overtook me. This was the house I and my children had been born in. My sister and my parents had died here. I had done everything to save it. I did not know how to live elsewhere.

I had to talk to Adrián, read whatever documents Remigio had left.

I had to wait nine days.

The morning after the novena, Adrián announced his visit, and I rushed to touch up Amalia's cleaning. Then I took a shower, donned a black linen dress, and waited.

Adrián behaved solemnly. He sat in the Louis XV armchair, lithe and upright in his black suit, his hands resting on his cane's ivory handle, his skull as lustrous as his shoes. He drank black coffee and asked about everyone's health.

Then he read the will.

In Adrián's voice, Remigio rose from the dead to spell out his last obligations and my many humiliations. The crude details of the funereal procession were there, complete with serenades to friends and lovers. A few debts needing settlement, nothing major. Then Adrián went on to lay out what went to the family. That is, Remigio's family. He may have imposed on me a lifetime of sacrifices, but not on himself. The parrandas, the whiskey-laced midnight yells. All that scandal—as if I needed confirmation—had yielded several "small houses" for large-bosomed women from Miguel Alemán Avenue to Aquiles Serdán Street. Like it or not, this family extended beyond my four walls.

Adrián read steadily.

In keeping with my responsibilities, I will provide for all my children.

He looked up. Of course that does not mean they all are equal.

Each of the illicit mothers—I appreciated Adrián's emphasis on the word *illicit*—will receive a single cash payment, after which their dependence on my assets will end.

The compassion in Adrián's eyes was hard to bear. He placed his hand on mine.

I cannot imagine how difficult this is for you, Clavel. But I want to emphasize the good news.

He produced a stack of bank statements and another of land

titles. Everything Remigio had earned in fourteen years, everything I had toiled for, all that was left after subtracting his
parrandas, lovers, and children without-the-walls, was now
in my hands. And it was not a pittance. The house and, to my
surprise, thousands of acres of coastal lands went to the family.
Just the cash in the bank was plenty to offer the children a life
more comfortable than they had known. I repressed a smile. To
believe Remigio, we had teetered on the edge of ruin, but here
was enough to rebuild the house. To educate the children. And
for me, the peace of mind I lost the day I met him.

Remigio was many things, Adrián said. But above all, he was a
gentleman. He even thought of Amalia: she will have employment
in this house as long as she wants.

A gentleman indeed.

Adrián made the meeting brief. He glossed over several
passages to spare me the jargon. He locked the will in Remigio's
desk, deposited the key in my hands, and cradled them in his.

These are difficult times, Clavel. But I am pleased that Remigio
can provide properly for you and the family. He worked all his
life to accomplish this.

Then he left me to a heady flood of shock and release.

That feeling lasted one day. With the children finally in school I
found a moment of quiet to read the will at my leisure. I entered
Padre's dusky library, where he had sold my youth. The window
casings were shut since the onset of Remigio's illness. I walked
in almost total darkness, reached the desk lamp and pulled the
chain. I sat in the office chair, reeking of Remigio's sweat and
tobacco. I unlocked the drawer where Adrián had placed the
will and relished this first-time access to the desk. How many
other places dominated by my husband were now mine? I would
discover them in my own good time.

I opened the document at the end. Next to the hard zigzags
composing his signature, I saw Adrián's flourishes in green ink.
The will was short—five typewritten pages. It contained my name,
those of my children, our domicile. The names and addresses
of the other women and children. I counted the mothers, three,

and the children, eleven. I tallied the allowances assigned them. The total exceeded my household budget for several years.

But it wasn't those names and addresses, not even those figures, that confirmed that my husband had been little more than an adversary.

Everything Adrián had said yesterday was true. The children would be educated and Amalia protected. I would receive a generous budget for the household.

I felt weak. Was this my only mention in the will?

I reread the document. I tracked each asset and beneficiary. I scanned the will for mentions of the house I had contributed to this marriage. I found my name toward the end, in one of the passages Adrián had not quoted.

> My two daughters, Mariana and Luisa Sánchez Celis, and my adoptive son Alonso Celis Coulson will receive all necessary monies to support their education until the completion of their university studies or the age of twenty-five. My widow, Clavel Celis de Sánchez, will assure that they are properly provided for.

A rush of gratitude filled me seeing Remigio treat Alonso as a son.

> Mariana and Luisa Sánchez Celis will receive on Luisa's eighteenth birthday: 1. title to the home on 64 Aquiles Serdán Street; 2. the balance of my savings and stocks as supervised by my attorney Adrián Landeros; and 3. the 25,000 acres of coastal lands starting on Kilometer 22 of the road North of Ayotlan (statements and deeds attached).
>
> My wife, Clavel Celis Coulson de Sánchez, and our maid, Amalia Godínez López, may reside in Aquiles Serdán 64 for life. Clavel Celis de Sánchez's current household budget will receive an increase of 40 percent. Thereafter, she will receive yearly increases of 8 percent on mentioned allowance. For her services, Amalia Godínez López will receive her current salary, plus an annual increase of 5 percent, for life.

I switched off the lamp and sat in darkness. That is what the cathedral receives. Thanks to Remigio's neat banking, I could expect to live the rest of my life in my home, next to my daughters,

my brother, and Amalia. I would not have to trouble with managing my assets. Because I had none.

A cold tide rushed from my stomach to my chest, obstructing
my breathing. My husband's power to insult me had transcended
the grave.

For the sake of my afterlife a confessor would warn me
against the capital sins hatred and ire. But I had little time for
such counsel. I had my and my children's terrestrial well-being
to attend to. I opened my eyes to the dust and darkness of the
shuttered library. I turned on the lamp and stood up. As I opened
the door, the morning sun blinded me.

Remigio had lost his life, but I had mine.

Forty

The mahogany door slammed, giving way to more noise.

I felt elation those days when, hot and tired and loaded with bags of screws or upholstery swatches, I found my home drowning in the noise of hammers, shovels, drills. The last weeks of Remigio's life, we had had to keep so quiet; in the end, that lover of loud festivities had shrunk from every noise. Now he could not stop the house's updating, the noise, the expense. He was troubled—and troubled me—no more.

I did it. I took all I could from my allowance and persuaded Adrián to cosign a loan. In a matter of weeks I set the work in motion. One might have expected me to modernize the house, but instead I turned it into its true self. In the ancient kitchen I brought the coal-fired stove, the bread oven, and the iron griddle back to working order. Refurbished shutters, wrought iron gates in whimsical designs, porcelain sinks and faucets, bathtubs and tiles. Everything that needed repair was now as when new, two hundred years prior. The walls repainted in the colors Luisa recommended: mustard, sand, cobalt, rose. The sweet girl surprised me with her sense of taste. Now, the grime of decades removed, the house was airy, lofty. I enjoyed checking on the workers' progress, directing small refinements. I was exacting but fair. Most frequently, my response to detail was a nod of approval.

I walked into the heart of my world—the garden. Four wide, cool corridors surrounded it and in turn were surrounded by many rooms. The garden was now replanted with gardenias and orchids. In the center stood the limonaria tree I cultivated despite all. Rescued from neglect, it offered better shade and fragrance.

Amalia stood under the tree, looking up into its fronds. She clutched a branch and placed a foot on another. Niños—her voice authoritative, fitting for the twenty-something she was. But her posture was that of a child.

The children climbed down. They saw me before Amalia. She turned to me, blushing.

We're done with homework, said Alonso.

They seemed largely untouched by their father's departure, but this was no surprise. He had seldom spent more than the midday meal with them, and he had not invited their conversation. Mijitos, I regularly admonished, Padre is tired. Be good and let him eat. He had been remote even before he fell ill.

You are finished? Show me, doña Clavel said with enthusiasm and curiosity.

They dusted off their clothes and sat at the iron table strewn with their books.

Alonso showed her a diagram. This is slow-intercept.

La señora nodded with a small smile. You're doing calculus in eighth grade?

The girls are doing fine too, I said. Just a little more grammar for Mariana and some reading for Luisa. You want to read for Madre, Luisita?

She read a paragraph of "Cinderella." Her voice was small, confident.

La señora stroked her pigtails. You're a good reader.

Mariana interrupted. Can I explain the pluperfect subjunctive? This is what you do. You say the verb in the participle. But first you combine it with the auxiliary, which has to be in the—

She watched her mother as she talked.

Good. Doña Clavel said, stroking Luisa's hair. It's time for a trim.

Good? Mariana asked, a sadness in her voice. I lowered my eyes.

Doña Clavel fanned herself. I'm pleased with your progress. Is Catholic school worth the trouble?

Luisa nodded. But they make us pray.

Is that a problem?

Luisa pouted. They laughed at me because I got stuck when I led the Hail Mary.

I patted her hand. We'll go over the prayers, dear.

Doña Clavel set her hand on my shoulder. Thanks, Amalia. For supporting me and the children in these times.

Oh, doña Clavel, I know it's—

She turned and started off. I'll be in my library.

¡Madre! Mariana shouted after her. Can we get music lessons?

Remember you said . . . ? Alonso asked.

On the new floor tiles doña Clavel's heels produced a crisp echo.

After homework I went to my bedroom and was reminded of the change the renovations had brought. A cheerful maize color, the walls were a far cry from the discolored stucco. Tiles now covered the cracked cement where I had knelt a terrifying night eleven years ago; new window panes replaced broken ones. I did not have to turn on the lightbulb until night, so bright was my room. It took me some time to stop feeling watched.

My very own room. Some employers might fail to renovate the servants' quarters, but not doña Clavel. I was fond of my room even when it had threatened to crumble around me, but now it was a haven, a place where I could be.

I took a key hanging from my neck and unlocked my armoire. I made space on the shelf for my novel *Fortunata y Jacinta.* Little María with her yarn braids sat on the shoebox. The red felt triangle of her smile held the innocence I had brought here.

I locked the armoire, hid the key under my blouse, and walked out.

At the library door I hesitated. Two months after don Remigio's death, his smell was still in the air—even after doña Clavel replaced his cigars, his filing cabinet, and his engravings of warships with tapestries, porcelains, fresh flowers.

Pasa, Amalia.

No need to knock—doña Clavel knew when I stood behind a door. She sat at her husband's desk, her hands warmed by the lamp. She had always expressed authority, but now she had a new self-containment. She looked older but more beautiful. She wore simple black dresses and pulled her hair back tightly, emphasizing her large eyes and almond face. She was a striking woman in her prime.

The first report cards are excellent, Amalia. See Alonso's human biology paper.

She stood up and crossed the room with a few strides. Her body, too, had changed with her husband's absence. She stood up from sitting as if into a dance. She had even begun to smile. She took the paper from a bookshelf and quickly flipped to the last page.

He got a 10.

I looked over the closing paragraph I had helped him compose.

He worked hard on the nervous system, I said. The new school has really excited them.

We must not let our guard down, though. Education is the only way.

Doña Clavel was back at her desk, the earnestness aging her instantly.

All they have is what they make of themselves. There's just so much I can give them, alone as I am.

Regretfully, I said. But la señora is young, will eventually remarry.

She was thirty, thirty-two years old? The chignon on her nape lengthened her neck. Her arms glowed.

She shook her head. I would be mad wanting a man to restrict me again.

I was startled at this confidence.

Holding me hostage. He refused to let me go out for months when I was pregnant. Not to visit a friend. No one could come here either. He locked me up, saying that a pregnant woman can't show herself in public. I was a prisoner in my home.

That was a difficult time, señora.

Doña Clavel looked pointedly into my eyes. Something palpitated in my throat.

Two times he held me here. First with Mariana. And then with Luisa.

I was used to rehearsing la señora's vision of the family history. I had to let her invent the child, and herself, even me. Every day, I had to aid her in creating the lie if I wanted to stay here. La señora spoke as though justice had been made. And I? I was grateful for my daughter's good health, her talent. For seeing her grow. I loved the other children too. So I put my resentment away and wished doña Clavel would finish this recitation already.

She was waiting.

I looked at my empty hands. I said, Twice. La señora was like a prisoner, during her two pregnancies.

Doña Clavel nodded. He was no husband. No companionship. No support. But now I do not need anyone. I can live on my own.

La señora can run the house, raise your children.

Doña Clavel smiled as though reading the words "your children" written on the walls facing her. Her voice softened.

I have done it all with your help. Don't think I ever forget that. She reached across her desk and pressed my hand. You are my partner.

Señora, I wanted to ask. The children want lessons. Luisa would like art.

Art.

Alonso wants to learn guitar, and Mariana mentioned piano.

Doña Clavel straightened herself a bit more. What they need is to study. If they want to stay in Catholic school, they have to keep the best grades. Do they want to go back to la federal?

Señora, they would be devastated. They love the order and challenge in their new school.

Then they must steward their assets. It would be a tragedy to see them in ten years with nothing to call their own. On the street.

Did she know what being on the street meant?

Alonso is almost a man now. One day he will be head of this family. The girls need to marry decent men who will respect and support them.

They understand that. Alonso is smart; he can do anything and everything. Music would make him more—educado. And did doña Felicia not say that all girls need to show their grace? She taught you embroidery. An artistic hobby would round out their education too.

She thought for a moment.

We'll make it a test. If they keep their grades, they can start lessons. But if they ever regress, it's the end of the frolicking.

Gracias, señora.

She looked me in the eyes. You have nothing to thank me for.

I understand.

Indeed I understood. Those were not my children.

And so weeks later, Alonso, Mariana, and Luisa passed their mother's trial. From that moment the house brightened with Luisa's colors, with the crystalline notes of Mariana's piano, with Alonso's ardent arpeggios.

As the cool December winds dissipated the odor of paint, varnish, and solvents, the Sánchez Celises took possession of their lovely house. They were a family in control of their destiny living in the most inviting home, kissed by the breezes swirling at the foot of Nevería Hill, cooed by doves and cheered by songbirds—the most fragrant of limonaria and guava on the coast of Sinaloa.

Forty-One

So our life went after Remigio nos dejó. He left us. He let us. Live. When Mariana turned sixteen and started with the singsong of studying abroad, I did everything I could to help her. She was so ready, with her hard-earned scholarship. Nothing could be better for that girl than time off from this old town.

That afternoon, back from dropping her off at the airport, I marveled at Amalia's speed in organizing the mess my daughter had left in her wake. People call her Muñeca, but she is not the tidiest. Allowed to take only two suitcases, Mariana repacked several times, agonizing over which items she could do without. As we rushed out, I turned back to see scarves dangling from open drawers, books and music records littering the floor. A teddy bear lay abandoned for the sixteen-year-old's life she would lead in Brooklyn. But in the time it took Alonso and me to put her on the plane and drive home, every single item had returned to its shelf.

Amalia had become a good housekeeper. Training her had required the eye of the master, but the effort had been worthwhile.

I pulled a photo album from the bookcase and sat on the bed. On the last page I gazed at my daughter talking to Rotary Club dignitaries after the recital that won her the scholarship. There was the poised girl, politely answering questions. I leafed back to find her a ten-year-old picnicking at the Culiacán River, a seashell at her ear, addressing Alonso from one end of the table to the other as if on the telephone. They were funny, those two. Inseparable. On the beach, a sand carving by Luisa depicted the three children talking on respective seashells. How good it was for them to have each other.

Mariana at a recital, so composed in the white gown and blue sash. The adoring audience looked on with Osvaldo on the first row. He was not a boy anymore; he must be twenty? He loved her so transparently. Today at the airport his eyes had welled up.

I'll wait for you, I overheard him say.

There were many pictures of the young couple. Sitting on a towel on the beach, walking hand-in-hand. Sixteen years old, and Mariana behaved like an adult. One more thing that tied her to me. I had nothing against this novio. But they had studying and growing up to do. I would help them. Those two had an ally in me and did not even know it.

How Mariana had changed over time. The awkwardness, the oversized feet, the cylindrical waist of childhood replaced by that hourglass shape.

Then there was esa muchacha—¿cómo se llama? In my mind Mariana answered—Fernanda. And yes, I would reply—like the Catholic king. There stood the Indian girl from afar, with the wry smile and black lassos for hair. One had to credit her for leaving her tribe to earn her education on scholarships. Her family was smart to send her to civilization.

But couldn't she find more appropriate friends? Why Mariana?

There they were, wearing gala gowns. My daughter in aqua, bathed in sequins, the Indian in a flapper frock the color of flames.

A bout of nausea overcame me. *That* was Luz Landeros's gown—she had worn it to the Carnival Ball decades back, the night the fire engulfed my sister.

My mind went dark. The orange dress swayed to a maddening mambo, surrounded by glittering banners and fireworks. Indistinct shapes whirled, elbows bent, high-heeled feet kicking sideways and back. Then a whoosh, and my sister went up in flames. Wailed for the first time.

I shut the album. The gown was Luz's. The pain of that night was mine. What right did that Indian have?

I held the album to my chest. I opened it again, found a number of blank pages, shaded rectangles marking where photographs had been. Had Mariana taken them to the States? There was one more picture of the two. Draped loosely, the orange gown played up the Indian girl's shape. Those breasts, so erect, the nipples practically at armpit level, barely concealed by the dress. The chest like a washboard, polished like ebony. Her torso was turned toward Mariana, one hand on my daughter's shoulder, the other on her hip. Fingers like earthworms on the creamy skin. The immodesty of those hands.

Mariana kissed Fernanda's cheek. Her lips parted slightly as they touched the black skin, a bead of wetness on her tooth. How could she?

I saw my hand holding the photograph. I was not nearly as dark.

I looked up at my daughter's mirror. On the image was the sunny room, the polished wood, the cheerful decorations. My daughter's books and medals.

Then I looked more deeply into the glass and saw gray walls, broken tiles, a frayed bed cover, and my face of sixteen. Madre rubbing my cheek.

Try this new cream, Mijita. You'll see soon how good it will be.

My mother had died hoping my life would be good. And I had grown up expecting just that. But I had not received beauty or protection. My husband had stepped on me on his way to affluence.

I would do anything so that my children would not suffer as I had.

I raised the photograph to my face. Slowly, carefully, I ripped it in two strips. I dropped one into the paper basket.

Forty-Two

Dust particles danced on the sunbeams streaming from the window. They bounced on the beat of my E and G strings. Then the door opened and the dust swirled.

It was Clavel.

Can't you wait, Clave? Villa-Lobos ends up clubfooted if he doesn't finish his Bachianas.

She nodded, cleared a pile of music papers from a chair, brushed the dust off.

I have to ask Amalia to clean this room better.

Oh, don't. She's got the entire house to do. I like to leave my things out. I can do my own cleaning.

She opened her fan, swung it. Alonso, I need to talk to you. Now that you finished your master's degree, have you thought what you want to do with your life? We're lucky there are good people to help you on your path.

I have my path, Clave de Sol.

G-clef, the leading voice—her nickname was perfect.

I'll keep teaching, the concerts. Classical and jazz. Building a name takes time.

That's all been good during your studies. I saw *Excélsior* call you successor to Enrique Tórrez. Is he really the best guitarist in México?

I felt my face blush. *Excélsior* always exaggerates.

I am proud of you. You can keep it up if you manage your time. But now that you have graduated, isn't it time to get a job?

Clavel, I have a full-time job at the university.

She closed her fan with a crisp snap. Teaching is a good hobby for the children of moneyed families. I hope I haven't given you the wrong impression. You might think we can live off what Remigio left us, but we can't depend on one source of income. En este país you can't predict what will happen to your savings—or to the bank. It happened to our father. One moment you think you're set; the next, politicians and bankers fiddle with exchange rates, and your money is good for wrapping peanuts at the market.

That's why I have my own income. I don't take anything from Remigio's money. Your money, I should say. Adrián assures me you are safe. I need very little, and I cover it from my salary. Should I put more into the household budget?

Of course not! I never asked you to give me that money.

Then I don't understand, Clave.

My chords fanned into soft arpeggios, like echoes of themselves.

I am talking about the family. Mariana, in New York, bleeding money.

Her fan sped up.

Just do me the courtesy. You can play in your free time. You're not married, have no children, but one day you will want your own family. Now is the time to build a patrimony.

I played a few louder chords. What would you want me to do? With a final strum I crossed my arms on the instrument.

You can work at something solid. Why not talk to Chepo Menard? I hear from Adrián he needs a manager for one of his restaurants.

Did he not ruin Adrián's house by building those towers two meters from him? Are they friends?

I wouldn't say friends, but they have mutual interests. You see, people sometimes have to put aside the timidities in their hearts and be practical. People need foresight.

Tell me about that, Clave de Sol.

About foresight?

What's in your heart.

I realized I had never known. I began Bach's Chaconne.

In my heart? There is worry. I have been alone most of my life. Without you we are a handful of mujeres solas. Look at Mariana. It's been five years since she left for New York, has no plans of settling down. Luisa, with her paintings. Neither seems to think of marrying. Maybe it is my fault; I should have made you understand. But here we are, and we need you.

The chaconne's dense, insistent chords seemed to contain my sister's anguish. I kept my eyes on the intricate movements of my left hand. The brooding, yearning melody, ever changing yet the same, echoed Clavel's voice. I played an ascending scale on a long crescendo.

As I neared the top of the scale, I looked up, and my heart skipped. Clavel was standing near the window, her face bathed in tears.

I had never seen my sister cry. She was my surrogate mother, the unwavering head of this family, the strongest person I knew. And her tears were not unfounded. The documents Adrián had shown me when I turned eighteen revealed she owned nothing, not even our parents' home. How Remigio had come to hold the title no one explained. On who knows what untold spite he had bestowed the home on his daughters rather than on her. Even I, his adoptive son, enjoyed more largesse. Thanks to him, I had music, the meaning of my life.

I walked toward her. I placed my hand on her forearm.

I'm sorry. I had not understood.

She pushed me gently aside, pulled a handkerchief from her strap, blotted a makeup smudge. In an instant she recovered her poise.

How old was she—forty-two? Would she always be as unflinching? I was an orphan like her, but I had had a childhood—a happy one. Clavel had never let me feel alone or insecure. Who had stood by her?

She had never asked anything of me. It was as if she had banked all chances to petition me, kept them stashed like seeds, protection for a bad year. Now the dreaded famine might come.

I picked up some books from the floor and placed them on the shelf. Could I acquire the house from my nieces? I imagined Clavel's joy as I placed the title in her hands. But how? My university job offered a modest salary; wage increases were infrequent. I would be old before I accomplished such a goal. It was like limping after a fast-moving target.

I can try with Menard. But you have to know—I'm not dropping my performances. If Menard is fine with that, I'll try working for him.

Will you! My sister smiled in a hopeful way. She touched my arm, a faint tremor in her fingers. Have you seen Karina, dear?

Last month, during a concert in Guadalajara. She brought so many friends they took up a whole row. Then we had supper. She is doing well.

She's become a beautiful young woman.

I chuckled. Now, now. All in good time. And I have a new adventure, don't I?

You'll see how good it will be. Doesn't Amalia say, Alonso can do it all? I'll always support your performances. And you'll feel satisfaction watching your accounts grow. In having a future. You won't regret it!

She hugged me. It was the first time in years.

I know I won't, Clave de Sol.

Forty-Three

Chepo Menard ate and talked at impressive speed. He finished the caviar appetizer, chased a few stray eggs on the table-cloth, licked his finger. A wine stain grew on his unused napkin. Adrián Landeros showed no reaction. Like the ghost of doña Luz, the translucent curtains caressed the breeze time and again. The beauty of the house and of the beach persisted, even surrounded by the towers of Hotel Careyes.

This pinche town is dying, Menard said.

How can you say that? You better than all know Ayotlan's potential.

That was before the devaluation. Now look at the Malecón. Many hotels are half empty, many up for sale, trash and crumbling plaster. The prices are so depressed, all you get are spring breakers sleeping eight to a room and bathing in beer. How are we going to earn a living?

You know we can, Chepo. We have to ride out this slump.

Where to—bankruptcy? The tourists spend their money else-where. Wake up, Adrián. This mine is exhausted. We built the best, but it was out of style before the paint dried. Mmta!

He shoveled forkfuls of shrimp into his mouth. He wiped tamarind sauce off the plate with his bread.

It's time for new investments, friend. There is money to be made.

Adrián raised his wineglass to his lips, too polite to point out that Menard alone had made the decisions he was calling ours. He did not seem to notice he was the only person eating. And me? I was sealing my fate that night. I waited for the boss to get sated and turn his attention to me. Then I would be a rock rolling downhill. I sipped ice water, analyzed the sounds around me. The

187

waves' crashing had a deep timbre; their rhythm was regular until a larger wave broke the pattern, spewing crowded chords like a cymbal. Registering the ocean's dissonances kept me calm. The only other person who knew this game was Mariana. What would she say when we spoke next—when I told her that art was great, but money?

And Karina? She and I had never talked about our dreams. What dreams would I share with her now?

Look at Cancún, Menard went on. They have big hotels to keep tourists focused. Kayaking, scuba, nightclubs, cabaret, water parks. Where is that here? You know I've tried.

Adrián's face darkened. Apparently this was a decade-long discussion.

You'll see, old friend. One day you'll come around.

So far you're doing a great job. How long have those coffins stood there?

In the window to the left I saw the shadow of Hotel Careyes Adrián's trees tried to conceal. On the right, another building lurked behind foliage.

Alonso here was a boy when you played that trick on me, *friend.*

Menard laughed. A wet morsel flew out of his mouth and landed on my wrist. Adrián glanced at me. I controlled the impulse to wipe it off.

I said, I remember when it was built. In fact I saw you there once, don Chepo. We were playing at the beach. I was about thirteen years old. Karina, your niece, came to the construction site to say hello to you.

The darling, he said, smiling.

Now this place is not lost. All we need to do is finish the original project. Give tourists what they want—

And what is that?

You don't suppose they want to mingle with Ayotlecos? They want to fly in, ride in airtight taxis to their airtight hotel, see the gate close behind them, and roast their asses. A week later, they'll fly back to their airtight countries and freeze their cojones off.

Adrián brought his glass to his lips.

Menard continued. They don't care about the Mexican curios and the local color. They want to be served by quiet, clean people. And they will pay.

I excused myself. In the restroom I spent some time filing the fingernails on my left hand. It calmed me.

Back at the table, Adrián seemed to have ridden out the rant. Chepo addressed me.

I hear you are discreet, know how to listen. That's good for the business. He knitted his eyebrows into a tangle of black and white.

For a restaurant?

You hear a lot of gossip there. Who lost money, who slept with whom, who fell down drunk, who died and how. You listen.

If the job is being quiet, I can do it.

Then you come and tell me. Especially if the cops show up.

The cops.

They shouldn't stick their noses where they're not called.

He brought his index finger below his eye; then he touched his palm to his lips. Watch and shut up. The cops never know unless someone sings. And we don't like to sing, hey?

My shoulders contracted.

You'll pick out the champagne and the cognac. Keep the customers happy.

Bueno.

If you see anything weird, grab the phone and give me a call. Luego luego.

Orale.

So that's that. When are you showing up?

Where?

There, where else? He pointed out the window.

I had never been in that hotel.

If I took your offer, I'd need to put in my notice at the university, finish the semester. I have a concert tour in México City, Puebla, Querétaro. It ends in two months.

Menard laughed, slapped his own thigh. If? If! Two months! Next week, boy. Send your students a note.

I did not say a word.

He got up. The chair scraped the floor with a jarring sound. I have to pay my respects to the white god. Compadre, talk to this escuincle.

Adrián patted my forearm. Try it for a year, he whispered. What harm is there? Clavel and the girls need you.

I was embarrassed for Adrián. I had not understood how important this was to him.

If the job is managing the room, I can do it. I like to see people enjoy themselves. I can give up teaching, but not the concerts. Menard needs to know that.

Adrián seemed relieved.

About the concerts, he said when Chepo returned.

You want to do concerts? he boomed. Give me your schedule. We'll have to train someone for when you're away. What do you tell the boss?

He manipulated his crotch before sitting down.

I smiled. Bueno—you're the boss.

Chepo's nose glistened under the chandelier. He peered at my hands. He said, Those fingernails have to go.

They're for playing guitar.

Ah ah. The cops will think you're doing cocaine, and that would not be good.

He rubbed his nose. He glanced at Adrián.

No, it would not, Adrián said with a quick smile.

I nodded.

And just like that, I, a musician and a man, became a restaurant employee. A yes man, and a spy.

Forty-Four

Ways of living: driving while Bach. Following the brilliant
Lydian scale to the mysterious Locrian. Getting my cues
for the weather from Vivaldi. If music was absent, try turning
every possible noise into an instrument. When I jumped from
my car into the noisy street, I imagined what a marlin might feel
when yanked onto a trawler's deck. On my way to work I had
to park in front of Adrián's house. To cross the street, I had to
push through a crowd of young people dressed in blue T-shirts
with a logo of wavy lines. They told me to Save Playa Careyes,
as if I did not care. They shouted about historic buildings. In my
past life I would have heard their grievances, lent a hand. But
there were only twenty-four hours in one day.

As I entered the restaurant, the air conditioning jabbed at
me. Worse than the temperature drop, even worse than losing
the music for the street noise was the shock of Muzak in this
cold enclosure. Silence would be better than this simulacrum.
Surely Menard could understand that quality music enhanced
the dining experience, but it was too soon to suggest changes.
I was learning what made the room flow, to anticipate what
needed attention. And fighting the sickly feeling that I was in
the wrong place.

I had seen Menard several times in the past weeks. He walked
into and out of the back office but hardly spoke to me. That, he
had said, was a sign of his trust.

Buenos días, señor Celis.

Alonso, Juliana. That's my name.

Alonso, señor Celis.

Juliana was stubbornly formal, which must have helped land
her the hostessing job. She showed me the reservation book—not

full, but better than last week. I checked on the waiters. The office door was closed, and that Omar guy was not blocking it with his rifle. That and the staff's relaxed ways told me Menard was not in, but it never hurts to be sure.

I did my rounds of the wine cellar and the kitchen. I approved the day's specials and updated the stocking list. Then I went out again: crossed the crowd of youths and tried to ignore their shouts. In my car I gave over to the passion of *Iberia.* I would need two trips to transport the supplies in my car, more than two hours. But it was so much better than riding next to Omar's Kalashnikov.

I saw the assault rifle when he took me around to meet suppliers on my first day. He climbed into the truck parked on the sidewalk, blocking the restaurant's door. The truck was red with hand-painted flames on its fenders as though from burning wheels. Omar took the rifle from the passenger seat—shotgun rides shotty, he said.

Check Kala out, kid. She is loaded, but don't worry; the lock is on.

Beautiful wood. Is it tiger oak? Like my guitar's.

Like it? You might learn to use men's things. Look through the viewfinder.

That would mean aiming at something.

Mmta. OK, kid. Throw Kala next to my spear gun. They keep each other company.

He gunned the engine, and the truck jumped. When I hit my head against the glass, he laughed as if at a big joke.

I learned to steel myself in his presence—I focused on the work, joked more, said less. But Omar enjoyed catching me by surprise. He would appear behind me and growl, How goes it, boy? He stood guard at the boss's. Cuadrado—feet planted apart, brandishing the spear gun or the rifle. He would catch my eye, give a big grin.

Quihubo, jefe, he would say.

He probably reported on me, but why? And what? My duty was to serve customers, my only power my courtesy. My hope was to get through the day. What was there to find out about me?

The best time of day was two in the morning.

Buenas noches, Mister Celis, said Juliana, in jeans and a sweatshirt, the gym bag with her formal clothes and shoes hanging from her shoulder. Good night, I said, holding the key to the front door. Sure you don't want a ride? No, she said like every night. It's just two blocks to my house. So I locked the door, dimmed the dining room lights, and climbed the spiral stairs to the loft. My office was the best place in the restaurant, its window offering the only natural light available to staff. To my right, I saw the saline spray of Olas Altas. On the left, I had Adrián's mansion. I sat at my desk, covered no more with wine lists and payroll, and gave myself two or three hours of practice. The music inspired me to look in one or another direction. With composers like Lauro or Villa-Lobos I fancied swimming in the churning ocean, whereas Bach invited me to balance my gaze on the pruned laurels, on the spirals of mermaids and seahorses carved in Adrián's terrace.

I turned my desk lamp off and relished the darkness. I did not need light for Villa-Lobos's études. What a different feel there was now, absent the customers, the anxiety. In the presence of Menard and his associates the staff parted like the waters of the Red Sea. The first time he hosted a room full of businessmen I went to introduce myself and offer a special wine. *Blow him the fuck up*! I heard as Menard unlocked the door.

Why would you blow up my nephew here? Menard joked with the deflection tactic I soon learned to recognize. You're like my nephew. No, Toncho?

My name is Alonso Celis Coulson. Encantado. I corrected the nickname Menard had imposed on me, hoping it would not sound like a correction.

Other words I heard: crush, cut, liquidate. But what those men would obliterate was not the deal or the problem. It was repeatedly él and ellos: tear *him* apart; hack up *those guys.* In Menard's world, people seemed obstacles toward dominance.

Was it metaphor, or real wrongdoing? The only person I knew who might have an answer was Adrián, but he was unreachable. No one worse suited to express an unfavorable opinion, even of his enemies. Adrián believed in polite gesture, gentle word, impeccable dress. Discretion was his shield against the vulgar and the cruel.

But lately his steadfastness appeared under assault. Once Menard shouted, You've been standing in my way too long. I am finishing the damn thing I started—with or without you. A haggard Adrián left the restaurant. On the street the activists accosted him, chanting louder. Some of them held on to his house's gate and talked to a reporter with a video camera. Ashen, Adrián pushed them aside, brandishing his cane. What could they defend against Ayotlan's defender?

Menard's power was his money. But where did he get it? The books were clear—in the past year the restaurant had broken even *once*. The hotel and his other properties were half empty. Yet he was always buying and building. It was clear tourism was neither the source nor the objective. This was Sinaloa, 1990, for crying out loud.

I slid up the glissando of Villa-Lobos's prelude. How close could one get to crime and stay clean? I could deal with the cooks, waitresses, bartenders, Juliana; offer customers a good meal. What did I know of what went on in the back office?

I could survive as long as there were nights every night. And above all, the trips. When traveling, I had only rehearsals, master classes, recording sessions; music shared with hundreds, and no one watching me. Bathed by floodlights, I closed my eyes, filled the hall with beauty, let the audience follow the tendrils of my melodies.

On the streets of large cities no one recognized me. I loved walking in bustling neighborhoods, eating street food, exploring hardware or stationery stores, because they had nothing to do with me. Once in México City, I took a long walk around the Ciudadela and got lost for hours. As I asked directions back to the hotel, I thought how easily I could disappear. I could grow a beard, color my hair. Take new students and gigs, establish my reputation under a new name. Clavel and the girls would visit me far from it all.

Bach's Chaconne pulled me back to here. The full moon cast lovely shadows on Adrián's stone carvings. Nothing relaxed me more than Bach combined with the aromas of the ocean and the sight of beauty. If only music could bend life to its rules.

But life refused. It was there in the echo of footsteps and a clinking of metal. Two shadows approached Adrián's house—a young man and a woman in blue T-shirts. They carried chains in their hands. I watched, playing mechanically.

> *It is the stick, it is the stone. It is the end of the road.*

That is how easily Bach gave my guitar to Antônio Carlos Jobim.

Down there, at the end of the road, those two looked in all directions. The man stood, his back to the gate of Adrián's house. The woman brought the chains to him—they were handcuffs. And she locked him to the gate! She took another set of handcuffs and, in a reverse Houdini number, managed to chain herself to the gate as well.

It is the stick, it is the stone.

They stood at the end of the road, looking left and right, like fools. I put my glasses on and took a look at their T-shirts. The logo read "Salva Playa Careyes." The one worn by the activists who had accosted Adrián days ago. The ones who had talked to some reporter, as they clung to the very same gate.

Caingá candeia, é o Matita-Pereira

Whoever their Matita-Pereira was, he was not showing up. And whatever those pranksters were up to was not my business, but it was Adrián's. I took the phone and dialed his number. It rang in counterpoint to Tom Jobim's bossa.

It's the wind blowing free
It's the end of the slope
It's a beam, it's a void
It's a hunch, it's a hope

It rang many times. I played mindlessly—a workout for the fingers, my mind on that suspicious, innocuous couple.

É a noite, é a morte, é um laço, é o anzol
The night, death, a rope, a fishing hook.

I took the phone and dialed again. It rang eight, twelve, sixteen times.

A roar came from around the corner. A red pickup truck parked across the street.

Taxi!

I threw myself at the cab, but it swerved around me. The driver pointed at the sign on the roof with the word "Libre." The sign's light was off; the taxi was off duty. This was the second cab I had tried to hail after I discovered my car's starter dead. It was Saturday, four in the morning; revelers were leaving nightclubs. Where were the taxis?

I walked on the shaded parts of the Malecón. I would get to the airport and catch a flight to Chihuahua. I would arrive two days before my tour, use the time to draw up a plan. I checked my watch. Seven minutes had passed since I'd left the restaurant. Twice Aguas de Março.

I kept an eye on the street for the miracle of a taxi. Miracles can happen. I could make a deposition. Public monuments laws protected historic buildings. Environmental laws protected coastal habitats. People cared about those things. They would listen.

An endless ringing echoed in my ear. I had just spent an hour hanging from the phone while two fools stood chained to Adrián's gate. Then came the truck with the flaming wheels. Omar and a potbellied man jumped out. They each carried a roll of duct tape. The young people smiled and said something I could not hear. With a grin on his lips Omar cut a strip of tape, and the fat man did the same. As they taped their mouths, the protestors started pulling and straining as if they could uproot the iron bars behind them. Like in a dance, Omar and the other guy worked on the young man first. The fat man stood on his feet and held on to the gate, his belly crushing the young man against the iron bars. Omar rolled a long strip of tape around the man's knees, then another around his ankles. He bound his torso and arms together, added tape to his mouth. Soon he looked like a half-dressed mummy.

They went to work on the woman. She was smaller, but they took longer with her—she writhed. They groped. They taped below and above her breasts, as though fashioning a bra, then squeezed as if milking her. The tape covered the logo on her T-shirt. Above one strip read "Salva." Below, "Careyes."

Then Omar bared his teeth and threatened to bite her. Her muted moan and the men's laughter were a blow to my stomach.

My hand shook on the telephone. Where was the reporter those fools must have called? And where would I find an officer that Menard did not own?

When they finished taping the woman, Omar took a metal cutter from his truck. He cut the man's handcuffs from the gate and reinforced the tape around his hands. Then he taped the man's eyes shut. The gordo leaned toward the man's feet and heaved them without warning. He toppled with a groan, terrified. Omar caught the falling torso with his arms as though a hay bale. The young man let out a louder groan as the gorillas dropped him on the truck bed, his body convulsing. The same terror and damage followed for her. She moaned like a wounded tiger.

The gorillas wiped their hands on their jeans and walked toward the truck. Omar stopped at the door, looked up at my window. As imperceptibly as I could, I pressed the button on the telephone's cradle, hoping the dark would conceal me.

Omar glared. Then he turned around, jumped into his truck, and drove off.

I jumped too. I gathered my papers, my guitar, the bag with my jeans. I was about to leave the office when I heard movement. Omar was again at Adrián's gate. I sat in my chair.

A bulldozer, a bobcat, and a truck with a telescoping arm arrived. Omar took a key out of his pocket and opened Adrián's gate as if he owned it. The workers drove the machines up the driveway and onto the lawn. The bulldozer uprooted an ancient bush as if made of paper.

Omar walked back where he came from.

The wrecking ball swung and met the two-story windows overlooking the bay. Glass rained like confetti in an endless racket, strangling the flighty curtains like the ghost of doña Luz. They crushed limestone and granite. Squirrels, rabbits, birds escaped from ancient trees shaped like peacocks and goddesses. Walls fell. Soon only detritus remained.

I had to leave.

The familiar roar came back. The pickup truck rolled slowly past Adrián's house, as though checking for a job done well. In the truck's bed, the blinded youths writhed like swordfish on a trawler's deck.

There were now three youths on that truck.

I carried my guitar on the Malecón and prayed for a taxi. I had to survive a few hours. As soon as my plane landed in Chihuahua, I would file a complaint with that prosecutor. Camargo was his name. It was a miracle he had taken the phone at three thirty in the morning.

Then I would live for music. I would find a way to stay away. Alive.

I walked, I ran, focusing on the shriek of speeding cars, the squeals of late-night revelers, the chirping of the early birds. The street's song was brash, but not unadorned.

Then there was a wail.

It was an unstopping honk, its pitch and loudness rising steadily as it approached. It ululated, it wailed in waves until it turned the corner. It came from an old, red Impala, sputtering its poison of blue smoke. Its lament led a procession of cars that were, in a way, all the same.

A VW Beetle pierced the Impala's cloud. It was rusty red.

A scarlet station wagon with ruddy wooden panels.

An illegal taxi that ignored my call. Bloody red.

A Ford Galaxy, crimson.

The wail ceased, and a red truck stopped next to me. Flames painted on its fenders.

Hey, Mister Celis, need a ride?

Forty-Five

I walked into Alonso's room. Not a sign of him—not a dirty ashtray, all his papers in the same disarray. Just another desolate day without my brother.

Ever since he started the job at Menard's, he had no time to spare. He worked. He traveled for performances. He would come home at five or six in the morning, sleep until eleven, breakfast, then back to work. We seldom shared a meal. Sometimes it was hard to remember where in the world he was.

I missed Mariana too, living in the States for almost six years. Yes, it had been hard to have her so far. But her cheer, her discipline and drive, had been impossible to contain. She was flourishing at the music school. We all eagerly looked forward to every summer, prepared for her arrival. I would rally Osvaldo, Mariana's friends, and their novios for a welcome reception. Amalia would cook the red mole and the mango flan; ready the pantry with the papayas, watermelons, and guavas she liked to feast on. Alonso procured duets to play with her. Then Mariana arrived with flushed cheeks and moist eyes, enjoyed everyone's love, corresponded her own sweetness. But it was all short-lived.

Once she had hardly been home for a week when she left for a trip to the Durango highlands. Since then, a few days into the summer, we knew what to expect: I am going to the Copper Canyon. Or the Michoacán woods. Or the Veracruz hills. Fellow students would fly in and meet her somewhere in the Republic. American girls and boys, and other nationalities. And off she went, a bandanna on her head and sunglasses on her eyes. She came back a few days before summer's end more freckled than ever, hugged everyone a tearful goodbye, and off to New

York. Luisa went along on just one of those trips. I had grown to accept that restlessness, knew to be patient. There would be time to bring her home, rekindle her relationship with Osvaldo, steer it to the altar.

With his excellent breeding, Osvaldo reminded me of Raúl Medina. Of course, I got in trouble when I told her. Mariana pointed at Laura's portrait: the one who abandoned tía Laura when she wasn't pretty anymore?

Then Luisa. The sweet girl preferred to stay home rather than socialize. I tried not to pressure her. In time an adequate man would come along. Meanwhile, I was grateful for her company, her easy compliance.

I was grateful, too, for Amalia, the most loyal of assistants, her drive to care for all of us. In her I had a right arm, a person holding my dearest secrets. It was easy to assume the house ran itself—until the day years ago when Amalia was called up to the mountains to see her father off to the cemetery, and the household nearly fell apart. The groceries were bought, but they were pricier and of inferior quality. I stumbled in answering the tax collector's questions. The children struggled to complete their school assignments. Amalia was brilliant. Sending her to the city, her parents had denied her an education, and yet she read well. I overheard her and Luisa talking about Roman sculpture. Another time, she and Alonso discussed early twentieth-century Mexican composers. Somehow she had become their interlocutor.

When had I heard them last? In fact, when was the last time I had talked to Alonso—had it been ten days? He always called when he traveled for his concerts. In those conversations he seemed closer to me than when he was home. We talked about the paradoxes of life for a "part-time professional musician."

Clavellina, he said. Life is fine, Clave de Sol.

I miss you, I would sometimes say, so softly that I wondered if he heard me. He would answer, What I miss is the sea. And your hollers, old hag!

Niño, stop or I'll spank you, I yelled above his laughter. Respect your elders!

I did not allow jokes from anyone but him. While the whole world treated me with deference, he treated me like a sister. Through his jokes I glimpsed a long thread of despair. Did he see friends? He hadn't mentioned Karina in a while.

Call me soon, I told him the last time. Call collect. Just call.

Ya, Clavela, Clarabella. I'll call you, all right. And don't worry about the phone bill. I'm rotting in money.

He would never have worked for Menard had I not pressed him. But if anyone, he could keep the balance between his art and what sustained us. Wasn't that part of maturing, taking on responsibility?

I pressed my temples with the thumb and index finger of one hand as I checked on Alonso's room. I had been checking for a week. Why hadn't he said goodbye? How could he be so inconsiderate, how could the restaurant do without him? Of course, he was a grown man; he did not need to answer to me. But he had never done this before!

I called the restaurant and asked for Menard to return my call. In his room I looked for an itinerary he might have left. He mentioned a tour to Chihuahua—two weeks ago? Maybe he'd left early one morning and did not want to wake me. Maybe he'd left a note, but Amalia had not seen one.

The headache was turning into a migraine as I paced close to the telephone.

The day faded without a call. I took five more aspirin and dressed carefully.

I hailed a cab. My vision was hazy, but I saw the driver reach back, pull the lock up, and say, Where to? That was the extent of his courtesy. I closed my eyes and did not open them until I was let out in front of Adrián Landeros's house. My heart sank. The air was clouded with dust. More than a week after this house's demolition, I could not get used to the idea that I would never again enjoy those gardens, that terrace. Thankfully, Luz was not alive to see this travesty.

But she would have prevented it.

I gazed through the gate at the colonnaded front porch and the one wall that was inexplicably still standing. I could hardly believe Adrián had sold the house. I wondered when he would be back in town—where he would live. Had money become such an issue that he would sacrifice his home? Better the earth had opened up and swallowed it whole.

A truck was blocking the entrance of the restaurant: one of

those monstrous vehicles one needed a ladder to climb into, flames painted on its sides.

The restaurant was an elegantly decorated place where women could meet. Or couples. In slate and lavender, with upholstered armchairs. Not what you'd expect from Menard. I sat at a table next to the window. The music was subtle and pleasant—surely thanks to Alonso.

¡Clavel! What a miracle, Menard exclaimed, rushing over to touch his cheek to mine. To what do I owe the honor of your visit? I concealed my surprise at his affection. As if he had not left my many calls unanswered. As if he had not just snapped his fingers at the hostess.

Have you had lunch? Would you care for a little sherry?

I prefer tea.

It was six o'clock. In the far corner, three women sipped coffee and nibbled on cake.

When the drink came, I took a sip.

It's about Alonso.

Menard scanned the dining room. He rubbed his nose, held his finger at his lips, and whispered, How can I help you?

Had he just shushed me?

My voice quivered. I haven't heard from him for a week. When is he expected at work?

A pulsating nail was piercing my left eye.

Menard looked left and right. He isn't here.

I waited.

W-what can I do for you?

Tell me when he left. Where I can find him.

He rubbed his nose. Alonso left about a week ago. Staff tell me he left with Juliana, the hostess. An indita from the south. They took their paychecks and walked.

What do you mean they walked?

I have it from Juliana's family that she took what she was wearing, nothing else.

He motioned toward the black-haired, meek-looking girl who had just served us.

Graciela here has been substituting for her. She's pretty good. I think we'll keep her, whether Juliana returns or not. Malagradecida.

Walked. Malagradecida. Why would he conflate the story of a disloyal waitress with Alonso? Un hijo de familia, the son of a decent family. My son.

The pounding in my head overtook me.

As for Alonso, I wish him luck with his music. Apparently he looks down on the humble work of putting food on the table. He chuckled at his pun. On these tables.

Liar. Greasy, hateful liar. I struggled to breathe. There were spots, holes in my vision.

I've had to advertise for his position. It won't be easy to replace him, I must say. He was charming. Maybe the music seduced him, do you think—or Juliana?

I stood up jerkily. If that is all you can tell me about Alonso's whereabouts—

I felt faint as I walked toward the door.

By the way, he left some papers and books. Would you like to have them?

I waited. Menard sent the girl upstairs.

He walked me outside, carrying a box of books and cassettes. We circled the truck. I had to reach out and touch it to keep my balance. Then I dusted off my hand.

Menard flagged a taxi and opened the door. He helped me into the back seat, placed the box of papers in the passenger seat.

He held the door open.

I will call if we hear anything.

He leaned in. He said, Alonso used to walk Juliana after work. We're not so surprised they disappeared together. Isn't that what men and women do—they find one another, and nothing else matters?

Amalia, please.

With difficulty I walked into the darkening house. The cathedral's seven o'clock bells pulsated in my head, tracing the pain as it radiated from behind my left eye to my forehead. It raked toward my crown, where it exploded in fireworks of agony. I vaguely remembered the ride from the Malecón. Traffic lights flooded me; car honks mingled with the cries of children escaping their parents' hands, running recklessly under the taxi's wheels.

Then there was darkness. My mind was a wasteland and my brother was in it. He walked away, growing smaller and smaller.

One hand carried his guitar. He circled his other arm around a woman's waist. I cried out. To my side, Luisa and Mariana whispered something to Amalia. I called out to them, but they ignored my supplications.

Visions of barbarous winds in a desert inferno flooded me. My brother was stranded, bereft of my protection. The wind howled through the crevices of animal carcasses. Caracara vultures waited on saguaros, readying themselves for the cleanup job at which they were experts—death's messy work. Alonso became tiny, then he walked into the beaks of those foul creatures. They flew away.

I leaned against a wall. I fumbled in my purse for my handkerchief, dabbed my forehead. I saw the rocking chairs, the begonias and gardenias hanging from the corridor beams, the dusky garden of my home. I would rest. Something had scared Alonso—he would never leave without a reason. I would find my brother and bring him home. I needed Amalia to fetch a narcotic from the clinic. To help me lie down. I needed my daughters.

Amalia had to be in her room. I walked in her direction. ¡Amalia! Was my voice stuck in my throat? I hobbled past the limonaria—the kitchen was on my right, the service area to my left. Just turn the corner and walk past the disused rooms, the laundry room and the storage. At the end I would find her. I walked within reach of the wall.

Then it was dark.

My eyes opened to an enormous bougainvillea petal. Behind it stood a giant breadcrumb; huge ants milled up and down, hauling it. A cool hardness pressed on my side. I needed Amalia—for what? I would close my eyes and rest for a moment. I breathed slowly, enjoying the cool on my flank.

Fireflies hovered in the dark; geckos made their kissing sounds.

Geckos live in the desert. Alonso was not home. What was I doing on the floor?

Terror raced through me.

¡Amalia! Meek moans reverberated on the walls. Was that me? How would I get up?

Holding on to a limb of the limonaria, I pulled myself to kneel, then stand. I felt a gentle rain, as if the tree were crowning me with petals. I pushed some off my forehead. I placed one foot after the other. That was it. That was all I had to do until I reached Amalia. The pressure in my eyes cleared a little. Did the cathedral ring nine o'clock?

I walked. Walking was an art.

Amalia's room was lit. She was there! Why had she not answered?

Amalia, dear, give me a hand. I'm feeling—I need—

Amalia was sitting on her bed next to a shoebox. On her lap was a large frame housing portraits. Many snapshots on the bedspread, like a collage.

Señora, you did not knock!

She scrambled to her feet, snatched the large frame, held it against her chest.

A poison flowed through my body. In an instant I was next to her.

What are pictures of my daughters doing here? I yelled. Give me my things!

Amalia cried. She leaned over. She tried to cover the photos with her body.

¡Señora, por favor!

Show me that. My fingers poked, pried. Amalia held on. But I was the mistress. Headache or no headache, dizziness or weakness. I held on. Pulled. I snatched the framed portrait. I stole one look and was revolted.

The frame was topped with the inscription "Quinceañera" in a tacky, hand-painted, bluebird garland–decorated cursive. It held the portraits of two girls. The picture on the left was black and white. It was Amalia with her braid wrapped above her forehead.

On the right was its simulacrum. The same blonde braid framing the oval face. The same eyes: large and blue; the same observant quality.

Below each photograph was a caption clumsily handwritten, imitating the style of the "Quinceañera" inscription above. They read "Amalia" on the left. And on the right, "María."

My hands squeezed the frame as if they could obliterate it. Amalia pulled. I jerked the pictures away. They fell to the ground; the glass shattered. We lunged to the floor, but Amalia was faster. She took the portraits, hustled to her armoire and shoved them. I forced my fingers between the dresser and the door. Amalia pried and pulled until I stumbled. With the key hanging from her neck she locked the armoire. I pummeled her shoulders.

She turned to face me, her forearms high around her face.

Thief! That portrait is mine.

I pursed my lips. I shot out. Spittle landed on her face, made the blood on her hands glimmer.

Give me that photo.

In the mirror the whites of my eyes were as red as Amalia's hands.

Mariana gave me that picture when she left for the States, señora. You can ask her.

I slapped. You don't tell me what to do!

Amalia lifted her hand to protect her face; I hit her head with my elbow. Then with my fist. Again, and again.

These are my daughters' pictures, I howled. Mine!

I turned to the bed. I clutched the snapshots in my bloody hands and turned to leave. A river raged through my aorta, my nape, the back of my left eye.

I turned one last time.

Let me remind you. All I need is to hire a locksmith to open any of the dressers in my house.

I stormed out.

I reached my bedroom in a whirl. I dropped the blood-stained photographs on the bed, sat in front of them, and took the phone.

In New York, the phone's bell pulsated in unison with the noises in my head.

Then it was all dark.

Part Three

Arribada

1991

Forty-Six

The full moon bestowed a fantastical glow on the vast beach. Luisa, Fernanda, and I would spend the night monitoring turtles. But little else was routine tonight. To reach this beach, we had flown into Oaxaca City, taken a fourteen-hour bus ride to Pochutla, then bounced in the bed of a pickup truck over the potholed road to Mazunte. After tonight's work we would meet with the Cosméticos Naturales de Mazunte cooperative—finally, like-minded people to compare notes with.

Some twenty of us stepped out of trucks in hushed excitement. Everyone wore long sleeves and pants despite the humidity. Some covered their faces with mosquito netting that gave their heads eerie elephant shapes. No perfume or insect repellent on this date, reina, Fernanda had said.

The long weekend was a vacation of sorts—away from the places where Alonso was no more. It was a break from the anger and hurt of living next to a woman who had lied, stolen, and cheated to pass as my mother. In the urn Fernanda had carved, Alonso's ashes quietly awaited the ceremony we would offer him. I needed rest from so much—even from the joy of learning how to call my true mother mother.

Fernanda's logbook was not the usual one. This had only some ten used pages but seemed much older, dog-eared and yellowing. The cover was labeled "La Escobilla" and decorated with the drawing of a straw brush tickling the carapace of a smiling olive ridley. Inside were fewer columns than in the book I knew.

Luisa asked, You don't count eggs?

Fernanda shook her head. Here we have a real arribada, the mother of all nestings.

I listened to their chatter.

What's the matter, reina? Fernanda asked.

She's obsessing about Menard. Not even here do you relax, hermanita?

How can I? Menard won't respect anyone. Even after amassing his wealth on their—

I kicked sand.

But we don't know who ordered the murder, Fernanda said.

Luisa nodded. Alonso made an appointment with a prosecutor in Chihuahua the night he disappeared.

Fernanda stopped.

His name is Camargo. He called the day the news came out about the murder. He gave Osvaldo the info on condition of keeping it from Ayotlan cops. Apparently Alonso called the prosecutor at three in the morning the night he disappeared. He told him about the demolition; said he knew names. He suspected that developers had skirted historic building and environmental laws to push the Careyes project.

Menard killed Alonso because he saw the house demolished? That's not a secret.

The prosecutor mentioned kidnappings and torture.

Fernanda stopped. Remember my friends the biologists, and Juliana, Belisa's cousin? They disappeared the same night.

I spat. That explains it. The pozole. The menu cards mentioning the Comcáac. Why would people at the dinner care about you, or leatherbacks?

Ya, reina. Fernanda circled my shoulders with her arms. I felt her tremble.

We've come so far, Luisa said after a moment's pause. Can't we forget this for three days? There is no Menard here. Tomorrow we'll go to Mazunte, check out the remodeling of the old slaughterhouse.

How are people adjusting to not living off the turtles?

Slowly. They disinfected and whitewashed the building. They'll make their factory there, their own Olas Altas.

Fernanda kissed my cheek. It'll be our little honeymoon. And I have a surprise for you.

She ran up a dune. At the top she threw her arms open, shouted, Do you know what Mazunte means? "Please lay eggs." It will be an orgy!

Indeed, that night the golfinas staged a reproductive fest. By the time we reached the intertidal zone—the widest I had ever seen—the little hookers were busy.

¡Golfina! I yelled. The turtle covered her nest, turned around, and labored toward the water. I was moved. This turtle had come to the place where she was born, a link in a chain of life from the beginning of time. She evaded the poachers and the long-line trawlers, she learned to sleep in decimated sea grasses, to evade plastic bags, and even to diet so she could keep her date with the future. She had just laid 218 eggs. Now she was back in the relative safety of the ocean.

I took a long view of the beach. On the slope where I stood some ten turtles surrounded me. Just beyond were ten more. Farther still, I saw some twenty. Then fifty. I panned the expanse and saw hundreds. The farthest ones seemed pebbles. My eyes could not make out the end of this beach, the largest I had ever seen.

Was the dark playing tricks on me?

The biologists' job tonight was less direct than before, but just as intensive. They did not transport eggs to a hatchery; just counting was challenge enough. Even walking was difficult on account of the many turtles. A student tripped over a nest and wiped crushed eggs from her sandal with little compunction. The turtle looked barely aware of the human presence.

So few in Ayotlan, and here there are hundreds!

I bet eight hundred, Luisa said.

A thousand, I replied. Could the law be improving things already? It's been in place only a few weeks.

No, chiquitas. La Escobilla is different. Here turtles come up only once a month, but in droves. The full moon calls them. I won't say how big this arribada can be. If you're off with your bet, I'll win. But don't assume this is an upswing. It will take decades to reach the numbers we had before the big fishing. Back in the sixties, they killed six hundred thousand turtles a year. Last year they got fewer than thirty thousand. And not because they weren't trying.

Mismaloya, Tlacoyunque, Chacahua, Ixtapilla, Fernanda chanted. Those used to be Moosni Otác's homes, and now all we have left are their Nahuatl names. But we still have La Escobilla. It will now be a nursery, not a slaughterhouse.

A vulture perched on a turtle's carapace and helped itself to the eggs plopping into the hole. I tried to shoo it away, but it trained its malignant beak at me.

Don't worry about animals. Just be sure no two-legged raccoons get their way. Right, Sargento?

We saw some fifteen men approaching, and Fernanda glanced at her watch—the patrol was hours late. I would have felt reassured to see Sargento Bermúdez.

You are here for the turtles?

The leader nodded. He looked like a fisherman, cradling a spear gun in his hands.

Fernanda extended hers. My name is Dr. Lucero.

The soldier passed his spear to his left hand, extended the right to her.

What's your name?

Obed Gandía.

Fernanda glanced at the insignia on his shirt. ¿Sargento Gandía?

He nodded and scanned Fernanda's clothing.

She went right to business. This is what you do: patrol the beach, stop any poaching attempt. We monitor enforcement of the turtle conservation law.

And you protect *us*, interjected Luisa.

The turtles are dancing! I shouted.

Hundreds of mothers were covering their nests. They tamped the sand with a pendular motion. And it was loud.

I held Fernanda, my hands on her shoulder blades. A rumble climbed up my feet, stronger every instant. It surrounded us like an earthquake. She tilted her head and kissed my mouth. The tremors ran up my body, accelerating the pulse in my throat.

You're not afraid of people anymore, reina?

I shook my head and smiled. Over Fernanda's shoulder I saw Sargento Gandía sitting atop a dune some twenty feet away. He hopped to his feet and resumed his patrolling.

Toward dawn, Fernanda checked her records. Rounding out, five thousand nests.

We cheered.

Our bets were off, Luisa laughed.

If all goes well, these are fifty thousand eggs borrachos won't drink for a hard-on. We can expect better outcomes if we sustain the patrol through the season. Sargento Gandía—the next shift is coming?

The sergeant nodded. Good night.
Good luck with the catch, she hollered.
The men nodded in her general direction.

After our colleagues left we walked toward the water and took off our shorts and shirts—this time we all wore bathing suits. I'd brought snorkeling gear. I pointed toward a wind-carved promontory.

I hear the reef around that point is full of sponges. I bet we'll find Moosni Quipáacalc.

I spat into a mask and rubbed it with seawater, offered it to Fernanda. Ready?

I'm tired, love. Fernanda yawned as she undid her braid and plopped on her back in the water, arms extending from her sides. Her hair floated straight in all directions, forming a circle like a huge, soft sea urchin.

I just want to float and drift.

Come on, party-pooper. What if we find Moosnípol?

Fernanda stretched her limbs. OK. Let's make it short.

Later we'll sleep, take time off after our meeting with the co-op.

I just hope it doesn't take up the whole afternoon.

Let's swim a little, Luisa said. Then, how about I visit with the co-op? You get yourselves massages or something. Get drunk, or go to bed.

I hugged her and said, Thanks, hermanita.

Luisa chuckled. For putting up with your craziness, sure.

For everything.

Who cared whether half or whole? Luisa was my sister, my best friend, my anchor to the world. A world buffeted and so changed in six months. Confirmation of Alonso's murder had carved a hole in my heart. But it stopped the anguished search and let us grieve. Above all, I was grateful to know my mother, and to have found Fernanda. What a bitter way to find love. And such love: one that gave me joy and fear in equal measure.

There was Menard's insistence in buying los terrenos del mar. I was anxious to clarify the murder. If indeed Menard was prepared to kill for those lands, I had to remove my family from harm's way.

The sky was rosy in the east. We coasted the first cove, swung around the point, and passed a coral cemetery where the water was warmer: white coral, no sponges, no fish, no snails. An underwater silence, piles of skeletons like a wet Chernobyl. No bubbles, no pops or snaps, no sand waterfalls. We passed the sickly ruins as quickly as we could and again found cool water, and schools of fish in agate, cobalt, mango yellow. Luisa waved at us and swam away.

See you on shore.

Holding hands, Fernanda and I sought the sponge and anemone forest where Moosni Quipáacalc might feed. An octopus slithered on the coral, and Fernanda picked it up. It wrapped its tentacles around her arm and poked her ear, made us laugh underwater. Then he tried to catch our bubbles. When she put him down, she showed me the purple marks of many suction cups.

Then everything changed. The sea turned dark as though a cloud had covered the sun. But the cloud was in the water, and it enveloped us. Then it pulverized. Every tiny section turned toward the sun and became millions of mirrors. It was a school of sardines: a glittering cloud, dense as a net, blanketing us in its nimble progression. I circled Fernanda's waist. Our bodies rubbed gently as we swam with one arm each. Around us an entourage of shooting stars, eddies upon sparkling eddies, making more, smaller eddies. And those, more.

They were showing us the way.

We followed them along the coast. I pulled Fernanda gently along. We slowed down, and the fish did too. Fernanda came to the surface, took her mask off, and yawned. I can't. I'll see you on shore, love.

I took my mask off too. I held her and kissed her like the first time. We stopped moving for a moment, and we dipped, kissing underwater. Around us, the fish made a circle of light. Then Fernanda swam away, and the silver cloud parted, some going with her. As I went around the point to meet Luisa, the other cloud followed me.

In the ocean we were always together.

I found Luisa, and we swam through the river of light. A black-and-gold moray eel flashed her needlelike teeth, then retreated into her den. And we caught our breath: between the eel and us rushed Golfina. Lost in the dance of silver, the turtle flew, her fins like wings, entangling dainty fish in her turbulence. She browsed the coral, unconcerned with the glittering sea, or with us.

I came up. ¡Fernanda, golfina! I listened for her. I heard the breeze.

With her shining entourage the turtle coasted toward open sea. One stroke of her graceful fins took her farther than many of our kicks.

I raised my face above water. The surface was a mirror. I called.

We swam. We followed Golfina, and the fish followed us.

We looked. Fernanda had to be somewhere.

We swam around a boulder into a small valley of sand and grasses surrounded by rocks and coral. There Luisa squeezed my hand in a spasm, pointed down.

The cloud of fish led us to long, black strands of sea grass floating from the floor five feet below. Luisa dove to reach the source of the caressing strands. The fish parted in whirlpools of light.

A scream grew inside me.

On the bed of swaying grass Fernanda rested. Her gaze penetrated my heart.

I rushed through the dark waters, ready to wrest my love from the ocean.

Then Fernanda dropped a rock she held on her chest and burst toward the surface.

I thought I would die there, waiting to scare you. She coughed and panted. She laughed.

Forty-Seven

We parked at the entrance to the beach. I stepped out of the car and looked up to a freshly painted sign: "Alonso Celis Coulson—Nueva Playa Careyes." And in small print, "Conservation International."

Luisa intertwined her arm with mine. I called Mamá, but she stayed back. Luisa and I led the group across the beach. It was a fifteen-minute walk among grass-crowned dunes on a walkway smelling of pine. Behind us, Mrs. Guzmán pushed Clavel's wheelchair. Directly behind, Osvaldo walked next to Adrián, holding the urn. Amalia and Fernanda followed.

Señorita Luisa, Mrs. Guzmán called. She struggled with the wheelchair.

I walked back and leaned over. Clavel looked up at me and shrunk.

I checked one wheel, then the other. I scraped the axle with my fingers.

I said, The sand is so fine it covered the rod.

Clavel said, Just push slowly and carefully, Mrs. Guzmán.

But I took the handles. Clavel craned her neck. I met her glance and nodded.

She smiled faintly.

The walkway nearly reached the water, and I parked Clavel at its edge. Next to her, Adrián pressed my hand.

Luisa and I took off our shoes. Osvaldo handed me the iron-wood urn Fernanda had decorated with the bejeweled Moosni Quipáacalc Alonso and I ushered into the ocean.

We were adorned for this ceremony with Fernanda's Comcáac makeup. We traced our fingers and wrists with gypsum lines reminiscent of the bones giving us shape. Four tiny silver stars shone on our cheekbones. We walked toward the surf and sang in low voices.

> *Ihapa iya ihapa*
> *Ihapa iya ihapa*
> *Ihapa iya ihapa*
>
> *It is true*
> *It is true*
> *It is true*

I could not think of more appropriate words to honor Alonso.

Luisa and I walked into the water up to our ankles. Purple and fuchsia and agate, our skirts fluttered in the breeze. A current tugged at our feet. Luisa poured a handful of ashes into the water, but the breeze blew them toward Pájaros Island across the bay.

Fernanda took my hands and placed them on the urn. The three of us submerged it in the rushing water, and the ashes spread. A school of fish flitted around my ankles. They nibbled from the particles that were Alonso.

That is how quickly he returned to life.

In the dawn light I scanned the raging Pacífico, this ocean peaceful only in name, hoping to welcome Quipáacalc and Moosnípol.

The sea churned.

Behind the Sierra Madre, a pale sun peeked. Above the water, a translucent moon persisted.

It was almost full.

Postscript

Back to the Islands, to the Land of Deer

Antonio Haas, in memoriam

Dear reader: If you have spent time in Mazatlán, you can probably recognize a number of features of the beautiful city in *Arribada*. I built the fictional town of Ayotlan with elements from La Paz, Mazunte, La Escobilla, Puerto Vallarta, and Mazatlán. But I have a strong bias for the Sinaloa port, as it has touched me the deepest.

Arribada means "arrival," and the novel is at different levels, including the personal, a story of return. I grew up in Guadalajara, never too far from Mazatlán, the place of many childhood vacations. My father was born and raised there, and twice a year, our large family would pile up in the station wagon or the Ford Galaxy and take the eight-hour trip north, past the Ceboruco volcano's moonscape and Plan de Barrancas, where I was sure our lives would fly out the car and down the ravine. But we always survived to enjoy the dunes, the waves and seaside walks, the sight of the ships from Asia, from Europe and the Americas, the evening skies ablaze, the lighthouse, our boisterous family, the stories of past and present relatives. My last visit as a young person included a Christmas celebration at a seaside mansion very much like Adrián's, where my friends, my cousins, and I stole sips from the unsuspecting adults' glasses and hid in the bedrooms to better acquaint ourselves with each other. Before us, on the beach, the castillo fireworks wheel spun and spilled sparks for hours. It did not harm anyone.

Time passed as I built my adult life abroad. When I returned almost two decades after that mythical Christmas, I looked forward to showing my toddler and my then partner the rolling waves, the neoclassic buildings, the dunes, the sunsets. And like Mariana, I was shocked to find many mansions under piles of rubble, expansive beaches thinned to a strip or outright underwater.

The heartbreak of this realization thrust me to write what would become *Arribada*. I wanted to understand how this town that prides itself on its monuments and natural beauty could allow its heritage to languish and decay. I developed the characters of Remigio, Adrián, and Chepo to represent different aspects of the decision makers' extractive, profiteering logic and Clavel's anxiously clinging to an exclusive, privileged society. I also created the younger generation to witness this, to struggle for agency, to try to effect change.

Readers mention my flair for loading my stories with implicit meaning, and I believe that tendency stems from my obsession with Kafka, Luisa Valenzuela, and Juan José Arreola. But I am here to spell out the historical and social contexts that feed my stories. In *Arribada* Mariana sounds the alarm in 1991 on the slow destruction of Ayotlan. Meanwhile, real-life Mazatlecos had been working since the 1970s to recover *their* historic center. Chief among the structures there is the Angela Peralta Theater (TAP, its Spanish acronym), a space very much like where Mariana announced her commitment to support workers and counter her elders' wealth hoarding. The site of many struggles, the real-life TAP is a symbol of its community's history and values.

In the mid-nineteenth century, a fishing village named the Islands grew in economic and political power and turned into a city named Mazatlán, the land of deer. Its entrepreneurs built their mansions inspired by Andalusian and Roman architecture—an example being Mariana's square home, with its four wings of rooms surrounding a verdant courtyard and a fountain. The large properties often occupied as much as one of the downtown's 180 blocks. And in their midst, the theater vied with the cathedral to become the cultural center, a meeting place for society, a symbol of sophistication.

In 1870, as construction of the theater neared completion, the developer, Manuel Rubio, died in a shipwreck while traveling to Paris to acquire furnishings. Soon after, the municipality denied his widow a tax break promised to her late husband, forcing her into bankruptcy. Doña Vicenta Unzueta had to sell the originally named Rubio Theater, but it survived to host the soprano Angela Peralta in 1883. The town congregated at the port to greet the Mexican Nightingale with the national anthem. In their enthusiasm, dignitaries unhitched the horses from her carriage and personally pulled Angela to her lodgings. This triumphal arrival, however, was the visit's last joyous moment, as the ship had brought to Mazatlán not only the troupe but also yellow fever. With the musical director mortally ill, Angelica di Voce e di Nome, as her Italian public dubbed her, had to run the rehearsal herself. In less than a week, half the musicians had perished, including the soprano.

Manuel Rubio's shipwreck, doña Vicenta Unzueta's bankruptcy, and the Nightingale's traumatic death may be seen as omens, yet the theater thrived until the 1910 revolution. Then started the hard times, as gleaned from the theater's marquee: operas, ballets, and zarzuelas disappeared in favor of pro wrestling and boxing matches, carnival bashes, and burlesque. In 1943, Teatro Rubio was turned into a movie theater and renamed Cine Angela Peralta, but the Nightingale's protection against the economic forces undermining it did not materialize.

Those forces came in the form of a craving for Americans and Canadians to spend their postwar wealth in *sol y playa*: the sun and beach Mazatlán has in abundance. The two iconic hotels—the Belmar, built in 1921, and the Freeman, in 1950—were relatively small and offered entertainment more suited to locals: black-and-white gala balls with large horn orchestras playing danzón and bolero, rather than the rock 'n' roll and, later, disco music that were the rage elsewhere. Wanting easy access to the beach from their bedrooms, tourists balked at walking across the street with beach towels and children in tow. In 1960 the first beach hotel was built north of Punta Camarón, the aptly named Hotel Playa Mazatlán. This was the beginning of the Zona Dorada, the long strip of hotels built on filled wetlands or directly on the dunes. Though the Mexican Constitution enshrines state ownership of coastal lands and guarantees Mexicans' right to enjoy them, private concerns can secure building concessions as long as they provide free access to the beaches. And build they did—quickly and abundantly. They offered the token beach access to locals, but myriad small insults often pushed nonguests away.

While Mazatlán focused on developing seaside tourism, its historic center was in steep decline. There, to allow better traffic flow, Benito Juárez Street was widened by shaving off the neoclassic mansions' facades. In 1964 Cine Angela Peralta was no more, becoming a factory for the open-air taxis called *pulmonías* (Spanish for "pneumonias") and carnival floats—two of Mazatlán's quintessential transportation forms. For better, for worse, for richer, for poorer—the theater named after the Angelic one stayed true to Mazatlán.

The downtown area reached such disrepair that the municipality considered demolishing it outright. But in 1972 a handful of real-life Marianas created organizations, such as the Patronato Pro Restauración, with the aim to rebuild and regain the area's and the theater's previous glory. But fearing competition, the tourism industry and municipal governments did not support their efforts. In 1975 the theater's structure was so weakened that the cyclone Olivia blew its roof off. The ruin invited petty crime; ficus trees grew on the stage, and vines climbed the balconies. Led by Antonio Haas, the group Amigos del Teatro Angela Peralta persuaded the mayor and state governor to purchase the property from its Spanish owners and rebuild it. As part of the fund-raising efforts, they offered a number of performances in 1987.

> The first cultural festival took place under an open sky, at the foot of the great Ficus. A rustic stage was built to accommodate a piano, a pianist and the soprano Gilda Cruz Romo. While she offered us a recital of Mexican romantic songs—*lieder tropical*—a full moon climbed behind the dilapidated wall and soared like a silver dove among the branches of the Ficus until, at the recital's end, it reached the clean, starry sky and glowed on the theater's every inch. Gilda sang well that night, but the moon stole the show.
>
> —Antonio Haas

Eventually, support poured from private organizations as well as local, state, and federal governments, designating the theater and downtown as historic monuments and national treasures. A coalition of governmental and nongovernmental organizations restored the theater and created galleries and conservatories for dance and music, painting and sculpture schools. The historic center was rebuilt. With the theater and schools came hungry students and their parents, attracting new cafés and restaurants, and this motivated the return of residents, who purchased and refurbished many surrounding homes.

Other private-public collaborations, such as the Historic Center Project Association, have seen to it that the downtown area remains a space for Mazatlecos to interact with each other and with tourists. Beyond their physical presence, the buildings have accrued immaterial value as places where relationships develop. I see the emphasis in the quality of life for Mazatlecos while welcoming tourists into their midst as one of this project's greatest achievements. And their winning strategy: the efforts led with participation of intellectuals, residents, touristic and commercial concerns, and governments.

I started this essay mentioning my return almost two decades after having enjoyed Mazatlán as a youth, and how what my second home had become triggered my writing of *Arribada*. As I return once again to Mazatlán—to research this postscript to my novel, visit with cousins, aunts, and uncles—I am glad to see the Nightingale's spirit glow in the Angela Peralta Theater. Downtown buildings are now repaired and painted in traditional colors, the sidewalks adorned with trees and flowers, the streets artistically lit, music everywhere. I also see that some lovingly kept facades are nothing but—like Adrián's home, a peek through exquisitely decorated windows reveals empty lots and open sky. There is still so much to do. Mariana would know where to begin.

I also saw, as my wife and I stood in line to buy artisanal ice cream, a ten-year-old girl wearing shorts over her leotard, her hair combed into a neat chignon, her feet in fifth position, rehearsing tendus while waiting for her treat. I celebrate ballet students like her, and the countless youths enjoying arts education, some of whom might dream of becoming the next Nightingale. I rejoice in their families' enjoyment of the plazas, restaurants, and homes, sharing the space with foreigners without having to relinquish it.

Could this model be applied to Mariana's other concern—the conservation and recovery of beaches, mangroves, and lagoons? Could the turtles come back?

Acknowledgments

Writing a novel is a mighty lonely task. And yet, a crowd has held me as I bring my little book into the world.

Ariane, deepest of readers, lovingly designed Arribada's cover and chapter illustrations.

My hadas madrinas believed in my book before it was, their incantations sustaining me through the years. Kevin McIlvoy "you will," Luisa Valenzuela "my witch," Luis Alberto Urrea "we need more of you," Dorothy Allison "do you know Macondo?" Ernesto Quiñonez "come to Cornell."

Solstice MFA Program's Sandra Scofield "unique," "you will publish it," and also "does this character have a body?" She took my manuscript, told me to put it in the trash and write it all over again. And taught me to trust myself and become a novelist.

Cynren Press's Holly Monteith received my book without an agent, without introductions or biases. Then she gave it a lovely shape and placed it where you, dear reader, could find it.

Before any agents or editors would touch it, many journals and institutions believed in Arribada. The Feminist Press's Louise Meriwether jury selected it as a finalist. Early versions of some chapters are housed, in English or Spanish, in Coal Hill Press, Flash Frontier, Solstice Literary Magazine, Connotation Press, Flyway, La colmena, Under the Volcano Anthology, Revista Luvina, Letralia, and Resonancias.

The following forums have welcomed and guided me: American Association of Writers and Writing Programs, Association for the Study of Literature and Environment, Breadloaf Writers' Conference, Feria Nacional del Libro de Escritoras Mexicanas, Latin American Studies Association, Macondo Writers' Workshop, Middlebury College's leave program and Faculty Development

Fund, Salzburg LGBT Forum, University of Vermont Honors Environmental Studies Program, and Vermont Studio Center.

In oblique ways, Arribada is my own family saga, and many of my loved ones lent it their spirit. My grandfather, abandoned by his own father, left second grade to support his family and went on to become a public intellectual and Mazatlán's defender. My grandmother Mamá Yoya showed me grace and resiliency in the face of adversity. Annie and la Condesa Lala, memory keepers. Mis nanas María and Nini mothered me. Ernesto Alonso's music lives on in my ears. An undying house, 2l de marzo 64 poniente. And my parents surrounded me with books and music and sent me to fly unfettered by safety nets.

Matías, Camila, Ariane: the loves of my life.

Questions and Topics
for Discussion

1. It is often said that once you leave home, you can never return, and home will never be the same again. Have you ever returned to a beloved childhood place you stopped frequenting for a long time? How was it changed, and what was your reaction in discovering those changes?
2. Identify a few beloved aspects of Mariana's hometown. What do they mean to her emotionally?
3. Many of the emotions in this novel are expressed through music. Did you recognize some songs or pieces mentioned in the narrative? Did knowing or discovering the music help you resonate emotionally with the characters' experiences? In which ways?
4. What are some aspects of Fernanda's work with sea turtles that stand out to you, and why?
5. Describe Clavel's attitude toward Fernanda. Can you explain what motivates her?
6. Now describe Fernanda's situation in the community where she lives. Which of her coping strategies do you notice, and what effect do they have on her and others?
7. In the second part of the novel, Clavel makes some extraordinary decisions that affect the lives of Mariana and Amalia. What does she do, and how does she explain it?
8. Describe the choices Alonso makes vis-à-vis his career. What motivates him, and what are the consequences of these choices?

9. In the end, Mariana makes several decisions that affect her family's wealth and well-being. Can you explain them from her point of view? Do you agree with them? Why or why not?

10. At the end of the story, how has this family been transformed, and what is its outlook going forward? Reflect about a character of your choice. What are the character's chances to find fulfillment, and why?

A full Readers' Guide is available from the Cynren Press website at https://www.cynren.com/catalog/arribada.